Gifted Generation Series

Book One

The Zealots

A novel

By

Reginald Wattree, Jr.

May you be zealous for God

Reginald Wattree Jr.

Purpose Publishing
1503 Main Street #168 ✖ Grandview, Missouri
www.purposepublishing.com

Copyright © 2015 by Reginald Wattree Jr.

ISBN: 978-0-6924294-2-6

Editing by Frank Kresen
Book Cover Design by Thaddeus Jordan

For permission and requests, write to the publisher:
1503 Main Street, #168, Grandview, MO 64030.

Author Inquiries may be sent to
giftedgeneration@mail.com

This book is available at special quantity discounts to use as premiums in youth development, educational and faith based programs.

In the last days, God says, "I will pour out my Spirit on all people. Your sons and daughters will prophesy, your young men will see visions, your old men will dream dreams.

Acts 2:17

Don't let anyone look down on you because you are young, but set an example for the believers in speech, in conduct, in love, in faith, and in purity.

1 Timothy 4:12

CONTENTS

PROLOGUE

In the near future; Palestine

All he saw was darkness, pitch black, blindfolded; with hands tightly bound with rope, his eyes were searching for light, but there was none to be found. He could hear frightening laughter, and background voices in an unknown language.

The heat from the summer day was causing his clothes to be saturated with sweat as dust, and sand clung to his skin. A gentle wind blew, bringing a few moments of relief, followed by more sand and dust adhering to his body. He never thought he would miss a cold shower as much as he did right now. It had been more than a week since water had touched his flesh. Oh, how he longed to bathe, to feel the water run down his body as the filth washed away.

Riding through the hilly terrain, he could feel every bump and pothole that God had created. Uncertain as to where he was being led, fear started to creep in. He had to remind himself that God would never leave him or forsake him.

"Hey, kid — stay strong. We are about to stop," Sergeant Summers whispered, briefly interrupting the young man's depressing thoughts. The truck stopped.

They had finally reached their destination, and he could hear footsteps marching toward him. All of a sudden, a violent push comes out of nowhere, causing him to tumble to the ground. One of the terrorists was yelling in Arabic at them with an aggressive tone, while another was unwrapping their blindfolds. The blinding sun hit their eyes, obscuring the face of the tall silhouette standing in front of them. The second terrorist spoke to them in broken English with a strong Arabic accent saying, "Don't worry — it will all be over soon." He cut the rope from their hands as they entered into a cave and were thrown into a holding cell.

After a while, the men guarding them finally left, leaving them alone to themselves. This was the first time he actually had a good look at Sergeant Jake Summers. He was a scruffy, muscular man whose crooked nose indicated that he had been in his fair share of fights. He had a strong, square jaw and a blond crew-cut, and he spoke with a southern twang.

"You know, most kids your age would have broken by now, under these conditions."

"It is only by God's grace, Sergeant," he replied.

"Please just call me 'Jake,'" he said.

"OK. By the way, my name is 'John.'"

"John, how old are you? And how did you and the other group of kids end up over here anyway?" Jake asked.

"I am nineteen, sir, and it's kind of a long story. I'm afraid we don't have time for long stories, sir," John replied.

"They're not going to kill us, at least not yet," the sergeant said. "They still need us for a ransom. I overheard them speaking. They don't know that I am fluent in their Arabic language."

John could only imagine how it sounded — him speaking Arabic with a southern twang.

"The plans they have for us are, to say the least, not good. We may be here a few weeks, maybe months. Don't fret. My troops are out there, looking. I am sure they have sent the spiderbots out to look for us."

"Spiderbots," John repeated.

"Yes, since we are being moved to caves, the air drones will not be able to detect our whereabouts. The spiderbots are little insect-looking robots with cameras that we use to get into tight spaces. They are virtually undetectable," the sergeant responded. And then, he added, "Are you a religious man?"

Somewhat startled by the question, John answered, "Yes, sir. I am a Christian."

"A Christian. Well, keep praying to your God that we get out of here alive," the sergeant said with a smug grin.

Out the corner of his eye, John could see that the sergeant was looking at him with a puzzling look. Sergeant Summers finally spoke and said, "I can't put my finger on it, but there is something different about you, kid. I am trained to be calm in these situations, but you have a peace about you that even I don't have. I am kind of curious as to why you are so calm."

The sergeant's question — "Why are you so calm?" made John laugh.

"What's so funny? I didn't tell a joke," the sergeant said, with a serious tone.

"If you only knew how I got to this point, sir," replied John. "I haven't always been like this. It is only by God's grace," John said again.

This intrigued the sergeant. "'God's grace,' huh? What about it? " he questioned.

"Well, to understand my story, we will have to go back four years. That's when I experienced this peace you speak of. It comes from the Prince of Peace."

This got the sergeant's attention. With a tinge of excitement in his voice, he urged John to go on. "Please continue — this sounds like a good one."

"OK. You see, my life-changing experience started in a small church in Missouri known as Life Changers Community Church or L3C. Let me tell you how it all began."

John began to expound on his story. The sergeant listened to John Mann's account as he journeyed back to four years previous.

Part One

Answering the Call

"Behold, I stand at the door, and knock: if any man hear my voice, and open the door, I will come in to him, and will sup with him, and he with me."

— Jesus Christ

CHAPTER

1

Four years previous

"Get up, boys. It's Sunday."

I could hear the faint voice of my mother yelling in my room, waking me up from my peaceful sleep. Slowly, my eyes opened, looking up at the pale popcorn ceiling. I found myself muttering, "Sunday. Why?"

For the past fifteen years of my life, I knew where I would be every Sunday. Always the same place — church. Sundays were hectic in my house, the Mann household. Even though this day came the same time every week, I was never prepared, hitting the snooze button at least two or three times, trudging along, trying to figure out what to wear. I wasn't motivated at all to attend church. To me church was another chore, a quota that had to be met.

My parents were very religious, naming my brother and me after bible characters. Philip was my brother's name. He was named after one of the evangelists in the New Testament. And I was named John, after one of Jesus' disciples. My dad was a deacon at our church, and my mom sang in the choir, so we had to be there a little earlier than others.

With Sunday came the scolding. My brother and I were always being reprimanded for not having any "sense of urgency," as my dad would say. He would give his usual speech.

"Boys, one day your mother and I won't be around to tell you when you need to get up and where you need to be. You will be making those decisions on your own. The habits you develop now will follow you into adulthood." I could recite every word he was going to say before even one left his mouth. We knew he was right, but breaking this habit wasn't easy. The pillow seemed to be even more comfortable on Sundays.

However, that day was a little different: There was no speech given, no look of disapproval in our parents' eyes, and no prodding from them hurrying us up. The only thing my mom said after she woke us that morning was, "I better see y'all at church today, or your dad will deal with you." Then, off she went, headed to church without us.

Still groggy from my sleep, wiping the crust from my eyes, I said to Philip, "Did our parents just leave?"

"Yup, gone," he replied.

Then it suddenly hit me — that's right! I almost forgot: We didn't have to ride with my parents anymore. Philip, who was a year older than me, had just gotten his driver's license the day before. We could ride to church on our own. What a pleasant thought that was.

It took Philip two attempts before he finally got his driver's license because he took his test with an older vehicle. Older vehicles required a series of additional tests where you had to control the car manually. A year ago, my dad had bought Philip a used 2015 Chevy Camaro ZL1, which turned into the motivation for Philip to get his license. As cheap as my dad was, there was no way that he was going to spend the money on a clean, efficient electric car or one of those solar-powered cars. Not to mention a flying car, which they were beta-flying down in Nevada. I couldn't wait to try one of those out someday.

No, we were stuck with an old Camaro. Most likely my dad, being who he was, was probably not going to buy another car for me next year. So this Camaro would belong to the both of us once I got my license.

The Camaro did have a nice, shiny exterior with a glossy, red-rock metallic color, but, then again, it still was a gas vehicle that got only 24 highway mpg — which was nothing compared to current vehicle standards. I wasn't sure how we were going to afford to drive this car with gas prices as high as they were. With the increased number of electric charging stations replacing gas pumps, filling up our car was an adventure in itself.

Everything was manual in this car — or, at least, it seemed that way: No voice recognition, no car-detection alert, no self-automation mode. I knew I shouldn't be complaining, because Philip sure wasn't. The look on his face was one of pride, to finally own a car. To him, this was a luxury. He didn't mind working on cars, but I couldn't say the same.

We got dressed, jumped into the Camaro, and finally arrived at Life Changers Community Church aka LCCC — or L3C, as most people called it. As we pulled into the parking lot, we could hear the music thumping through the doors — the sounds of praise and worship.

Rachel Matthews, your typical girl next door, was leading the worship with a song called "How Great Thou Art," an old classic hymn. Rachel went to our school. She was an average-looking, seventeen-year-old Caucasian girl, with green eyes and sandy brown hair — and the voice of an angel. My mother would always say, "Man, that girl can *sang*!"

L3C was located in Grand Lake, Missouri. This church was different from most churches. Unlike your typical congregations, that were segregated, with either predominantly white or black members, we had a multicultural church, with people of many ethnicities attending.

Also, unlike most churches, if you'd planned on coming to L3C and then afterwards planned on watching the afternoon Sunday football game, you'd have been sorely disappointed. Services there could get lengthy and go well into the day, surpassing the afternoon game time. It hadn't always been like this. Once upon a time, we could count on leaving church at the same time every Sunday, but things had changed.

You see, we'd just recently — about a year previous — gotten a new pastor. His name was Pastor Bruce Marino. An Italian man in his mid-forties, most considered him young for a pastor. Some members liked him, while others hated how he was changing things. All I knew was that, ever since he'd taken over, he took a long time preaching and lifting the offering, pleading with people to give.

Offering time was when I liked to sneak away to the restroom or even outside if I could get past the ushers and wait there until offering was over. I hated hearing about the church's needs and about what would happen to us if we didn't give — even though I knew that, if everyone felt this way, nothing would have gotten paid for in the church. I just wish there'd been a better way to raise money.

Philip and I entered into the sanctuary doors and headed to our usual seating area in the back of church. The back rows were where there was easy access to the exit and also where we could get a good look at everyone in the church. Since our parents were making us attend church, the one thing I could look forward to doing was hanging out with my friends in the back rows.

There was one person in particular I really wanted to see every Sunday. I could hear her sweet voice calling my name as we approached our seats. She was standing with her dreamy brown eyes, caramel skin complexion, and long wavy hair. "Hey, Johnny" she said, with her mesmerizing smile. When she smiled, the one dimple on her left cheek just enhanced her beauty all the more.

"Hey, Jazzy" I responded with a sheepish grin.

Jasmine Reed. "Jazzy" is what I called her. I'd known Jazzy ever since we'd been in fourth grade. I remembered when she was a new girl coming into the class. She'd stand there with yellow barrettes hanging from her two pigtails. She'd be clutching her Barbie lunch box, looking like she had stepped into another world. The teacher introduced her to the class, but no one was kind enough to invite her into their circle of friends.

One day in class, the teacher was passing out class work for us to fill out. I noticed that Jazzy didn't have anything to write with. While everyone was completing their worksheets, she just sat there quietly, too shy to ask for a pencil. So I reached over and gave her one of mine, and from that moment on, we connected and became good friends.

The strange thing is that, lately, our relationship had been changing. My feelings for her were becoming more complex. I didn't know why I was getting so jealous when other guys showed her attention. No longer did I see a little girl with pigtails and a Barbie lunch box. She looked different — all grown up, with a womanly figure that was filled out in all the right places. Sometimes I caught myself staring at her, and then I had to remind myself that this was Jazzy I was looking at, but I couldn't help it. I wanted to be more than just friends.

Another strange thing was, I was starting to notice her doing things that she normally didn't do in the past. For instance, I would catch her giving me random winks and smiles for no reason. This was putting me in an awkward place, not knowing if she was flirting with me or being playful. I thought, *Should I risk potentially destroying my friendship for a chance at something more?*

We sat at our seats in the back of the church. Many of the youth sat in the back, filling up a few rows. Philip, Jazzy, Pete, and I usually sat next to each other. Pete was my best friend, my partner in crime — really; he was like another brother to me. I had known Pete even longer than Jazzy. We had been tight ever since the second grade, pulling pranks on the teacher and sneaking into the movies together. Pete was the one who was always getting us into trouble and pushing the boundaries. With

Pete, I know that he would always have my back, and I could count on an adventure and a good laugh.

Laughing is what we did a lot — especially during praise and worship. Pete loved to joke about how different members of the church looked when they were praising God.

"Hey, there she goes, twirling around again in the middle of the aisle," Pete said, laughing, trying to imitate her movements.

"Who, Tameka 'Tutu'?" I questioned.

"Yeah, Mrs. Ballerina. Look at her. What is she doing?" he replied.

"Maybe she is auditioning for a play or something" I said, adding to his joke.

"Not with those moves."

"Or maybe she is just praising God," Philip cut in with a sharp tone.

"Whoa, man — what's up with you? If I didn't know any better, I would think that you like her or something," Pete replied.

"Yeah, man. Why are you trying to defend Tameka 'Tutu'?" I asked.

"I'm just saying, it looks like she is genuinely worshiping God," Philip answered.

"Look, I can understand if you like her, because, oh, my goodness, she does have a nice butt. Don't she?" Pete said, nudging Philip for a reply. "Tell the truth, I know what you are looking at, and it is not her worshiping," Pete said, embarrassing Philip a little.

"Whatever, dude. You are so immature," said Philip with a beet-red blush showing through his brown skin.

"Ew, boys?" Jazzy said with a tone implying her disgust about our conversation. "Pete and John — you need to stop talking about people, because one day it will come back on you," she said, rebuking us.

This, however, did not stop us from continuing our roasting of the saints in church. We spent the rest of praise and worship talking about the facial expressions on two college kids, Stephen "Deltoid Man" Ortega and Carl "Stank Face" Green. It was hilarious how Carl looked like he had just got a whiff of manure with the faces that he was making. Stephen's hands seemed to stay in the air during worship time. He had to have some strong shoulders. That's where the name "Deltoid Man" came from.

Making jokes about people was our normal routine every Sunday. I must admit that, really deep down, I secretly admired those who had the courage to freely praise God without worrying what others thought, because I didn't think that I was bold enough to.

My parents were somewhat strict about us paying attention during church. Every once in a while, I would catch my mother glaring at us from the choir stands with a look of disapproval, giving us the evil eye when we were getting rowdy in the back. My dad would not allow us to bring our digital tablets to church.

"You need to be listening to the preacher, not looking at that thing" he would always say. I tried to reason with him, claiming that I would use my tablet only to read the bible and take notes. His response was always, "You can do things the old-fashioned way — by bringing your bible, pen, and paper to church." *Who still does that, when you can easily do everything on one device?* I would think to myself, because I wouldn't dare say that aloud. That was my dad being strict, as always.

Praise and worship was over, the offering had been lifted, and the choir had sung. Now it was time for the preacher to preach. Today our pastor had invited a visiting pastor from out of town to preach. Surprisingly, he wasn't the stereotypical preacher who likes to hoot and holler or use dramatics, conjuring up emotions as though he was speaking compassionately to you. He wasn't the fake, smiling preacher, giving you a false sense of joy by saying, "Everything will be alright as long as you believe."

No — this preacher was a little bald man, a plain-speaking man, with no theatrics. He was a little boring at times and sometimes soft spoken, but he was actually holding my attention. I was impressed by his humility, and it seemed as though he really cared for God's people.

Normally, at this time of the service, I would be texting either Jazzy or Pete, since we were not allowed to talk above a whisper to each other. Because I couldn't use my tablet, I would normally use my phone or watch to communicate.

Pete sent me a text to look at Sister Jenkins bending over, with her low-cut dress, exposing some of her cleavage, and to look at Brother Ross, drooling as he slept in the choir stand during the sermon. I resisted the urge to reply or look at them. I was locked in and focused on what was being said. It felt like this preacher was speaking directly to me.

"You were born for a purpose, and this purpose can fully be known only through Jesus Christ," the preacher said. Those words pierced my heart and stuck in my mind. *Why was I created?* I asked myself.

The little bald man finally brought his sermon to a close and paused for a while, like he was thinking about something. Then, lifting his eyes, looking straight at me, he said, "Young man, God has a call on your life, but you are headed down the wrong path. You need to turn back to Jesus, or your end will not be good."

Is he talking to me? I looked back over my shoulder. *He must be mistaken*, I thought. Then he spoke again, pointing *directly* at me and quoting a bible verse: "There is a way that seems right to man, but its end is the way to death." His words sent a shiver down my spine and rang in my head, causing me to reevaluate my life.

18

CHAPTER

2

It was an unusually cool summer morning in Grand Lake, Missouri. The normal warm temperatures had, apparently, decided to take the morning off. The reddish-orange sun was beginning to peek its head over the horizon. There were sounds of birds chirping, refreshed and ready to commence their search for food. The aroma of hazelnut coffee filled the air.

I was in between the dream world and reality when I heard the beautiful sounds of the song "When We Meet Again" in the room across from me, which finally awakened me. Philip came into my room with his grease-stained mechanic's uniform on.

"Get up, sleepy head," he said.

"What time is it?" I asked in a scratchy voice, peeking out my window.

"Six-thirty."

"Six-thirty? It is way too early. My alarm hasn't rung yet. Why am I up?"

"I am about to leave, that's why. You betta get used to waking up early anyway, because in about two weeks, we will be going back to school," Philip reminded me.

"Where are you going?" I asked.

"Where does it look like I am going?" he said, pointing at his uniform and stating the obvious.

Philip was working as an apprentice under Mr. Roberts, a friend of my dad. He was letting Philip work part time at his auto-repair shop that summer so that he could make some extra money. Even though most of his money would probably go toward the high price of gas for his vehicle, he seemed to be content with his job. His job responsibilities were just keeping the shop clean and answering phones. Occasionally, Mr. Roberts would let him help out the mechanics if they were busy. Working on cars was my brother's passion, even more so since he had gotten his own car.

"Are mom and dad already gone?" I asked.

"They just left for work," he answered.

Downstairs, I could still smell — floating in the air, making its way to my nostrils — the pot of coffee my dad had brewed. I loved the smell of coffee but hated its taste.

"I am off to work, bro. Find something to do," Philip said as he left.

"Alright — see ya later," I replied.

I was sitting at the edge of my bed, with thoughts of the previous day still fresh in my mind. *Young man, God has a call on your life, but you are headed down the wrong path. You need to turn back to Jesus, or your end will not be good.* The preacher's words kept ringing in my head. I needed someone to talk to — someone to help me sort out my thoughts.

I texted Jazzy and Pete to see what they were doing. Jazzy was awake and replied:

Nothing — just watching The Morning Show. What's up?

There was no response from Pete, which probably meant that he was still sleeping.

I need to talk. Could we meet at our spot at the lake? Not sure if Pete will make it, I replied to Jazzy.

See you there. On my way, Jazzy answered.

I also left Pete a text telling him that we would be at the lake if he wanted to hang.

When we were younger, Jazzy and I used to always play at Clear View Lake, which was just a few miles from our homes. We even had a tree in the woods with our names carved into it saying, "Friends forever — John and Jaz."

As time went on, our visits to the lake decreased, and we used it only for emergency talks. I wasn't sure if this could be considered an emergency, but I needed to talk. I dusted off my old mountain bike that I hadn't ridden in some time. Since Philip had the car, my only options were to walk or ride my bike. Even if I had the car, I still wouldn't have been able to drive it. So the bike it was.

I finally arrived at the lake, and, to my surprise, Jazzy was already here. She was sitting on a large rock near the water, skipping stones. She looked gorgeous sitting there, with the wind blowing her hair back into the air. She was so focused on her task that she didn't even notice that I had arrived. I slowly tip-toed up behind her, stepping quietly over broken branches. I couldn't resist the opportunity to frighten her. So I eased my way behind her and gently tapped her on the shoulder, which caused her to belt out a terrified scream.

"John!" she hollered as she turned to see me. This caused me to erupt in laughter. "Don't do that — I almost fell into the water," she said as she gave me a hard punch to my arm.

"What's up girl?" I said, as I finally calmed down from my laughing. But she didn't respond. She turned her head away, ignoring my question.

"Come on — I know you're not mad at me for that."

"That wasn't cool, John."

"Okay...okay, I'm sorry. How did you get here so quickly?" I asked.

"Well, you seemed like you really needed to talk, and I was already dressed, so I left right after you texted me."

She was right. I really did need to talk, and I was glad that she was there with me. When I needed someone to have a good time with, Pete was the man, but when I needed to talk about more serious matters, Jazzy had always been the one I came to.

"So what's on your mind, John Mann?" she said, looking into my eyes with a comforting smile. We were both sitting on the large rock, looking out over the lake, where the geese were flying above, calling to each other.

"Well, you know, yesterday, when the preacher was talking to me? I can't seem to shake his words out of my head. I was thinking about what he was saying, about the call on my life, you know?" I said.

"That was kinda freaky how he pointed you out like that, John," she said.

"The funny thing was that I felt like he was talking to me the whole time during his sermon."

"So what do you think he meant when he said that you were going down the wrong path?"

"I don't know. I think that I'm a pretty good kid. I don't get into too much trouble. He couldn't have been talking about me." *Or could he?* The thought passed through my head. *Does he see something in me that I don't? No — this can't be,* I thought, trying to dismiss this thought.

He has to be a false preacher, I tried to convince myself, and, at that moment, something came over me, and I just started ranting: "You know, Jazzy, I'm not even sure any more about this Jesus thing. I mean, when I was younger, it was different. I used to love going to church and following my dad around. I even remember acting like I was preaching, with my hairbrush as a microphone, standing on top of my bed. I wanted to be a preacher so badly.

"Now I'm older, and I realize that that was a foolish dream. Most of the people in church don't even live a so-called 'Christian life.' No one can live up to God's standards." I was starting to feel the anger boil up in me, not knowing why, but I continued on my rant.

"They just come to church to feel better and then go out and do whatever they want the rest of the week. Hypocrites — that's what the church is made up of, and I don't know if I want to be a part of it.

"Just the other day, I saw Brother Ross stumbling out of the liquor store off of Main Street, and, the week before, I saw Sister Jones cursing out her kids at the grocery store. If this is what Christianity is all about, then I don't want any part of it," I said, fuming from all the suppressed emotions I had held inside about church folks.

A look of shock washed over Jazzy's face, wondering why I had just exploded into a long rant about people in the church.

"I've never seen you like this before, John. I didn't know you felt this way." Trying to sympathize with me, she continued, "I don't know much about this Jesus thing, either. I mean we were both raised in the church, and we've heard our fair share of sermons, but I don't see too many people living out what the bible teaches. I guess I believe there is a God — I just don't know if our view about God is right," she said.

I could tell that she was having a hard time trying to articulate her thoughts. I jumped in.

"Sometimes I wonder — if I had grown up in a family who were Muslims, would Islam be my faith? I probably would be believing in that," I said.

"Do you think we believe in Christianity only because our parents brought us up this way?"

23

"I don't know, but if the Jesus of the bible is real, I pray that he will reveal himself to me. Let me see somebody who is a true Christian. I want to know what is true."

"Amen to that," agreed Jazzy.

"Thanks for listening to me and letting me vent."

"That's what friends are for, right?" she said.

"Right, that's what friends are for."

We sat quietly for a while, just listening to the geese and watching the sunrise over the water. In the distance, we could see two deer passing through the woods. Jazzy broke our silence, still looking out at the sunrise, she asked, "What do you want to do after high school is over?"

"You're starting to sound like my parents now."

"Seriously — what do you want to do with your life?"

After a long pause, I answered, "Well, once high school is over, I can't wait to get out of this slow town and move to Southern California."

"Why California?" she asked.

"They have some of the top film schools in the country, and I am going to become the black Steven Spielberg of Hollywood."

"'Steven Spielberg' — who is that?" questioned Jazzy.

"He's a famous movie director. You know — *Jurassic Park, E.T,* and *Jaws.*"

"Oh, yeah — he made those old movies I hear my parents talking about."

"Yeah, those," I chuckled.

At this very moment, I wish I had brought my camera with me. The sunlight was reflecting off the water, shimmering right into Jazzy's face, causing a twinkle to appear in her eye. It was like a scene from a romantic movie, the sunrise and all — one that I couldn't have scripted. This was the perfect time for me to ask Jazzy about what had really been on my mind.

I summoned up enough courage and asked, "So, Jazzy, why don't you have a boyfriend?"

"Why do you ask?" she calmly replied, catching me off guard. Not the reply I was expecting.

"Well, you are a pretty girl, and I see a lot of guys coming to talk to you, but you don't seem interested in any of them."

"So you think I'm pretty, huh?" she said.

"No — I mean, other boys think you are. I mean, if I wasn't your friend, I might think you — are pretty."

Jazzy just started guffawing at me. I can only imagine how I looked, stumbling through my words.

"You look so cute when you do that thing with your nose"

"What thing?" I said, somewhat angered by her laughing at me.

"You know — how you scrunch your nose when you get nervous or when you're lying about something."

My cheeks began to blush.

"Whatever," I said, trying to dismiss her comment.

"I know you, John, and I think it is adorable. To answer your question: Maybe I have been waiting for the right person to ask me out," she said, pulling her bangs behind her ears and scooting closer to me. This time there was no doubt about the signals that she was giving me. If there had ever been a time to advance our relationship, now was the time.

"Jazzy?"

"Yes, John."

"I have something I have been wanting to ask you for a while." I said, pausing as my heart started racing. Suddenly, I'd become conscious of me scrunching my nose in nervousness. "Would ... would?"

Jazzy moved even closer until she was touching me hip to hip and arm to arm. "Would you like — ?"

"Hey, what's up, my people?" Pete said, interrupting my confession, causing Jazzy and me to abruptly pull away from each other. As a result, I went tumbling down the side of the large rock into the grass.

"What is going on here?" Pete asked, grinning at us.

Neither one of us had noticed that he had arrived. He seemed to appear out of nowhere. How much of the conversation had he heard?

"Nothing — we were just talking about stuff," I quickly said.

"I should probably be going. My mom will be messaging me soon," Jazzy said, trying not to look at us.

"But I just got here. I got your text. What is this 'emergency talk' supposed to be about?" Pete asked.

"I'll see you later, Pete, Johnny," Jazzy said, looking at me with a grin, showing her dimple. I timidly waved goodbye as she walked away. After she left, I turned, only to catch Pete glaring at me with a wide smirk on his face.

"Did you two finally realize that you like each other?"

"What are you talking about?" I said, acting clueless.

"Come on, John. Everybody knows that you two like one another. My advice: You'd better snatch her up before one of these other guys do. I know that Triston Stewart has had his eye on her."

"You're probably right," I said, finally resigning myself to my feelings.

"I know I'm right. So I guess this lake meeting is adjourned, huh?"

"Talk to you later, Pete."

"I came all the way out here for nothing?" Pete said with his hands in the air. "Alright. Later, lover boy."

I hopped on my bike to ride but before I could begin to pedal, my phone started vibrating. I checked my phone, and I had a text from Jazzy that simply said, *I would love to.*

CHAPTER

3

"Hey, dad."

"Hey, son. What have you been doing?"

"I just finished Aunt Jenny's video montage."

"The one for her fiftieth-birthday celebration?"

"Yes, sir."

"Do you know where your brother is?"

"He's in the garage, working on the car. What are you watching?" I asked.

"It's the Democratic National Convention. Senator Cordell Wright is about to accept his nomination. This should be interesting," my dad said sarcastically. The two things that usually make people uncomfortable talking about are religion and politics. These were the two things that my dad was passionate about, and he was not afraid to express his opinion on either one. This year happened to be a presidential-election year.

To me, politicians were nothing but a bunch of slick liars who don't keep their promises once they are elected. It doesn't matter who you vote for, anyway. It is already decided who will win. Someone or some group already has this thing planned out — at least that's my opinion.

My dad and I sat on the couch watching the TV. My brother was working on replacing the rims on his car, and my mom was cooking dinner and having a video chat with her friend Mrs. Wilson, Tameka's mom.

On the television, there were signs with the senator's campaign slogan saying, "United as One" everywhere. Balloons filled the convention, colored red, white, and blue. People were waving flags and everyone seemed to be having a good time as the music blasted.

A tall, distinguished tan-colored man with black hair and gray temples came from the back door, smiling. Senator Wright approached the podium with a swagger, a look of confidence. The music was booming while everyone was on their feet, giving him a standing ovation.

"Thank you...thank you...thank you," he said, waiting for the applause to cease. "To all my fellow Americans, to all those who are ready for a nation to be united and guided by peace and tolerance. With profound gratitude and great humility, I accept your nomination for presidency of the United States of America." The crowd roared with excitement as the camera cut to a woman in the audience jumping for joy. With his hands, the senator gestured to calm the audience down. After the long applause died down, he continued with his speech.

"Let me first thank all the candidates in this great party. I'm honored to represent you. I would also like to take a moment to recognize my lovely wife, the next first lady, and my running mate and next vice president, Jim Lackey." More applause came from the crowd.

"For the last four years, this nation has been taking steps backward. President Sandra Copperfield has only been isolating this great nation from the rest of the world by her unwillingness to convert to a more stable universal currency. She is promoting her religious bigotry through her faith-based initiatives, which are funding religious extremists. This must stop!" The camera panned to a little girl on her father's shoulder, nodding with approval and waving her little flag.

"In order for this nation to advance, we must be one, we must be willing to work with other like-minded countries, and we must be tolerant of everyone's beliefs. Who are we to deny Mary and Sue from raising a child in a loving home? Who are we to deny thirteen-year-old Sally treatment to terminate a pregnancy that could take her hope of a future away? What gives us the right to spew hateful dogma to those who don't think like us? I say no one. No one should deny two parents the right to raise children in a loving home regardless of their sexual orientation. No one should take a child's future away because of a mistake that was made. No one should feel harassed by religious extremists because their views are different.

"Yet President Copperfield, with her archaic belief, is trying to reverse the progress that we have made with the Marriage Act. She is trying to make Sally get permission from her mother before she is able to correct her mistake. Whose body is it anyway? President Copperfield is promoting religious-extremist groups through her faith based pro—."

"This country is going to hell!" my dad blurted out at the TV. "If this devil is elected, America is headed for its destruction." Turning off the TV, my dad was visibly upset by Senator Wright's speech. I really think he was more disturbed by how the audience seemed to be falling in love with this man and the media portrayal of him being somewhat of a savior to us. My dad looked at me and said, "The time is upon us when we will not be able to freely express our faith. Are you ready, son?" he asked.

"Time to eat" my mother yelled from the kitchen, interrupting our conversation. "John, go get your brother."

"Yes, ma'am" I replied.

I was glad my mom cut in because, honestly, I didn't know how much I was willing to be persecuted for something or someone I'm not sure about.

After I had called out to Philip several times, he finally came from the garage, trying to wipe his greasy black hands on his shirt.

Guided by the sweet aroma from the kitchen, we both tried to reach for a piece of chicken, but my mom quickly smacked our hands away. "Not until you wash your hands. You, too, honey," she said, looking at my dad, as he was about to bite into a chicken leg.

"Yes, dear," he replied. We all cleaned up and sat down at the table.

"Can you believe that Senator Wright?" my dad said, still fuming from the senator's remarks.

"I know, honey, but before we start talking about politics, let's bless the food," said mom.

"You're right. John, why don't you bless the food today," dad suggested.

So I began with my usual prayer — the one that I'd been reciting since I was five years old. "Dear Lord, thank you for this food, for the money to buy it, and for the hands that made it. Let this be good to our bodies. Amen."

My family tried to make the tradition of eating at the table together a priority. It didn't happen all the time, but the majority of the time, it did. That day was soul-food day at our house, my favorite. On the menu was fried chicken, sweet potatoes, greens, and butter rolls, with sweet tea as the beverage. My mom was a mean cook. With three ravenous males in the house, she knew how to quench our hunger and bring a smile to our stomachs.

"If Senator Cordell Wright ends up winning this election…" my dad said, clenching his jaws tight with anger, not wanting to finish his statement.

"What, dad? What do you think will happen?" Philip curiously egged him on.

My mom answered, "Well, dear, if he wins, that will mean the beginning of persecution against us, the church." I could tell that both of my parents were serious about their belief that doom was coming to America, especially to the church.

This caused my dad to go on one of his spiritual-political rants. "You see, boys, this is how Satan gets people to accept sin. First he gets you to laugh at the act of sin. Then he slowly presents sin in a way that you will accept it, even though you may not agree with it. The famous saying, 'It's OK for you but not for me' is a lie. Next, we become comfortable with sin. We are desensitized to violent acts, sexual images, and perversions. It doesn't bother us like it used to. Finally his last step is to have you believe that anyone who opposes this view is not tolerant but hateful.

"We, as a nation, are entering into the last phase. The United States is morally declining. We want to legalize sin. This is what the senator is promoting, and this is what we must fight against. He wants to eliminate God from this country. If he can't do that, then he wants to dilute the meaning of God, and anyone who disagrees with him won't just be opposing his opinion but violating the law."

I could see the fire blazing in my dad's eyes as he spoke with both fists clenched on the table. My mom, trying to lighten the mood in the room, said, "Okay, babe. That's enough about politics. You know, last I checked, God is still in control, no matter what events may happen." She placed her hands on my dad's balled fists.

"You're right, honey. God is in control," he said, relaxing a bit.

Switching subjects, my mom asked us, "So, how is school going?"

We were only a few weeks into the school year. Last year, my freshman year, I was entering a foreign land where time sped up, the hallways were bigger, with no compass to guide me to class, causing tardiness to be a regular occurrence. Nervousness bubbled in my stomach; I was a little person in the land of giants. Now as a sophomore, having one year under my belt, I knew the ropes. I was familiar with my surroundings and didn't have to ride the bus anymore.

I rode to school with Philip and sometimes Pete, when his mom let him drive her car. Pete had just gotten his driver's license. His birthday was late — a week after the deadline from the start of school. So, Pete, then sixteen, had always been one of the older kids in our grade.

That summer, I had grown four inches, now standing at a lanky 6'3". I had also let my hair grow out over the summer, styling an afro, which made me look even taller. I had to say that I was feeling pretty good about the upcoming year. I stood out above my friends, there was no more bus riding, and I had someone to call my lady. Yep, life was good.

"Everything is good," I answered my mom.

Philip almost choked on his chicken wing hearing me say, "Everything is good."

"I bet everything is good for 'Johnzmine,'" he said, with a laugh.

"'Johnzmine'?" my dad questioned. A light went off in my mom's head. She understood what Philip was saying.

"Oh, that must be the name that the kids are giving John and Jazmine at school," my mom explained to my dad.

"Yeah, 'Johnzmine,'" Philip repeated with laughter.

It had been weeks since my talk with Jazzy at Clear View Lake. That ride home seemed like I was pedaling in the air, floating on love. Jazzy and I were now dating.

I couldn't stop thinking about her, her contagious laughter, her gentle touch, and her distinct scent — like an ocean-breeze fragrance — which smells so good. Even though we had been friends for a long time, I still looked forward to seeing her face each day. It was official then. On my social-network sites, my status was now displayed as "in a relationship" for the whole world to see. This whole boyfriend/girlfriend thing was new to me. I'd never had a girlfriend before, and I couldn't imagine being with anyone else.

Our parents still would not allow us to go on dates alone. We had to be accompanied by a chaperone. Usually Philip, Pete, or Jazzy's step-brother would accompany us. We still managed somehow to sneak away in private at times, especially before or after school.

Walking through the hallways at school, Jazzy and I were insepa-rable. Thus came the name "Johnzmine." I hated the name, but Jazzy did-n't seem to mind. The kids in school viewed us as one person. I don't know why, but Philip thought that name was so funny.

"Speaking of girls," my mom said, looking at Philip. "I saw that you and Tameka were talking a lot to each other during our Wednesday class."

On Wednesday nights, our church normally would be divided into classes, according to age group. However, for the past six weeks, the pas-tor had asked all those in the congregation who were twelve years old or older to assemble together. Those who were younger would still have their regular classes. Pastor Bruce began his series called *The Last Days.*

The first three weeks of the series, everyone was assembled to-gether while the pastor explained what was to come of the church and why prophecy was so important. The next three weeks, Pastor Bruce de-cided to break the congregation up into small groups, to dialogue about what had been taught and to discuss what our roles were in the church. The pastor assigned leaders in the church to facilitate these groups. The elders, deacons, and youth leaders were the facilitators. The church was broken up into about ten small-group classes. In my small group, twenty-year-old Stephen "Deltoid Man" Ortega was my facilitator. He was one of our youth leaders. My group included Carl "Stank Face" Green, Ra-chel Matthews, Hannah Jay, Jazzy, myself, and a young couple who had just joined the church.

My dad was a facilitator for a class which my mother and brother were a part of. I didn't know that Tameka was in their class. Philip failed to mention this to me.

"Tameka 'Tutu' Wilson?" I blurted out.

Philip defended himself. "Man, she is alright, once you get to know her. We were just talking as friends, and, besides, she is two years older than me."

We all knew that was an excuse that he told himself to have as a reason not to like her. "She is two years older than me." I could tell Philip was embarrassed by my Mom's statement. I didn't know brown skin could turn red so easily from blushing.

My mom continued, "That Tameka is a good girl, a dedicated Christian, and, when, she dances, it is like she has fire shut up in her bones that she has to dance out."

Philip and Tameka Wilson? Now *I* was the one laughing at the kitchen table. *Wait until I tell Pete about this one,* I thought to myself.

"Young love," said my dad.

"Oh, the days," mom said with a whimper, looking off into space, reminiscing. "I remember when your dad had that same look in his eyes like you boys have... Oh, the days."

"Come on, honey — I don't have that look anymore?" dad questioned her.

Silence was my mom's response.

"Well you still make my eyes twinkle," dad said as he leaned over and planted a big one on her lips. After their long, disgusting kiss, my mom rose with a smile of embarrassment on her face. Every so often, my parents would do this — act as though Philip and I were not in the same room. All I could say was "Disgusting."

"Come on, dad!" said Philip, equally disgusted.

"Sorry, boys. I can't help that your mother still looks so fine."

"Stop it, Kevin," my mom said, red-faced, as she gave him another peck on his cheek.

"Really?" I said, rolling my eyes. They finally got the hint that we'd had enough of the lovey-dovey stuff.

"So what are we going to be talking about tomorrow in class, dad?" Philip asked, with excitement in his voice.

Over the past few weeks, a lot had changed with my brother. I wasn't sure what was going on with him. Ever since we had been going through this bible series on Wednesdays, his whole outlook had changed — like he was a new person. Just a few days before, I'd caught him kneeling down in prayer next to his bed before we left for school. All he talked about now is the bible and wanting to know more about Jesus.

He kept trying to get me to meet Stephen and Carl at our church. They were the two people we normally made fun of every Sunday. I didn't want to have anything to do with those super saints. Lately, Philip had been spending a lot of time with them, going to bible studies and praying. He was not even sitting next to us during church service anymore. He had moved closer to the front of the church, with Stephen and Carl.

"Well, I have been studying about the anti-Christ and his role in the last days. Pastor Bruce wants us to touch on this subject tomorrow." Dad answered Philip.

The way that my dad talked about Senator Wright and seeing how angry he got at the mention of his name, one might have thought that my dad considered the Senator to be the anti-Christ — the one who, in the last days, would rule this world and force everyone to take a mark to worship him.

"So, dad, do you think that Senator Cordell Wright is the anti-Christ that the bible talks about?" I asked.

He paused for a while and then answered, "No, I don't think that he is, but I believe that he is just a piece that will help usher the one who is the anti-Christ or "The Beast" into the world. This is why I am passionate about my stand against him. I can just see the agenda of a one-world government coming into fruition. We are approaching dark times, son. God is calling all believers to prayer, to stand their ground, and to fight for the faith."

CHAPTER

4

That particular Wednesday, the sun was shining bright late into the day, with no hint of bowing down to the night. It had been a stress-free day, riding shotgun in my brother's car, on our way to church, with the windows down, as the wind blew, caressing our faces. One advantage of riding in a slower vehicle is that you have more time to enjoy the ride and look at the beauty of God's creation.

Philip said, "I want you to meet Stephen and Carl after church today. Is that alright?"

"Why are you hanging out with those super saints?" I finally asked the question that had been bugging me.

"The only thing super about them is the one who lives in them."

"Oh boy, you are starting to sound like a preacher now. Man, what has been going on with you lately?" I questioned. "Ever since we have been going through this bible series, you have changed, man."

"I just realized that our time on Earth is short and that, whatever my purpose is for existing, I want to complete it. I just want to be pleasing in God's sight. When I meet God, I want him to say, 'Well done.' I am tired of 'playing church,' John. I decided either I was going to leave Christianity or go all in. I'm all in. Don't you see God is going to use the youth in these last days? I don't know how I know, but I can just feel, it and I want to be a part of this. I want you to be a part of this, too," he replied.

Philip spoke with such assurance and peace. One thing was undeniable, and that was that something really had changed in my brother. The once loudmouth, wise-cracking brother had settled down and now was into church.

I, on the other hand, was still not sure about Christianity. But I knew that I had nothing to lose if I talked with Stephen and Carl. Maybe I would get Philip off my back.

"Alright, I will listen to them." I reluctantly conceded.

That day was the last week of the bible series called *The Last Days* on Wednesdays. Stephen, my facilitator, was talking about something like how we as a church needed to humble ourselves and pray for this nation.

Jazzy and I were halfway paying attention to him speak, checking out our watches, counting down the time to when we could leave. All I could remember was Stephen stressing the importance of fellowship between Christians and how we would need each other even more in times to come. This seemed to prompt a question from the husband of the new couple in our group.

"Is it necessary to go church? Can't we still be effective Christians without attending church?" the husband asked.

Those were my thoughts exactly. Why do we have to come to church?

Even though Stephen was attempting to answer the man's questions, the answers that he gave didn't seem to suffice for the husband or for me.

Pastor Bruce was walking from group to group, monitoring how each group was doing. When he came to our group, he could see that Stephen was struggling to find the right answer to the husband's questions. Stephen, looking at the pastor, said, "Pastor Bruce — could you help me with this man's question?"

"Sure, could you repeat the question" he said.

The husband expounded, "Pastor, my wife and I have been looking for a church home for more than a year now. I definitely enjoy attending church here, but I can also stay home and get good teaching, too. There are a ton of bible resources, video streaming, virtual churches, and books available. Why come to church and leave the comfort of my home, when I can have my own personal relationship with God?"

The pastor responded, "You know, that's a good question, Marcus — right?"

"Yes sir," the husband replied. He was pleasantly surprised that the pastor remembered his name.

Pastor Bruce continued, "Well, Marcus, first of all, in Hebrews 10:25, God commands us not to forsake assembling together — we should exhort each other. When you become a believer, you are part of the universal church, which is Christ's body, but Christ also wants you to be part of a local church, where you can be edified, equipped, and replenished. Where two or three believers gather together, he will be in their midst.

Did you know that Jesus went to the synagogue, or church, regularly? It's true. Check it out in Luke 4:16. Now, if it was Jesus' custom to go to church regularly, what should you be doing?"

This seemed to satisfy Marcus' curiosity.

The pastor spoke again to our group. "God's church is called to evangelize to the unbelievers, to edify the believers, and to exalt the Lord. He has given each one of us gifts that are to be used to help each other in the church. I just want to encourage each of you to keep seeking the Lord, getting all that he has for you." As he was leaving, he turned and said, "Keep up the good work, Stephen."

"Thank you, pastor."

I guess I never looked at it like that. I mean, if Jesus, the Lord, went to church, I guess I should, too. This was the last day of our *The Last Days* series, and class was ending. After class, Jazzy left with her mom. I stayed to talk with Philip, Stephen, and Carl for a while.

"So, what did you think about our class?" Carl asked.

"I guess Stephen is an alright teacher," I said, jokingly. Not knowing how to reply, Stephen just gave a half-grin.

I must admit Stephen was different than I expected him to be. He was not as bad as I thought — a handsome guy, of Latin descent, with an olive skin complexion, clean cut, dark, wavy hair, and well spoken. It was strange that I'd never seen him flirting with any of the girls at our church. At first I had questions about his "orientation," — if you know what I mean. After talking to him, I found out that he was actually shy when it came to girls and so focused when it came to the things of God that he sometimes was clueless of the interest girls were giving him.

However, the person who surprised me the most of the two was Carl. I hadn't expected that he would be so comical. He told me that growing up as an overweight, freckle-faced, red-headed boy had made him an easy target for teasing from kids. He was still red-headed, freckle-faced, and overweight. That hadn't changed.

He had quick-wit humor and the ability to point out others' weaknesses easily. He said that, while he was growing up, they were his weapons of defense. He could go toe to toe with anyone in a "Yo mama" battle. I was just glad that he didn't do that anymore. If only he knew how many times Pete and I had made fun of him during church, I don't think that he'd have been so accepting of me right then.

Surprisingly, I actually had a good time talking with them. Before we ended our conversation, Stephen spoke to me.

"Hey, John. Do you remember when that preacher came from out of town about a month ago? He said to you that God had a call on your life but that you were going down the wrong path."

"I remember" I answered. How could I forget?

"Well, I was talking about today in class how we as Christians need to have fellowship with each other, so we can be accountable. John, I can see that God has something special for you, but you must surrender to him."

Now the truth had come out. *This* is why my brother wanted me to talk to these guys, as I suspected. Trying to get me to give my life to Jesus. Philip should have known better. We had been raised in the church, and this message was not new to me. Besides, I'd done that when I was nine years old.

However, Stephen didn't press the issue of my salvation. I wasn't sure if he could sense that I didn't want to hear what he was saying or if my facial expression was giving away my discomfort with the conversation. His last words to me were, "Bad company corrupts good character. Be careful with whom you choose to be friends."

Why he said that to me, I had no idea, but those words hit me like a ton of bricks — the same way the visiting preacher's words had. I felt like it was a warning that I needed to heed.

* * * * *

I will be @ your place in 10 mins. Be ready, Pete's text read.

"You riding with me today? Philip asked.

"Nah. Pete should be here in ten minutes. Go ahead and go to school."

"Alright. Don't be late, bro."

That day, I had agreed to ride with Pete to school since his mom had let him borrow her car — plus I hadn't spent much time with him. My relationship with Pete was kind of weird then. Sometimes I felt like I was abandoning him because lately I had been spending so much time with Jazzy. We hadn't hung out at all the past few weeks. So, that day, I had decided to spend some time with my best friend. Pete arrived at my house to take me to school.

"Yo. Wassup, Johnzmine?" Pete yelled from the car.

"Man, not you, too?"

"What? You don't like that name?" he chuckled.

"Funny — ha ha," I said sarcastically. "You would think people could come up with a cleverer name than that," I added.

"I hear ya."

"Anyways, where you been hiding, man?" I said.

"Me? You're the one who's been wrapped up in Jazzy World," he retorted, stinging me with his words.

"Sorry, man. This whole 'girlfriend' thing is new to me."

"It's all good. Hey, I have some friends I want you to meet today."

"Cool. When? After school?"

"Nah. During school."

"During?"

"Yeah. After lunch, we'll meet them near the gas station next to that new Mexican restaurant."

"So you plan on skipping class?" I questioned.

"Yeah — you down?" Skipping class is something I had never done or thought to do. "I know you hate Mr. Donovan's class," Pete added.

It was true. Mr. Donovan, my World History teacher, was dry as dust, but I could hear the faint voice of Stephen in my head: "Bad company corrupts good character." And I didn't even want to think about what my parents would do if they knew I'd skipped school.

"Come on, man. Have some fun!" Pete pleaded.

Without even thinking, I answered, "Alright, I'm down." I tried to justify my ditching class as spending time with Pete, but, inside, I knew it was wrong.

"Meet me at lunch today, so we can sneak out," he said.

My whole time in school that day, I was nervous and uneasy about my decision to leave early with Pete. Now the time had finally come. It was lunch time. Passing through the hallways, it felt like every teacher was looking at me or looking through me. Did they know what I was about to do?

I went through the lunch line and got my lunch. I wasn't even sure what food was on my plate: Some kind of meat — possibly Salisbury steak — with vegetables. Not being able to identify lunch food was a common thing, ever since they'd started enforcing the "No Junk Food" policy at our school. I spotted Pete at our table.

"You ready to do this?" he said.

"I guess. Who are we meeting?"

"It's a surprise. When the buzzer sounds for lunch, exit out near the gym, and meet me at the car."

"Alright." This morning, Pete had parked his car across the street from the school. This was so he would not be stopped by security when entering and exiting the school parking lot.

The buzzer sounded. I paused for a moment as I heard the same soft voice saying, "Bad company corrupts good character." *What am I doing? I shouldn't —.*

"John...John!" Pete said, snapping me from my thoughts.

"Let's go...come on!" he urged me.

Knowing that I should not be leaving, I strode toward the exit doors anyway. I arrived near the gym exit. I snuck out before anyone could see me and before another thought could come to my mind — a thought that would convince me to stay at school.

I was outside the building and dashing toward the light-blue Toyota Camry parked at the church across the street from the school. I entered in on the passenger's side, where Pete was greeting me with a joker -like smile.

"Yeah, that's my boy!" exclaimed Pete, elated by my decision to join him. "How does it feel — your first time skipping class?"

I just laughed, as the adrenaline was flowing through my body. I knew that this was wrong, but I had to admit that it felt good. The mixed emotions of excitement and fear rushed through my body, heightening my senses. Doing something that I shouldn't felt so good.

We drove away from the school with the radio blaring to the popular song of the year called "It's My Life — I Do What I Want." Pete had always been a little mischievous, but, that day, he had a different look about him. It was like he believed the song that was playing, leaning back in his seat with a proud look. What was happening to my friend?

"Where are we going?" I asked.

"Like I said, we're going to meet some friends."

"Who?" I demanded.

"Whoa — chill, alright? I just want you to meet Todd Combs."

"Todd, the one who is part of that gang called 'The Renegades'?"

"Gang," Pete laughed. "Nah. It's more like a brotherhood."

"Why do you want me to meet them?"

"I'm trying to help you out. You see this?" Pete pulled out a wad of cash. "You hang with these guys, and you can get this, too. Maybe you can buy that new camera you always talk about."

"How could you — "

"Hey, we are here. Let's go," Pete said, cutting me off before I had a chance to finish my question.

We arrived at an old, paint-chipped, abandoned building with boarded windows and rusting rails. Trash was everywhere, and the smell was repulsive. Across the street was a new Mexican restaurant that had just opened. We pulled to the back of the building, where four other teen-agers were huddled, leaning against the wall in a conversation.

"Yo, T-Dog," Pete yelled to Todd.

"My man, P-Money" he replied. *"T-Dog" and "P-Money" — what kind of names are those? "T-Dog!" How many gang members are called that? It's a pretty generic name. And "P-Money"! What is Pete — some kind of big dealer, pimp, or something?* I was trying to contain my laughter.

"Is something funny?" a voice said. "Who is this dude?" one of the four boys asked, looking at me with an intimidating look. I noticed that he had a long scar across his face, like he had been in a fight with a switchblade and lost.

"Yeah, P-Money: Why you bring this chump here?" another boy said.

All of a sudden, I was starting to feel threatened as the boys approached me. The boy with the scar was just inches away from my face, looking at me eye to eye.

"I thought this was supposed to be a private meeting," he said to T-Dog.

"He's cool. This is my boy, my partner since grade school," Pete spoke up as the scarred-face boy started reaching for something in his back pocket. I clenched my fists, anticipating a brawl to occur.

T-Dog jumped in between the two of us. "Everybody relax" he calmly said. "So this is your friend, huh?" T-Dog said to Pete.

"Yeah. He's cool."

"He betta be" he said giving me a wry smile. "Today is your lucky day. I brought you gifts." T-Dog reached into his worn, ripped coat pocket and pulled out a paper bag. Inside the paper bag is several small plastic bags with something blue inside them.

"Is that what I think it is?" one of the other boys said.

"Yes, it is — a fresh batch." T-Dog pulled out one of the blue items from the small plastic bag. This, my friend, is what we call '*Blue*.'"

Blue was a potent drug that had recently overtaken the Kansas City area. It was a round, quarter-sized, paper-thin, blue-looking wafer. I'd heard it said that it was a mix of a lot of different drugs. All it took was one to get you addicted. The wafer was placed on your tongue and dissolved, giving you an instant high lasting for about an hour.

"This *Blue* is going to bring me *green*," T-Dog said, rubbing his fingers together as the other boys joined in on his laughter. "Would you like to try this?" T-Dog said to me, dangling the plastic bag of *Blue* in my face. "The first one is free," he chuckled.

I could feel the pressure from the group of boys, and I could see Pete joining in with their plot. I thought, *What has happened to my friend? This is a totally different Pete than I knew. Why was he trying so desperately to fit in with these losers?* I couldn't understand.

God has a call on your life, but you are headed down the wrong path. The preacher's words kept repeating in my head.

"Nah. I'll pass," I said.

"I thought you said your boy was cool," T-Dog said to Pete, speaking to him like I wasn't present. "Why don't you show him how it's done, P-Money?" the scarred-face boy said. I could see the nervousness on Pete as he tried to conceal his agitation. Sweat rolled down his face as he reached his trembling hand into the small plastic bag and pulled out the thin blue wafer.

"You want to be one of us? Take it!" T-Dog demanded of Pete.

Pete slowly brought the wafer to his lips, but, before he could place it on his tongue, I knocked it out of his hand.

"Yo! What are you doing?" I pleaded to Pete.

"Wussy! Give it here," said the scarred-face boy as he swiped the wafer off the ground and placed it on his tongue. In a matter of seconds, he fell to the ground and suddenly started convulsing, shaking as his eyes rolled back into his head and foam built in the corners of his mouth.

"What's going on?" Pete frantically said.

"He must have gotten a bad batch," T-Dog said. "You can stay and see what happens, but I am out of here" T-Dog and the other boys hustled to their vehicles, leaving their friend behind.

"Let's go," Pete yelled to me. We both ran in panic as the boy was still bouncing up and down on the ground, with more foam oozing out his mouth. "Are you just going to leave him?" I asked."Get in the car," yelled Pete.

CHAPTER

5

The man on the television spoke: "Good evening from the Pavilion in North Texas. I'm Clive Duncan from the GSTH news network. I welcome you to the first of three debates between President Sandra Copperfield and Senator Cordell Wright. Tonight's ninety minutes will be about domestic issues."

That day was the first debate of the presidential debates, and my family was gathering around the TV to view the debate. Dad was in his favorite chair, the recliner with two worn-down arm sleeves Mom was lying across the sectional, and Philip was on the floor, finishing up his homework. I was on the two-seat couch with my tablet, checking my social sites.

"Here we go. Let's see what you have to say, Senator," Dad said, leaning forward as the moderator spoke again. "I ask that, here in the Pavilion, you remain silent. There should be no distractions, so that we may hear our candidates. The only exception that I will make is now as I welcome President Copperfield and Senator Wright."

The crowd let forth a thunderous applause with whistling as each candidate entered, shook hands, waved to the crowd, and then approached their podiums.

After the applause, the moderator said, "I would like to welcome you both. Let's start with the topic of our economy. Let's begin with this question. What is the plan for future job growth in this country? Mrs.

President, you have won the coin toss. You will answer first. You have two minutes, Mrs. President."

A carved-ebony woman, with neatly silver locks, President Copperfield stood erect, pausing a moment before presenting her case. Her face relaxed as she let out a gentle smile.

"Thank you very much, Clive, for this opportunity. I would like to thank Senator Wright and thank the Pavilion for your hospitality. Four years ago, I gladly accepted the challenge of leading this great nation. One of my goals was to bring back jobs to the United States of America. In order for America to become the strong nation that we once were, we have to become producers again — not just consumers. Over these past four years, employment has increased, and unemployment has decreased from 12 percent to 5 percent. My administration has been bringing jobs back to America by creating new jobs and not sending our businesses overseas.

"We plan on continuing these strategies by encouraging Americans to pursue a higher education by reducing student loans and offering debt forgiveness to those who earn it. Our goal is to have a well-educated and skilled nation. So to answer your question, my plan is to continue with this strategy because it has proven results."

"Okay, Senator. You have two minutes to respond. What do you say?" said the moderator.

"Well, thank you, Clive. I would also like to thank the Pavilion for hosting this event and to thank the President. Mrs. President, I cannot deny that you have made some improvements to the status of the American people. Jobs have increased, and unemployment has decreased, but I'm afraid that your plan is only a temporary fix for the United States. Even though more jobs have come to America, the American dollar is steadily decreasing in value. People will have jobs to work, but the money they receive is only losing its buying power, causing more to work longer and harder trying to make ends meet.

"I say that we must consider joining with our allies and converting to a more stable system, the universal dollar, called 'Sync'"

"One world government is what it sounds like to me," dad blurted out. Talking to the television, for him, is a regular occurrence.

"Shh..." mom said with her finger over her mouth. "Trying to hear what is being said."

My dad just rolled his eyes and bit his lip as he struggled to keep quiet. I, personally, had had enough of all this political talk. I tuned out and decided to text Jazzy to see what was up.

Hey, what u doin beautiful? I texted. Two minutes later, I got a reply.

Nothing, handsome. Just watching this boring debate with my mom and stepdad. It's on just about every channel.

Yeah, me too. I will be glad when all this is over, I replied. Then I added, *I have been thinking about u.*

Aw.

I have something I want to give u. I will be by tonight.

Tonight? It's late.

I know. Just listen for me, OK?

OK.

Time passed, and, after several outburst and interruptions from my dad, the debate finally came to an end. The way things were looking, this first debate seemed to have gone in the senator's favor. The news reporters at GSTH were praising Senator Wright for his stage presence and eloquence in speech. They said that President Copperfield was stiff and not engaged as much as they would have liked.

I finally decided to head to my room for bed — at least that's what my family thought. Once everyone had fallen asleep, I grabbed my jacket and snuck out my bedroom window. Outside my window was a sturdy tree that I used for my escape. My bike was on the side of the house, ready to go. I hopped on it and headed toward Jazzy's house.

I arrived at Jazzy's house and turned into stealth mode, as I sidled around the house to the back, where Jazzy's room was located. Jazzy's bedroom was on the second level, accessible from a nearby tree. I climbed up the tree and gently tapped on her window. I was trying to be careful not to wake anyone, but I also wanted to make sure that she heard me. I whispered, "Jazzy."

After a long pause, I whispered again, with a louder voice, "Jazzy." A lamplight came on, and I saw a silhouette approaching the window. I moved back to the side of the window, trying to hide, not sure who was coming. The window opened and someone looked out.

"John, is that you?" I exhaled at the sound of her familiar voice, relieved that it was Jazzy at the window.

"Hey."

"What are you doing here?" she whispered, embarrassed that I was catching her in her sleepwear. Her pajamas had drawings of little kittens all over them, her hair was wrapped, and she was without makeup. She still looked lovely to me, even without makeup and a hair wrap.

"I told you I was coming. Can I come in?"

"No! My parents would kill me if they knew I had a boy in my room. Wait a minute. I'm coming out." One minute turned into ten. She finally came out the window, wrapped in her jacket and her long wavy hair released from the hair wrap.

"What are you really doing here, Johnny?"

"I just want to hang out with my girl."

"At this time in the night?" she replied.

"I'm just tired of always having a chaperone. I want to spend some time with you, alone — not with your step brother, my brother, or our parents. Me and you — that's all."

Jazzy smiled and lay her head on my shoulder as we both sat on her rooftop, looking out onto the brisk, open field that was in her backyard. She rubbed her hand through my hair.

"What are you doing with your hair?" she asked.

"Nothing. I am just letting it be free."

"You need to trim it or braid it, something."

"What — you don't like my style?"

"It just needs to be manicured" she politely said, even though I could tell that she had more to say.

"How much of the debate did you watch?" Jazzy asked.

"Not much. You know how my dad gets when it comes to that stuff."

"I know — your dad is hilarious," she laughed and then continued. "You know, Senator Wright is a very smooth talker. People are starting to take his side."

"Well, Principal Strudel needs no convincing. He has always been on Senator Wright's side" I said. Principal Strudel was our school principal, and, like my dad, he was not ashamed to express his political views even though he and my dad were total opposites in their views.

Jazzy perked up and began in her gossip about our principal. "Principal Strudel and his boyfriend — partner, or whatever they are — are proudly wearing their buttons that say, 'Vote the Wright Way.' I heard that he is trying to get all the teachers to wear them, too."

"'Vote the Wright way'?" I said, trying to decipher what she was talking about. It finally dawned on me that it was a play on words. "Wright — right. Oh, I get it. That's kinda clever." I said.

"As much as he promotes the Senator at our school, you would think that he is a part of his campaign."

"Isn't it illegal to endorse a candidate at school?" I asked.

"I think it is, but no one is going to test Principal Strudel. He and his partner, Mr. Boots, strut around the school like they should be revered," she replied.

It was kinda weird at our school — how this scrawny, old, nerdy principal has so much power. It was also weird that he was dating the head of our school's security, Mr. Boots. "Mr. Boots" was the name that the kids at our school had given him because he is always wearing combat boots to the school. Weird fashion, weird relationship between them, but no one wanted to challenge Strudel's authority. Just weird how we just accepted this and moved on.

While we were talking, I felt a buzz from my phone. I checked to see what message I'd just received.

"I know you're not looking at your phone while we are talking," Jazzy said, with an attitude.

"Sorry, it's a habit. Check this out, though."

Jazzy looked at my social site. There was an animation of a pimple-faced boy with his swollen tongue hanging out his mouth. The caption read: "CAT GOT MY TONGUE." The boy was drooling, trying to talk.

"Oh, my goodness. That is hilarious," I commented.

"You know who that is, right?" she questioned me.

"Yeah — it's that Trevor kid in school."

"So, you know that he can't help the way he talks," she said.

"I know, but it's still funny. Besides, I didn't post it. Your secret admirer Triston did," I said somewhat jokingly with her, about how Triston had always wanted her.

"Ew, Triston's a jerk. Besides, you look just a little better than he does," she said, joking with me as she squeezed my arm.

"Oh, I do, huh? He is a jerk and not as good looking as I am, but that animation was funny," I said, causing her to chuckle as we both laughed.

Jazzy's mood suddenly changed as she grabbed my hand and decided to change the tone of the conversation.

"So how are things between you and Pete?" she said, with a look of genuine concern.

It had been nearly a month since the incident at the abandoned building — how we left the scarred-face boy there to die. I later found out that his street name was "Slash" and that Jazzy's step brother Randall knew him well.

When Pete and I got in the car to leave that day, I'd decided to make an anonymous call to the cops, letting them know that there was a medical emergency at the building. I later found out that the paramedics barely made it in time to save his life. However, as a result of the temporary loss of oxygen to his brain, Slash had some memory loss. He was in a coma for two weeks, and, even though he had recovered, he was still using. He was addicted to that powerful drug called *Blue*.

Since that day, I hadn't said much to Pete. I still couldn't get over why he so badly wanted to be a part of this loser group. What kind of friends would just leave their own to die like that? I was also upset at him for the danger that he brought me into.

So Pete was the last name that I wanted to be hearing right then.

"I don't want to talk about him," I answered roughly.

"Now John, you and Pete have been friends since forever."

"I trusted him, Jazzy. I trust — " I couldn't finish the words, as I felt the anger and tears coming.

Jazzy drew closer and gave me a comforting hug. "Try talking to him, Johnny. See what is going on. Don't just throw away your friendship. Promise me that you will at least talk to him. Don't shut him out," she said.

I hated it, but she was right: I had been knowing Pete since I was seven years old. I guessed I could at least talk to him.

"Maybe — I'll see," is all I could muster. Uncomfortable with where the conversation was going, I switched subjects. "Enough about me. What has been going on with and your

stepdad lately?"

"Can I say, 'I don't want to talk about him,' like you did?"

"Nope."

"Okay. In the year since my mom married this man, things have changed between us. I used to be able to come to my mom and talk about anything. Now I feel like I am second. He is always trying to tell me what to do — like he is my real dad — and my mom does nothing. She always takes his side on everything. She loves him more than me."

She leaned into me with her shoulders shaking up and down, weeping uncontrollably. I hadn't seen Jazzy like this before. The hurt was evident.

"I'm thinking about moving down to Texas, with my real dad, but — " she said.

I already knew what the "but" was.

It was me.

I was the one who was keeping her there in Grand Lake. I knew it sounded selfish, but I didn't want her to move to Texas.

"You have to do what is best for you," I said, even though I didn't really mean it. "Stay here" was what I really wanted to say.

"I can't leave you here," she said.

"Wherever you go, even if it is to the moon, I will find some way to get there," I said as I squeezed her.

With her tear-filled eyes, she smiled and gave me a peck on the cheek.

"Hey, that reminds me: I've got something for you. Close your eyes. Come on — close them!" I said.

"Okay."

I reached inside my coat pocket and pulled out a ring that I had been working on, created from my 3D printer at home. It was a paper ring coated in gold. In the middle of the ring was a heart, with the initials "J&J" inside it.

"Open your eyes," I said. Jazzy slowly opened her eyes and was speechless. "So what do you think?" I asked.

"I love it. You're so sweet."

"Are you crying again?" I said, surprised that she was so moved by this paper ring.

"Maybe, someday, I will give you a real one," I suggested.

"I love it, Johnny. 'J&J' — John and Jazmine," she said, smiling at the ring. "I have something for you, too."

"You do?" I questioned.

"Close your eyes!" she said excitedly.

"OK."

I could hear Jazzy's breath, smell Jazzy's breath, and then feel Jazzy's breath against my face. Suddenly a warm, soft touch pressed against my lips. I opened my eyes and was pleasantly surprised by a long, passionate kiss. I didn't want her to stop. A rush of hormones started to flood my body. A tingling sensation invaded my core as my blood rose and my heart fluttered. This was the first time that we had kissed in this way. In my hasty attempt to draw closer, I lost my footing and almost slipped off the roof, causing a loud *Thud!* A few moments later, I could faintly hear a voice calling.

"Jaz — are you okay? Jazmine," her mother called to her room.

Jazzy rushed into her bedroom, jumped into her bed, and pulled the blankets over herself.

I jumped to the side of the window to hide. I was about to make a leap for the tree until I heard Jazzy's mother opening her door.

"Is everything okay, dear?" her mother said. Jazzy, acting as though she was waking up from her sleep, said. "Huh? What's going on, mom?"

"I thought I heard a loud thump up here."

"No, I don't think so. It may have been the cat. You know how Bailey gets at night."

"I suppose so," her mother said. As her mother was turning away, she noticed that the window was open.

"Honey, why do you have the window open? It's freezing. Let me close it" she said.

Still on the roof, I could hear Jazzy swiftly jumping to her feet. "*No* — it's okay. I'll close it."

"Okay, honey. You are acting strange, child. Why are you sleeping in your jacket?"

"Good night, mom."

"Good night, sweetie."

I couldn't see her mother, but I could imagine her giving Jazzy an inquisitive look. Her mother exited her room and closed the door. Once the door was closed, Jazmine rushed to the window.

"John...John, are you there?"

"Right here."

"That was close. You better get out of here," she said. Before I left, she leaned over and gave me one last, lingering kiss. "Thank you," she said.

Halfway down the tree, I could see but barely hear Jazzy mouthing the words, "I love you, Mr. Mann."

Once I hit the ground I mouthed and signed the words that I had been dying say to her for some time.

"I love you more."

CHAPTER

6

I was lying in a bed that was not my bed, covered with sheets that were not mine, in a room that I vaguely recognized. I heard a sweet voice saying, "Ready or not, here I come." The voice was a familiar voice, one that I would recognize anywhere. It was Jazzy's. I saw her coming into the room, wearing a silk robe.

I was on the bed in great anticipation, waiting for her to come to me. As she walked toward me, excitement rushed through me, and sweat began to trickle down my forehead. Then, suddenly, I heard a loud buzzing noise, ringing violently and shaking me to the core, causing me to open my eyes. When I did, I found myself looking at the ceiling in my room, with the alarm clock sounding.

It had been just a dream — a dream that I desperately tried to get back to. I closed my eyes again and again, trying to return to that place, but it didn't work.

Instead, I awoke that morning feeling filthy, guilty, and ashamed of the dream that I'd just had. If my mother had known of my dream, she'd have been ashamed of her little boy. Last night, on Jazzy's roof, our first passionate kiss had triggered something inside me — a lusty inferno. Now I had only one thing on my mind — the same thing many boys do at my age: Sex.

"I'm leaving in thirty minutes if you are coming with me," Philip yelled into my room. I lay there, trying to shake my thoughts.

"I'm coming. Wait up," I said as I rushed to get ready for school.

We arrived at school, and, during most of my time there, I was still somewhat distracted by my thoughts. Every day after Jazzy's Algebra II class, I met with her and walked her to her next class, which was near mine. That day, I was a little nervous for some reason. Maybe I was feeling a little dirty about my dream of her.

She exited her room, and, as our eyes met, she released a warm, bright smile at me — the kind of smile that showcased her full dimple. I noticed that she is wearing the ring that I'd given her, hanging from her necklace.

"Hey, handsome," she said and gave me a big smooch on the lips, which only fueled my lust even more. Principal Strudel, who was monitoring the hallways, saw us kissing and rushed over to us to reprove us.

"That's enough, you two. Get to class. Get to class, I say."

We finally unlocked lips Jazzy went skipping off to her class, and I headed to mine.

Lunch had finally come, and I was starving. On the healthy-choice menu that day was baked chicken, rice, and green beans. Not bad compared to some of our other meals.

Some buddies of mine, Gary and Eugene, were at the table.

"Hey, John: Check it out," said Gary as he pulled out a bottle of orange juice.

"What's so special about your orange-juice bottle?" I asked.

"Why don't you take a sip?" Gary said.

"It's okay. Go ahead," said Eugene.

I hesitantly took a sip and discovered that it wasn't orange juice but orange soda — a luxury that hadn't been allowed in our schools for some time, ever since the ban on junk food.

"Cisco is selling them. Me and Eugene are going to get some more. You want some?"

If you needed anything in our school, Cisco Carr was the man who could get it.

"Sure" I said. "Give me grape," as I passed some cash to them.

While Gary and Eugene were going to get the sodas, labeled as 100% fruit juice, I saw Pete walking by. Jazzy's words came to my mind: "Talk to him. Promise you will." Since the incident a month ago, Pete and I hadn't talked, and he hadn't been sitting at our table at lunch, either. *Now would be a good time to address our silence,* I thought.

"Hey, Pete why don't you come sit with us?" I asked Pete.

He was startled that I was talking to him. "Who, me?" he said.

"You are the only Pete I know."

"Alright — why not?"

Pete grabbed a chair and sat at his usual spot at the table. I could tell that he was surprised that I chose to talk to him.

"How have things been, friend?" I said.

Pete — not one to beat around the bush — cut straight to the problem, addressing the elephant in the room.

"Look, John. I'm sorry. It's my fault that I got you involved with those guys. After that day, I realized that those guys were up to no good."

"So, what are you saying? You're not with the Renegades anymore?"

"That's what I'm saying." Pete replied.

"Well, then, it looks like I got my friend back," I said with a huge smile. "I missed you, man."

While we were talking, Gary and Eugene arrived at the table. "Hey, Pete — good to see you, man." Eugene said.

"What's up guys?" Pete responds.

"Here you go, John." Gary said as he slid me two grape juices that were actually grape sodas.

"Here you go, Pete," I said, giving Pete one.

"Ah, this is some good stuff," Pete said.

"Why are they depriving us of this great pleasure?" said Gary, as he leaned back with his orange soda after taking a big gulp.

"Hey, Johnzmine — what's up with you and Jazmine anyway? Have you banged her yet? You two been dating a while now," Eugene said bluntly, catching me off guard with this abrupt questioning. Not knowing what to say, I said nothing.

"Yeah, I know you have. I saw you and Jazmine locking lips in the hallway today and that look she gave you," Gary said, shaking his head up and down, smiling.

"That's my boy!" Eugene added nudging me with approval. I don't know why I didn't say anything. Maybe I didn't want anyone to know that I was still the v-word, commonly known as a "virgin." So I just let them think that Jazzy and I had done the do. I was pretty sure that Gary and Eugene were still virgins themselves.

Gary wanted more details about Jazzy and me.

"So how is it — I mean how was it?" he asked.

Pete, sensing that I was getting uncomfortable with the talk, jumped in. "Hey, leave the man alone. What he and Jazzy do is none of your business."

The lunch buzzer rang, and I was glad that Pete had come to my defense. This was the friend that I'd been missing — the one who'd always had my back. After lunch, Pete pulled me aside and said "Hey, you and Jazzy haven't — you know?"

"No we haven't. I'm still a lonely virgin," I said with a sigh.

"Nothing's wrong with that," he said, which I was sort of surprised to hear from him. "What are you doing tonight?" he asked.

"Nothing — ahh! I forgot — today is Wednesday, church night. By the way, where have you been? I haven't seen you in church in a long time. It is not the same making fun of people without you, man," I say, laughing with Pete.

"I do miss that," he said, and then he explained why. "My mom said that I was old enough to make my own decision about whether I was or wasn't going to serve God. She wasn't going to force me to go to church anymore. That was all I needed to hear, so I stopped coming to church."

"Well, I still have to go. I can't imagine my parents giving me that option," I said.

"Hey, what's happening to your brother man? He turned all super saint on me yesterday, asking me about my relationship with Jesus and about me coming back to church and stuff. What happened to Philip?"

"I know, man — you see what I have to deal with every day."

"Hey, it was good talking to you again, man. I'll catch up with later. I need to get to class," he said. As we departed, I thought it kind of odd that he is going toward the gym when his class was in the other direction. I thought, *Could he? Nah...*

* * * * *

"Could everyone turn in your bibles to 1 Timothy 4:12," said Youth Pastor Joel Jackson, a husky Caucasian man in his mid-thirties with a receding hairline, who was still trying to hold onto his wispy red Mohawk. His long-sleeved shirts couldn't hide the multitude of tattoos that canvassed his entire body — especially the ones on his neck and hands. They would always be a reminder of his days in a biker gang. Pastor Joel had had a rough past. He had come from the prison to the pulpit, from a biker to believer, and from gangs to God. Now he was standing in front of us in a raspy voice, saying, "I need everyone to turn to 1 Timothy 4:12."

Wednesday night bible studies were back to normal, since our bible series was now over. Pastor Joel was teaching all the high schoolers and college kids today, while other youth leaders were attending to the other age groups.

Unfortunately, my girlfriend Jazzy was not able to make it to church that day. Visiting her grandfather in the hospital — she said, something like that. Her not being there was probably for the best. When school ended today, Jazzy and I met up, and I couldn't keep my hands off of her. I was testing the limits to see how far I could go and where I could. I didn't get very far, though, because Randall, her step brother, was hating on me. He'd come to pick her up. So, that day, I was forcing myself to pay attention in church, since I had no other distractions.

"Philip, could you do us the pleasure of reading that passage in Timothy?" The Youth Pastor asked.

"Sure" Philip replied. "1 Timothy 4:12 reads, *'Don't let anyone look down on you because you are young, but set an example for the believers in speech, in conduct, in love, in faith and in purity,'* he reads.

"I implore each of you to heed this verse. Don't let anyone look down on you because you are young. God has a call for each of you, and he has a plan for you even at your young age now. Set an example for your fellow believers with how you talk. Speak words that will encourage, not tear down. Live a Christian life with your actions and love. Have faith and live a pure life. Pure life, this is what I want to speak about to-day — purity.

"The bible tell us to flee youthful lust, to flee fornication. Joseph is the perfect example of one who did just that. The bible tells us that he was seduced by his master's wife saying, 'Come to bed with me.' Now Joseph was young and handsome, well-built, the bible tells us. Probably looked like you, Stephen." Pastor Joel said jokingly, embarrassing Stephen and causing a few girls to giggle and smile. Pastor Joel continued, "This was something that went on repeatedly, but he told her that he couldn't do such a sin against God.

"One day, when no one was around, she grabbed him and said, 'Come to bed with me.' I'm sure that his master's wife probably looked good, also. After all, she was married to one of Pharaoh's officials.

"Joseph was in a dilemma. His master's wife wanted him, and no one was around to witness what they could do. This was a perfect opportunity for Joseph, a young man whose hormones were raging, I'm sure. Now, right before him, was a beautiful woman who wanted him. How could he resist? But no, Joseph fled, not even entertaining the thought. He didn't reason or try to stay and fight the urge — he just ran. So I say to you, 'Flee youthful lust,' I say."

It felt like Pastor Joel's words were directed at me. How did he know that this temptation was on my mind? While I was pondering his statement, another boy in class said what I was thinking.

"Pastor Joel, what if you are in a place where you can't flee and the temptation is beyond your control. Sometimes I feel that sexual temptation is too strong for me. Why does God tempt us with things he knows that we are going to fail at? If I was Joseph, I know I would have sinned," the boy said honestly.

Even though a lot of kids were laughing at his comment, I knew they really felt the same way, myself included.

Pastor Joel took a moment and told the boy to turn in his bible to James 1:13-14. "Could you read that, please?" he asked. The boy stood up and read, *"When tempted, no one should say, 'God is tempting me.' For God cannot be tempted by evil, nor does he tempt anyone; but each person is tempted when they are dragged away by their own evil desire and enticed."*

"You see, God doesn't tempt us. We *choose* to participate in sin, because we want to," Pastor Joel said and then turned and looked at me. He asked if I could read 1 Corinthians 10:13. I stood with my tablet. Wednesdays were the one time dad allowed us to bring our tablets to church. I searched for the verse and read, *"No temptation has overtaken you except what is common to mankind. And God is faithful; he will not let you be tempted beyond what you can bear. But when you are tempted, he will also provide a way out so that you can endure it."*

Those two bible verses stuck with me, and, on the way home, I was having a war in my mind. I was thinking about how Jazzy looked and how being close to her made me feel. And then I would think about the words about "fleeing youthful lust."

Philip could see that I was quiet the whole way home and questioned me. "Pastor Joel taught a good lesson," he said.

"Yeah, he did." I said solemnly, still meditating on his words. While I was deep in thought about Joseph and how he said that he didn't want to sin against God — not against his master, Potiphar — but God, Jazzy called.

"What's up, Johnny?" she said cheerfully.

"Hey, Jazzy."

"Why do you sound so sad?" she asked.

"Ahh, it's nothing — just thinking about church."

"Well, how was it?"

"Alright, I guess."

"Okay, why don't you meet me at the park tonight and talk about it?"

"Tonight? It's kind of late."

"I know. Doesn't this conversation sound familiar?"

That got a smile out of me.

"My mom is working a double and my dad — step-dad, I should say — is out of town. Randall is in the house with some nasty girl. I need to get out. Meet me at the park tonight. We can talk alone again," she says.

Flee youthful lust, I say. The words of Pastor Joel rang in my head.

"Johnny, are you still there?" Jazzy asked.

"Yeah, I'm sorry. I'll see if I can get away," I said, dismissing the pastor's words.

Philip turned and looked at me with a convicting look. With one eyebrow raised but not saying a word, he still managed to make me feel guilty.

* * * * *

Where are you? Jazzy texted. I was standing behind Jazzy, watching her sit on the park bench and contemplating my actions: *Should I sit next to her or flee?* If I sat next to her, I was afraid that I wouldn't be able to control myself.

Before I could make a decision, she turned and spotted me.

"There you are. What took you so long?" she said.

"I had to wait until my parents went to sleep. My dad wanted to talk today." I wished my dad *would* talk to me about what was really on my mind. The topic of sex was straightforward with him: Simply don't do it until you get married. My mom avoided the subject completely and passed it off to my dad. They had never shared any of their experiences of growing up as a teen dealing with sex. I knew my dad hadn't been a Christian all his life. I'd heard a few things about his past.

"So how is your grandfather doing?" I said.

"Not my grandfather, my grandmother — and she is doing better. Are you okay, John? You seem a little distant."

"I'm good."

"Tell me what church was about."

I didn't want to get into what had been taught. "I can't remember. Same old stuff — you know, 'God loves us,'" I lied, even though I had been deeply affected by the lesson.

"Okay, whatever," she said, changing the conversation. "All my girlfriends love your ring."

I could hear the excitement in her voice. She placed her hand on my knee and bumped into my side.

"I'm glad they do — I'm glad you do."

"I know it's just paper, but it's so thoughtful. By the way, I also have something for you."

She pulled out a ring very similar to the one I'd given her — with "J&J" in the center of a heart, but this ring was covered in silver, not gold.

"Wow! How did you get it to look like my design?"

"Randall helped me. He's good at that kind of stuff."

"Thanks," I said, genuinely, as I leaned over and kissed her cheek.

"Do you know what our rings mean?"

"No, but I'm sure you're going to tell me."

"Ha, ha. You see you gave me a gold ring, which represents success, prestige, and sophistication — all of which you are to me. And I gave you a silver ring, which represents fluidity, emotionality, sensitivity, and mystery. That represents me. See, we are both carrying each other next to our hearts," she said, holding her ring from her necklace next to her heart.

"If you say so," I said looking at her strangely. I wanted to say, "What in the world are you talking about, woman?" But I was wise enough to be quiet. Sometimes I couldn't understand her, but I still loved her.

As though she'd heard my thoughts, she looked at me and asked,

"Do you love me, John?"

"Of course, I do." She closed her eyes, leaned in, and gave me a kiss on the lips. I kissed her back. Jazzy placed both of her hands on my face, kissing even harder. I couldn't control it anymore. My hormones were racing. I grabbed her with one thing on mind:

Tonight was going to be *the night*.

I pressed closely to her, and I could barely hear her saying something. She said it again, this time a little louder.

"No — not here, not now," Jazzy said, but I couldn't stop. My urge was too strong.

"Come on, Jazzy. You love me — right?" I desperately pleaded to her.

"I do, but—" she said softly.

At the very moment I was reaching for her, I see three deer running, right in front of us — two does and a young buck. This time of the year is mating season, and the young buck was set on one thing: Getting his prize. The two does jumped a ragged fence, but the young buck charged out unaware that he was about to run into this loose-wire fence. The wire from the fence wrapped all around the buck, tangling his antlers and cutting into his flesh. The huffing buck looked possessed. His eyes met mine, and it was like looking into a mirror.

I was like the young buck. Like an animal, concerned only about getting my needs met. Not even aware that I was walking right into a trap. The distraction of this deer interrupts us. ***But when you are tempted, he will also provide a way out so that you can endure it.*** The very scripture that I'd read only hours before came to my mind. This was my way of escape. Did I want to take it or not was the question.

CHAPTER

7

Pastor Bruce stood at the podium. A weary man with dark circles under his eyes, he looked like he had the weight of the world on his shoulders. The gray in his head seemed to be winning the battle, outnumbering the black. They were overtaking them one by one, multiplying, and taking up residency on his scalp. He was nearing the end of his sermon, with his hands extended to the congregation. He made his plea.

"Dear saints — *now* is the time for salvation. Some of you will say that you need to straighten out the mess in your life first before you come to Jesus. Let me ask you a question:

"Do you clean your clothes before you take them to the cleaner? Of course not. That's why you take them to the cleaner — to be cleaned by a professional. They can clean your clothes better than you. They are able to remove the tough stains, straighten out the wrinkles, and have your clothes looking new again.

"Jesus is the cleaner. He can straighten out the mess that you have made. He can straighten out your past wrinkles. He can clean up the tough stains in your life. The bible tells us in Isaiah 1:18, *'Come now, let's settle this, says the LORD. Though your sins are like scarlet, I will make them as white as snow. Though they are red like crimson, I will make them as white as wool.'* He wants to make you a new creature. The bible also tells us, in 1 Corinthians 5:17, that *'This means that anyone who belongs to Christ has become a new person. The old life is gone; a new life has begun!'* So I say, let him do the cleaning because he is better at it than you are."

75

I could feel the sincerity and passion that our pastor was speaking with. My head was down, and I was sitting in my usual place in the back of church. It felt like Jesus was inside me, trying to claw his way to the surface of my heart. Jazzy was next to me, holding my hand. I could see a tear rolling down her face. She was touched by this as much as I was.

That night at the park could have had a different outcome for us if the deer hadn't interfered. I was totally committed to satisfying my desire, and I knew that Jazzy would eventually have given in to my advances. I was like an animal, and it took an animal to make me see that.

When the deer passed, we both decided to part ways also. The next few days with me and Jazzy were awkward, as we tried not to mention our potential hookup that night. I could only imagine what could have been. Neither one of us had had protection that night at the park, and the thought that she could have gotten pregnant terrified me.

Eventually, we spoke of that night and agreed that it would be for the best if we didn't meet alone at night again. I guess being chaperoned is not all that bad after all. Now, hearing the words of the pastor, his words pierced my heart, and I knew that I needed to return to Christ. But it was like my feet were stuck in cement, and I couldn't move them. Even though the pastor was calling for everyone to come to the altar for repentance, I couldn't seem to make that move.

I looked at Jazzy and could tell that she was just waiting for me to make the first move, but I never did. The church service ended, and I could still feel the uneasiness of my stubborn refusal to move forward. I tried to convince myself that I don't need Jesus to clean up my life. *I am OK,* I told myself.

Driving home from church with Philip, it was a cool crisp day outside, as the leaves blew aimlessly in the air. My heart felt like the outside — cold and aimless like the empty wind and the lonely leaf. Lately, my brother seemed to have picked up a sixth sense about things concerning me.

Philip spoke. "Hey, bro — you know God is knocking at the door of your heart. Only you can let him in, though. Don't ignore his knocks, because if you don't answer, one day he will stop knocking."

I felt a sudden sinking in my heart — the feeling you have when horrible news is received or when sudden danger appears. That was how I was feeling at that moment. I turned to speak with Philip.

"I know that I need to repent, and I want — ." Before I could finish, my phone rang, and I looked and saw that it was Pete calling me. I pressed the "Ignore" button and continued with my conversation. "Philip, I want — ." My phone rang again.

"Don't answer," Philip said.

"It's Pete again. It must be important. I have been meaning to talk with him anyways," I said as I answered the call.

"What's up, Pete?"

"My man. Guess what?"

"What?"

"I have two tickets to see *Soulless Corpse*. You want to go?" he asked. *Soulless Corpse* was only the most highly anticipated feature movie of the year. It was directed by one of the best movie directors out there, Sabal Singh. I'd heard that the cinematography was awesome.

"You know it," I enthusiastically replied. "When?"

"Tonight. I'll pick you up at eight. Alright?" Pete asked.

"I have to let my parents know, but I'm sure it will be alright," I said.

"Cool — see you at eight."

"Alright. Talk to you later."

After my conversation with Pete, we pulled up to the house, Philip was looking at me like he wanted to continue talking about something.

"What were you going to say to me, John?" Philip asked.

"What?" I said.

"Before Pete called, you were going to say something about how you 'needed to do something,'" Philip said, trying to jog my memory.

"I don't remember. Maybe we can talk about it later. I need to ask mom if I can go see *Soulless Corpse* with Pete tonight," I said excitedly.

My dad was still at church, counting the offering contributions, but my mom was at home. Philip and I entered the house. Mom was in the kitchen, preparing her favorite Reuben sandwich for lunch.

"Hey, boys," she said when we got to the kitchen.

"Hi, mom" said Philip.

I chose to skip the greetings and get straight to the point. "Mom, can I go out with Pete tonight?"

"Where are you boys going?" she questioned.

"To see a movie. He's coming by."

"I haven't seen Pete in some time. How is he doing?"

"He's fine mom. Can I go?" I said, eager to get an answer.

"Well, it's okay with me, but you'll have to ask your dad before you can go. He may need you to do something."

She would have to say that, wouldn't she?

With my dad, I never know what kind of answer I will get. He normally doesn't care if I go out, as long as I come home at a decent time. But, sometimes, on Sunday, he'd have Philip and I doing chores.

Finally my dad arrived home after what seemed like hours of being away. Before he even got a chance to put his coat away, I presented my request.

"Hey, dad."

"Hey, son."

"Have I ever told you what a fine job you are doing as a dad?"

My dad raised one eyebrow and looked at me, knowing that I was buttering him up for something. "What is it that you want, John?" he said.

"Well, Pete is picking me up."

"To go where?"

"We may go see a movie."

"What is the name of the movie?" he asked.

Why is my dad asking all these questions? He never does this! Most of the time he doesn't care where I am as long as I am with Pete or Philip and we come home before curfew, but today he is interrogating me like I am a suspect.

"*Soulless Corpse*" I answered.

"*Soulless Corpse*? What is the rating on that?"

"Rating?" I said, surprised to hear him say that — another question that he never asked about. I don't know how many times Pete and I had gone out to the movies, and he'd never asked us what film we were looking at and what the rating was. What had gotten into him?

"I'm not sure, dad."

"Well, let's see," he said as he pulled out his phone and looked up the movie. He read the reviews aloud to me. "*Soulless Corpse* — a bloody thriller that will keep you awake at night." He read another review. "Don't drink too much before you come because you may wet your pants," one critic wrote.

"Yeah — that's what I'm talking about" I said, not realizing that I'd said it out loud.

My dad just raised his eyebrow again and continued reading. "*Soulless Corpse* is rated "R" for violence, nudity, language, and sexual content." He just looked at me, and I dreaded what I knew was going to follow next out of his mouth.

"I'm sorry, son. I can't allow you to go see this" he said.

"What? Why?" I pleaded.

"It's rated "R," and you're fifteen, not seventeen. Even if you were seventeen, do you think that this is a film that you should be looking at? This is not something I believe a Christian should be partaking in."

Disbelief — and then anger — boiled up in me. The words just came out. "Who says that I am a Christian anyway? Just because you can't handle it doesn't mean I can't." Before I could catch my words, I'd blurted out what I meant to say in my head, not aloud. Instantly, I knew I had done something that I shouldn't have done.

I looked and saw my brother and mother nearby, with their jaws dropped and mouths wide open in disbelief of what I'd just said. My dad just stood there, stunned at my response. He finally looked at me, and all he could say was, "Go to your room."

I don't think that I had seen my dad look so disappointed with me ever before in my life. I didn't question him anymore. I just turned and went to my room, knowing that I had just royally messed up.

I lay in my bed reflecting on the words that I'd just said to my dad and pondering my true beliefs. *Am I a Christian? Do I really believe in all this stuff I was raised to believe in? Do I even believe in religion, God?* I believe there is a God — there has to be. *But how do I know if*

Christianity is the only way? While I was soul searching the meaning of life, my phone buzzed.

What's up? You still going? Pete texted.

I can't go.

What? What happened?

My dad.

This is a once-in-a-lifetime opportunity. Can't you sneak out?

I stared out the window, contemplating sneaking out.

What do I have to lose? I am going to get punished anyway for talking back to my dad. I might as well enjoy this day while I can, I thought.

I will meet you @ the corner @ 8 I replied.

Time was creeping along; minutes seemed like hours. I stayed in my room looking at the reviews of *Soulless Corpse.* This made me want to see this movie even more. "A tortured soul returns from the dead seeking out those who publicly humiliated, bullied, and ultimately led her to commit suicide years ago. Now she has returned, seeking out each and every one who has ever posted a hurtful comment or humiliating image of her on social media. With no emotion, no conscience, and no mercy, this soulless corpse is out for revenge," the narrator said in the movie trailer in his deep, epic-movie voice.

That was it. I have to go now, I thought. I put my clothes on, stuffed my bed with pillows to make it look as though I was asleep, and waited for the clock to strike 7:55 pm. I was about to climb down the old rugged tree outside my window. Then, I heard someone at my door. Philip burst through my door and caught me red-handed, with one foot out the window.

"Man, don't you know how to knock?" I said, angrily.

"What are you doing, John?"

"Why do you care?" I yelled back.

"Hey, if you leave, I'm not going to lie for you."

"Come on, Phil. Don't tell dad."

"Really, John. Why are you doing this? This is not you. I know that you have been sneaking out at night. Last week I came to your room and found that you were gone. If you leave this time, I will not keep it a secret."

I was shocked to hear that he knew about me leaving in the middle of the night but hadn't said anything. While Philip was talking, I received a text from Pete.

Where r u @?

"So, what are you going to do, John?" Philip asked. Pondering what decision I should make, I replied to Pete:

Sorry, man. I won't be able to make it.

OK, man. Your loss, he replied.

"You did the right thing, bro. Philip said.

I couldn't believe I was doing this — turning down an opportunity to see the movie of the year. It had been a roller coaster of a day. From the pastor making me feel bad to my dad declining to let me go see only the best movie of the year. I'd had enough for today and decided to turn in early. *Bed, here I come.*

* * * * *

I found myself looking at a cool, refreshing, purple grape soda behind the frosty glass door in the convenience store. All of a sudden, I heard a loud scream. I turned to see what the commotion was all about. Others started to scream. That's when I saw three men with black hoods and masks in front of the store. The masks had a sinister, life-like human skull. It was like I was looking at the angel of death. A sudden fear engulfed the area and dread swept over me about what may come.

One of the men yelled "Everybody get down." The voice of the man sounded more like the voice of a teenager. A red-headed woman screamed in terror. This angered the teen, and he pistol whipped her, pushed her to ground, and yelled again. "I said, 'Everybody get down'!"

I was frozen, paralyzed with fear, still standing in the same spot trying to process what was happening. Strangely, the robbers didn't say anything to me like they had to the red-headed woman, even though I was standing right in front of them. It was like they were looking right through me. One of the robbers was guarding the door, looking out, with his gun cocked by his neck above his shoulders. Another was taking control of the customers, making sure that each one of them kept their face down to the ground. The third guy looked like he was the one in charge. He began walking toward me. He reached in his pocket. His pocket — I had seen that pocket somewhere before. That worn, ripped pocket looked eerily familiar, but I couldn't recall from where.

He drew a gun from that worn, ripped pocket, a long silver one. He was right in front of my face now but didn't say anything. He only continued to walk at me. I braced myself for contact, but he went *right through me*. Right through me — like a ghost! They couldn't see me. Was this a dream or something? I tried to grab his gun, but my hands just went through his. What was going on?

The leader yelled to the cashier, "Open up, and give me all your money!" While the cashier was fumbling around the register, he yelled again, "Hurry up, and don't try anything. I will shoot you!" The cashier finally got the register open. The robber at the door looking at his watch yelled, "Hurry, man — we have to go!"

The leader answered back "Not until I get everything." Even though I couldn't see the robbers, it was clear that they were teenagers by the way they talked and moved. Once the money was stolen, they all rushed out of the gas station. But before they left, the leader turned and fired a gunshot right at the cashier, hitting him square in the chest.

"What are you doing, man?" the robber at the door yelled frantically. The cold-blooded shooter answered, "He was reaching for his gun." I ran to the cashier and found blood splattered everywhere. The middle-aged eastern man lay lifeless, with his eyes rolled back into his head. "Furu" is what it said on his Fast Gas name tag. I rushed to the front doors and see a light-blue car zooming up to the entrance. The robbers scurried to get into the vehicle. This car looked oddly familiar, too.

I exited the gas station and ran toward the car to get a closer look. The one who was driving the car looks extremely nervous and terrified. He didn't have a mask on like the others, but I still couldn't get a good look at who it was. So I ran to stand right in the path of the oncoming car, hoping I am still ghostlike. The car's light beams were shining right in my face as the car was speeding straight at me. I finally got a good look at the driver. To my surprise, he turned and looked directly at me.

Pete...Pete? No, it couldn't be.

CHAPTER

8

I stumbled out of bed, perplexed about what I'd seen last night in my dream. It felt so real. I can still smell the food, the gas, and the blood that was splattered everywhere. Poor Furu. I was like a ghost peering into an actual event but unable to change the outcome. What was the meaning of this?

I awoke before my alarm went off, and I could smell the familiar smell of hazelnut coffee in the air. I trotted down to the kitchen, where I found my dad sitting, drinking his coffee, and looking at the morning news. We never did discuss my smart-aleck remark from the previous day. I knew that we would have to address this soon, so I pulled up a chair to sit at the table with my dad.

"Good morning, son," he said.

"Good morning, dad."

"Do you understand why I didn't let you go to the movies?"

"Yes sir," I replied. I understood, but I still didn't agree with his decision.

"Look son. You know where I stand when it comes to God, but you must decide where you stand. *God doesn't have grandchildren — only children* (one of his famous sayings). "Your mother, brother, and I are Christians. We are children of God. Just because you go to church every Sunday and have a family who loves God doesn't mean that you are going to be in heaven. You, son, have to accept Christ for yourself. I can't make you become a believer. You must do this on your own. Do you understand?"

My dad spoke with a twinge of sadness in his voice. I could tell that the comment that I'd made to him yesterday about me not being sure if I was a Christian was heartbreaking. But he was addressing me with love. I was expecting to be yelled at — not this.

"I understand, dad, I said. When he finished speaking, my mom and brother came into the kitchen. We were all getting ready to start our work and school week.

On the television, I see a flashing prompt come across the screen saying, "Breaking News."

"Turn up the TV" hollered Philip.

A young, beautiful news reporter appeared on the screen. She spoke:

"This just in, authorities are investigating a string of overnight armed robberies. Multiple gas stations and fast-food restaurants in the Grand Lake and South Kansas City area have been targeted. Police say that a group of what seemed to be three juvenile males robbed two gas stations and two fast-food restaurants. They were dressed in black hooded jackets and wore a mask of a skull. There was one fatality in the string of robberies. Standing with me is one of the witnesses to the fatal robbery at Fast Gas in Grand Lake."

A woman with red hair was standing next to the reporter.

This can't be!

It was only a dream, I kept telling myself, but this was the same woman in my dream. The woman began to describe the incident.

"Three men burst into the store yelling, 'Get down." That's when one of them smacked me in the face and shoved my head into the ground." The woman turned her head so that the camera could get a close -up of her bruised face. "I didn't dare look up — that is, until I heard a loud gunshot and seen that they'd shot the cashier. I heard him giving them the money. Why did they shoot him? He gave them the money." The woman voice escalated as she began to break down, and she started sobbing uncontrollably. The camera panned back to the news reporter as she tried to gain control of the situation.

"As you can see, this account is still fresh in our victim's mind. If anyone has information, please call the TIPS Hotline, 111-555-1111. This is Jenny Gray, reporting from Grand Lake. Back to you guys."

"What is this world coming to? Dad said. "I guess I better get to work" he continued.

"Me, too," mom replied. "You boys behave in school today. Love you." Mom added.

"Love you, too," Philip answered as our parents left. I was still standing and looking at the television, in awe of what I'd just seen.

"I was there," I said out loud. Philip looked at me strangely.

"You were there? What are you talking about?" he said.

"I was there at the gas station when this happened," I said, pointing at the television.

Philip laughed and said, "No. You were here. Right?" He paused and then repeated, "You were here — in your room. Right, John?" This time, his voice was louder, and he was showing a straight face and a look of uncertainty.

"Yes, I was here — but I saw the whole thing in my dream" I answered and then proceeded to describe the entire event in detail to him. This blew my brother's mind — how my description of what happened could only come from someone who'd been there. Even though I was convincing to him, he was still somewhat apprehensive as to how I knew all of this.

"You didn't sneak out, did you? You were asleep in your bed."

"Sound asleep," I assured him.

"Then, maybe God is trying to tell you something, John."

"Like what?"

"I don't know. You have to ask him," he replied.

We were running late, so Philip and I hopped into the Camaro and headed to school. I couldn't wait to question Pete when I saw him, but the whole school day passed without me seeing him there. The next day came and went without any sign of Pete at school. I was starting to get a sick feeling in my stomach that this had been more than just a dream — more like a reality.

I finally decided to call Pete's house since he hadn't been answering any of my texts. Mrs. Woods, Pete's mom, answered the phone.

"Hello."

"Hello, Mrs. Woods. Is Pete around?"

"Oh, yes, dear. He's here, but he's not feeling very well."

"Do you mind if I come by to see him?" I asked.

"Well, I'm sure he would love to see you. It's been a while since you've been here."

"Yes, it has. Can I come over now?"

"Sure — I guess so."

I had to find out if my dream had just been an eerie coincidence or if there was some truth to what had happened. I grabbed my dusty bike and rode that way.

I arrived at Pete's door.

"Hello, John. It's been a long time since I seen you, sweetie," said Mrs. Woods.

"Hello, ma'am"

"Pete is in his room" she informed me.

Pete saw me approaching and perked up. "My man. Wassup? I have to be sick for you to visit me?"

"I guess so. What's going on with you?"

"I don't know. I think that it was that food I ate at the theater a couple of days ago," he said rubbing his stomach.

"So you went to the movies Sunday?" I said.

"Yeah. Since you abandoned me, I went by myself. It was the best movie I have ever seen. The ending — well, I won't spoil it for you. What happened to you?"

"I told you — my dad wouldn't let me go."

"Do you do everything your parents tell you?" Pete said with a smug look.

At least he was at the movies. Good. He couldn't have robbed the stores then. I felt a little relief, but something still didn't add up. I had to question him more.

"It's been two days, and you're still having issues with your stomach. Maybe you should see a doctor." I suggested.

"Doctor? No I'm feeling better already," he said as he sat up.

"Alright. Will I see you at school tomorrow?"

"See you there." As I was leaving, Pete spoke again. "Hey — this weekend, me and you. No excuses. Lunch is on me. I have a lot of things I want to talk to you about." Pete had a look of sadness in his eyes that he was trying to mask — like a burden that he wanted to tell someone about.

"Alright, man. No excuses. See you this weekend," I replied. Pete got up and walked me to the door. For someone who was supposed to be sick, he sure looked spry and healthy. Before I left his house, he said something strange to me.

"John, you should have been there Sunday," he said, soberly.

"At the movies?" I questioned.

"Yeah — that, too."

* * * * *

"So, where do you want to eat? Lunch is on me," Pete said.

"Alright. Let's go to the Marketplace," I replied.

"Drewman's?"

"Yeah. They have one of the best deli shops in town."

"Alright. Drewman Marketplace it is."

After many failed attempts to reconnect with Pete, we'd finally made good on our promise to meet this weekend. There was a lot on my mind concerning Pete and the person he was becoming. Even though he was not admitting to his involvement with the robberies, I had a sinking feeling that what I saw had been more than a dream. This horrific event actually happened, and Pete had been a part of it. But, for the time being, I tried to put this aside and enjoy our time together. Two old friends just hanging out.

We arrived at the marketplace, and, surprisingly, the place wasn't as hectic as it normally was. We entered into Manny's Deli and were able to move through the line relatively quickly.

"Hey, isn't that Rachel Matthews at the cash register — the one who sings at L3C and is a senior at our school?" Pete asked.

"I think so," I said. We were still some distance away from the register, so, it was hard for me to recognize anyone. When we approached the register, a green-eyed, sandy-brown-haired gal was smiling.

"Welcome to Manny's. May I take your order?" Rachel asked. It was probably a scripted line that she said at least a hundred times a day. I could tell she was trying to identify us.

"Don't I know you guys from somewhere?" she asked.

"We go to the same school and church," I replied.

"That's right. You're Philip's brother, right?"

"That's me."

"Are you guys coming to the youth meeting? Recording artist Vision will be there next week," Rachel said enthusiastically.

"Please — I don't believe in those fairy tales anymore, and Christian artists are whack," Pete said with disgust, as though he was offended by her question.

"What about you, John? What do you think?" she said as she turned to me. There I was — again faced with the question about what I believe.

"I would like to order now," I said, deflecting her question.

"Okay. I'm sorry. What would you like?" Rachel said as her enthusiasm was quashed and she reverted to being business-like.

"Give me the Italian Sandwich, with no onions, please."

"Would you like any sides?" she asked. I looked at Pete, trying to determine how much he was willing to spend.

"Go ahead, man. Get whatever you want."

"OK. I would like a bag of chips and a grape soda."

"You and your soda," Pete chuckled.

After we'd ordered, we sat down. Pete saw a girl from church eating with another girl.

"Hey, isn't that your brother's girlfriend over there?" I looked and saw Tameka eating with Hannah. "Tameka? No, I think she has him stuck in the 'friend' zone."

"That's a shame for Philip. She has a killer body," Pete said, looking at her with a lustful eye. "What about that other girl, the Asian one? She's a knockout. Who is that?"

"You are talking about Hannah. Remember? She moved here a year ago. Her parents are missionaries — the Jays."

"I don't know how I missed her at church. If I knew she was there, I might have stayed," he said with a smile.

After a long talk about people in the church and people in our school, I finally confronted Pete. "For someone who just overcame food poisoning, you have a healthy appetite."

"What are you trying to say, John?" Pete replied.

I cut to the chase and asked him directly. "Where were you Sunday night?"

"Well, I went to the movies alone, because someone abandoned me," he retorted.

"After the movie, where did you go?

"What is this? Am I being interrogated?"

I was getting angry that Pete was still lying. I could feel my voice escalating. "I saw you. I saw you driving the car at the robbery." The words finally come out of my mouth, loud enough for the people next to us to hear. The look on Pete's face was one of fright. He knew that I knew. He was busted and couldn't lie anymore.

"Hey, calm down," he whispered as others were starting to look at us. "Let's go to the car and talk."

I shook my head in agreement, and we went back to his car. Once the doors were closed, he began to panic. "How do you know about that?"

"I saw the whole thing in a dream."

"Did you tell anybody?"

"My brother, but I'm not sure he believed me"

"You got to keep this a secret — okay?"

"I don't know, man. Why were you involved in this?"

"It wasn't supposed to go down like that. Just one robbery — and I didn't have to do anything but drive the getaway car. But they got greedy and kept going. Then he killed that guy." Pete's lip started to quiver as he reminisced. Then he let out a booming cry — a cry of regret. No more masking his pain. He'd finally broken.

"Let's go to the police. Tell them your story. You didn't rob or kill anyone."

"I am still an accomplice, and I fear for my life. Todd threatened to kill us if we snitched. He's not the type that would bluff."

"What — Todd? So you lied to me. You're still part of the Renegades? Man, take me home."

I just wanted to go home. This was too much for me to process.

Pete started the car, and we got on the highway. "Do you have any tissue? I have to blow my nose." I asked.

"Look in the glove box. Wait—"

But before he could finish his sentence, I opened the box, and a bag of *Blue* fell out. I looked inside the box and saw a long silver pistol. I was furious. "What is this? Are you using too?" I said, boiling with anger. *How could he be so stupid?*

"I'm not using — just selling. And that pistol is not mines. It must be Todd's."

"So you have drugs on you and the murder weapon from the robberies. Just get me home," I said, exasperated.

"Look, John. Not everyone has a good life like you. I look at you, and you take so much for granted. You have two parents who love you and a girlfriend who adores you, and you still make it seem like your life is so hard. What do I have? I've got a dad I've never seen in my life and a mother who is working double and triple shifts just to make ends meet. She leaves me home alone all the time, for me to survive on my own. The one thing that I could depend on was you, but, ever since you and Jazzy started dating, you abandoned me, just like them.

"At least my guys the Renegades treat me like a brother, which is more than I can say for you. You left me, man, for a girl. So don't act like you're all high and mighty."

As Pete was finishing his rant, I looked up and saw red and blue lights flashing from behind. They kept getting closer and closer. Cars were pulling over, letting the cop get through. Pete pulled to the side to also let the cop pass. But he didn't. Instead, he pulled up right behind us.

"Oh, Lord! This can't be happening!" I said, raising my hands to heaven.

"Hurry up and put everything back in the glove box," Pete yelled.

The policeman slowly approached Pete's car. He tapped on the window, and Pete rolled it down.

"Is there a problem, officer?" Pete said, calmly.

"Sir, we're doing a highway check for cars matching the description given to us in a recent robbery, and your car fits that description." Someone on the police radio began to speak. The policeman said to us, "Give me one second, sir. I need to take this call," as he went back to his car.

Once he'd left, Pete looked at me and said, "I'm not going to jail."

"Pete, don't do anything stupid. Now is the time to tell the truth," I said. The police officer was on his radio for a long time, and his facial expression had changed from nonchalant to stony-faced. This time, he approached with a more cautious walk, with his hand near his gun.

"Sir, I need to see your license and insurance," he said. Pete was hesitant because his license and insurance were in the glove box.

"Sir — your license and insurance, please," the officer said, more forcefully.

Pete looked at me like he was going to do something stupid. I shook my head, silently pleading for him to reconsider.

The officer grasped his gun and said once more, "I am not going to ask again. License and insurance." Pete reached for the glove box. Then he suddenly did something totally unexpected — he slammed on the accelerator. The officer rushed back to his car to chase us.

"I'm not going to jail," Pete said again, with tears forming in his eyes.

I was totally dumbfounded. We were in an all-out police chase. What had I gotten myself into? There was a bag of *Blue* in his car that is worth a lot, Pete was driving his mother's car — the getaway car — and the murder weapon was lying right in his glove compartment. Things were not looking good.

"Why?" I tried to reason with Pete to turn himself in, but he was a different person now, not the Pete I knew. We were weaving in and out of traffic. I could see a police chopper above. *We are certainly doomed now*, I thought. I looked at my phone and saw "Breaking News. Police have identified the getaway vehicle and potential suspects in the fatal robbery that occurred Sunday night. Right now they are in hot pursuit. There appears to be two suspects in the vehicle. If you are on Highway 49, please be advised." The alert had been broadcast to all mobile devices.

"Pete, *please*," I pleaded with him. "These chases never end well. They have the choppers on us, and everyone has been alerted."

"I'm not going to jail," was the only thing Pete would say.

Looking out in front of us, I could see that the police had placed a spike strip about 100 meters in front of us. By then Pete was zooming at 120-plus mph.

There was an exit coming up right before we were about to meet the spikes. I could see that Pete was going to try to exit off the highway.

"You won't make it!" I exclaim.

"I'm not going to jail," he yelled one last time and then suddenly swerved right, onto the exit ramp, making the car go airborne. As the car was about to hit the ground, the only thing I could think to say was "Jesus save me!" The car tumbled, and everything went black.

CHAPTER

9

"Where am I?" Nothing but a gray, desolate place. I looked down to see a cracking, dry ground, with tumbleweeds blowing across the surface. When I looked to my right, I noticed two gates. One was old and narrow, and the other one was wide and shining. Inside the first gate. I saw only a few people traveling down a hard, rocky road. Inside the other gate were an abundance of people cruising down the road on this path.

While I was trying to figure out the meaning of these gates, I heard a voice behind me say, "Which one?"

I turned to see who was speaking. There was a man who had a compassionate smile. He repeated, "Which gate are you going to take?"

I was confused by his remark. The wide gate definitely looked pleasing, but something just wasn't right about it — how easy things seemed to be. The people inside that gate were smiling on the outside but looked troubled on the inside.

The other gate was unappealing. The path looked hard, with many obstacles. But the people inside the narrow gate, for some reason, had an inner peace, even though the road was rough. I was puzzled by all of this.

The man spoke again to me.

"John, through this narrow gate, it is hard, and the path may be rocky, but at the end of it is life. This wide gate is pleasing to one's eyes, and many are on it, but its destination is destruction."

It felt like I knew this man, like I'd met him before. He was looking right through me. With his loving, warm eyes, he spoke once more.

"John, there are two paths but only one way. I am knocking at your door, but I can't come in unless you let me. If you don't answer, someday I will stop knocking."

"Jesus? Are you J—" Once I realized that the man who was speaking to me was Jesus, in a blink of an eye, I was transported to a different place.

My eyes slowly opened, and my vision was foggy. As my vision began to clear a little, I immediately felt pain traveling through my body. Someone was standing in front of me.

"Are you an angel?" I said to the beautiful creature standing before me. My vision was getting clearer, and I could see that the angel in front of me had a familiar face —

"Jazzy?"

"Yes, John. It's me!" said Jazzy, with tear-filled eyes. She called for my family and the nurses.

"Ahh — my head! Where am I?" I said.

"You're at St. Paul's hospital," she answers.

"How long have I been here?"

"It has been three long days."

The accident?

Things were starting to come back to me.

Pete?

"Where is Pete?" I asked.

"Pete is — "

"John!" my mother said bursting through the door to the room, excited to see her baby boy still alive.

"You had me scared, bro," Philip said.

"God answers prayers," Dad added.

For the first time, I could see what Pete had been talking about. My family loved me, and Jazzy was there right beside me. And all this time, I had been taking them for granted, thinking about my needs only.

The doctor stepped into the room and started checking my vitals and asking me a lot of questions. While he was checking my health, I tried to move my hand. I could feel cold metal around my left wrist — and the shiny handcuff connected to it.

"John, on a scale of zero to ten, what is your pain level — zero being no pain and ten being unbearable pain," the doctor asked.

"Six," I said.

"OK. You're looking good. You're a lucky kid," he said.

I looked at the doctor, realizing that I had to acknowledge that God had let me live for a reason. I said, "No, sir. I am *blessed* — spared only by God's grace."

After I heard what had happened during the accident, it became even clearer. The car flew through the air and tumbled at least ten times before it finally stopped.

Jazzy showed me the video of the police chase and the horrific accident. How did I survive that? It was because of God — and God only. The car was unrecognizable, smashed and broken into several pieces. I'd been unconscious for three days but with no internal injuries and no broken bones — only minor bruises and a massive headache. They'd had to cut me and Pete out of the car.

"Pete? What happened to Pete?" I asked everyone in the room. Everyone's faces suddenly dropped. I panicked. "Is he — "

The doctor placed his hand on my shoulder to calm me down.

"Your friend? Your friend is still in critical condition. We are doing all we can, son." The doctor looked at me again and said, "You are still weak, and you need to get some rest." He ordered everyone out of the room, leaving me with just my thoughts.

I lay, handcuffed to the bed, restless. I was assuming that the doctors were asking the police officers outside my door to wait until I'd gotten some rest before questioning me, but I couldn't sleep. So I reached for the remote to scan the TV to see what is on. To my surprise, just about every channel was showing the second presidential debate. "What the heck? I have nothing else better to do," I muttered to myself.

They are in the middle of the debate. A young white man who is an undecided voter asked the senator and president a question.

"This question is for the both of you. I am a twenty-year-old college student. From what it sounds like, Senator, you want to get rid of religion in school. You say that we will have the freedom to worship — just not the freedom to practice our belief. So does that mean I can't pray or speak of my God in school? Why are you so adamant about changing this law?" the student asked.

"Well, son, I can understand your concerns. I am not pushing the elimination of religion. I just think that there should be limits on its expression in this country. We are evolving, and some of our old practices should be revised and improved upon," the senator said.

"Mrs. President, your response," the moderator said.

"Young man, I want to commend you for having the courage to stand and ask this question. Unlike Senator Wright, I believe the founding principles that have governed this country through the years is what makes this country unique. If the senator gets his way and eliminates the freedom of religion — or 'limits religion,' as he says — he will also be eliminating or limiting the freedom of speech. We cannot have freedom of speech if we don't have freedom of religion. We will not be able to voice our opinions. You, son, will not even have the freedom to ask the question that you have just asked," the President replied.

I could just hear my mom saying, "You go, girl."

Surprisingly, I actually stayed up and watched the entire debate. It seemed as though the President had made a strong showing, coming back from her lackadaisical first debate. I finally crashed, with the TV still running in the background.

The next morning I awoke to two police officers towering over me. One was in uniform and the other was in plainclothes. The plain-clothes cop was Detective Rodgers. He drilled me with questions about my involvement in the string of robberies and why I'd been in Pete's car. This seemed to go on for hours, until they were finally convinced that I'd had nothing to do with the robberies and just had been in the wrong place at the wrong time.

It also helped that they'd gotten word that a member of the Renegades had confessed, ratting out Todd as the shooter who'd murdered the gas-station clerk. Todd, Bobby, Rashad, and Pete were the suspects guilty of the robberies. I'd finally been cleared of all charges.

The next few hours, I was alone again — alone with my thoughts. The throbbing from my headache decreased. It was, at best, tolerable.

Why didn't I die? I reflected upon my life and how I got to this point.

Did I die? Did I see Jesus? If that was Jesus — those loving eyes, that gentle voice, and that smile of compassion — then I was faced with the question: Why did he send me back? Why was he giving me another chance to pick the right gate? More than ever, it was clear to me how God had been calling me. The past few months, he'd been knocking at my heart.

First, there was the visiting preacher who came to my church to warn me that the path I was taking was the wide gate that leads to destruction. Then, there was my talk with Stephen; he was warning me about the company I was keeping. Then, there was Pastor Joel's message about fleeing fornication right before I met up with Jazzy. If I hadn't heard that word, I think that Jazzy's and my relationship would have been different.

Even though my brother seemed like a thorn in my side, he was there to prevent me from potentially being a part of a crime. Who knows? I could have been with Pete when all those robberies had gone down.

The list just kept on going, from the pastor, my dad, and even Rachel Matthews confronting me about what I believed in.

All of that, just for me, Lord?

Just for me?

I finally get the message. I realize I need you, and I am ready to answer the knock, to answer the call. Now is the time. I have always known that I didn't fit in. I was always an outsider to the world and to the church. To the world, I was a church kid. I tried to fit in but never did sound right cussing, no matter how much I tried. I tried to act tough, but I had not been exposed to the street life. I didn't grow up that way, but, I didn't fit in in the church, either. When the church had hype songs with banging beats, I might have participated, but, when it came to slow worship music, I was on the outside looking in, while everyone else was entering into God's presence.

How could I have been so blind? A flood of emotions was starting to overwhelm me. The faucet of grief had been turned on. Tears streamed down my face. Pride had clouded my judgment. I thought that I could do this life thing on my own. Now I was at a point where I knew I needed Jesus. I didn't need any more warnings, no more pretending. I had finally come to a point where, like my brother, I want to be all in. I want to be a committed Christian, to see what this Christian life was all about.

The one who made my life knows best how I should live it. I folded my hands, bowed my pounding head, and began a prayer that I should have prayed a long time ago.

"All I can say is, 'God, you are good. I am sorry for being so selfish. Lord, I am sorry for not listening to all your warnings. If you can still hear me, could you come into my life again? Could you forgive me of all my sins? This time, Lord, I want to serve you with all I have. Please save me and live in me. You are Lord and have died for my sins — I know. I believe you rose again from the grave and one day will come back for us...'"

As I was praying, the same feeling came over me that I'd had when I was nine years old, standing on top of my bed, preaching. Peace — an indescribable peace. A sense of belonging. I felt his presence just lingering in the room for about thirty minutes. I didn't want him to leave.

Joy — pure joy — engulfed me. I couldn't wait to tell someone of my conversion. The first person who walked through that door was going to get an earful of Jesus. Someone was coming...

* * * * *

Caves of Palestine

Meanwhile, back in the dingy caves of Palestine, the night was growing late, and the sergeant's bloodshot eyes were getting heavier and heavier. John wanted to continue on with the story, but sleep was starting to overtake him, also. Their captors turned out the lights, exhausted from the stress of always being on guard; never knowing what could happen next was wearing on them mentally. They agreed to continue John's story the next day. "Just when it was starting to get good," the sergeant said, fading into sleep. Watching the sergeant lie on the cold, dusty floor, John began to pray.

"God, please save this man. I believe you put me here just for him. Use me, Lord. I am a willing vessel." John also began to think about his family and friends. He pictured his mother being a nervous wreck over the uncertainty of his condition. John also knew that his friends were praying fervently for his release. That is what he was holding on to — hope.

Part Two

Cost of Discipleship

"There is no success without sacrifice. If you succeed without sacrifice, it is because someone has suffered before you. If you sacrifice without success, it is because someone will succeed after."

— ***Rick Joyner***

CHAPTER

10

Four years before

"Mom has prepared your favorite meal," said Philip.

"Lasagna?"

"You know it. Hey, the doctor should be here any minute now." Almost as soon as Philip had made the comment, Doctor Rosenberger appeared. Doctor Rosenberger had a business-like demeanor, a matter-of-fact kind of guy. He wasn't mean or rude, just friendly enough, not much for small talk. Came only to do his job.

"Well, it looks to me that you are ready to go home, young man." he said in a nonchalant manner.

"Can I see Pete before I go?" I asked.

"Well, your friend is still recovering in the ICU. We can let you see him only if a family member accompanies you, and I'm afraid Mrs. Woods just left for the day."

"Come on. He's my best friend, practically family," I pleaded, hoping the doctor would give in.

"Sorry, son, but I'm afraid it doesn't work like that. Comas can be tricky. Pete could wake up tomorrow, six months from now, or — ." Doctor Rosenberger paused a beat and then continued, "or never; we don't know." That's when the harsh reality hit me: Pete may never wake up.

"But you, my son, are lucky. Take it easy when you get home; let your body heal completely," the doctor said as he went about inputting my discharge information into the health system.

"No, sir. Not lucky. I'm blessed," I said proudly to the doctor. Not questioning me, Doctor Rosenberger just nodded his head in agreement and said, "OK — blessed. You are a blessed kid," he said, acknowledging my comment.

My mom sent Philip to pick me up from the hospital so she could finish making my favorite meal, lasagna with meat sauce, garlic bread, and a salad, with grape soda to drink, of course. Philip and I got into the old Camaro.

"Glad to have you home, bro, and I'm glad that someday I will see you in our final home," he said pointing to the heavens. Earlier that day, I had accepted Christ in my life or rededicated myself to him again. I'm not sure what you would call it, but I was glad I was in God's family.

Philip was overjoyed with the news, jumping around the hospital like he'd just won the lottery. I wasn't expecting that. Jazzy, on the other hand, was a different story. She was the first person to walk through the doors after my conversion. The news of my salvation was met with some opposition. I wasn't expecting that, either. I don't know how I was expecting her to react. I just know that I wasn't expecting her to be so skeptical of my decision.

While in the car, I shared with Philip my confession to Jazzy. "Hey, bro. After I'd given my life to Christ, I was excited and ready to tell the first person who walked through the door about him. Jazzy was that first person, but do you know what she said?"

"No. How did she react?"

"She said, 'I guess you reconnecting to God is a good thing and all. And I know this week has been a traumatic experience for you. This could cause you to question your life, but don't go all super saint on me, John.' She said it to me with sort of a disappointed look on her face. It was weird. I don't know how to feel about it."

"Hey, don't worry, bro. Just pray. It's all in God's timing. I was praying for you, and it took you a while, but look at you now," Philip said, reassuring me.

"I guess you're right."

* * * * *

Upon returning back to school, after my stint in the hospital, I was greeted with loads of homework and projects due. Of course, Mr. Donovan, my World History teacher, had us doing an essay about the Thirty Years War. The research for this assignment seemed like it was taking thirty years to complete.

However, there was one class that I looked forward to getting back to and that was my video-editing class. One of my projects was to complete the video highlights of this year's Grand Lake football team. I had already recorded most of this year's season and gathered some additional footage from other students. Now I just needed to edit the video into a gripping highlight reel.

Mr. Spring, my video-editing teacher, agreed to let me stay after school today to get caught up on my assignment. He opened the video room and let me in. He went to the faculty room, planning on returning a couple hours later. If I finished early, I was instructed to come get him so that he could lock up.

After an hour and a half of replaying footage and making difficult decisions on what to keep or cut, I thought I'd finally produced a satisfactory reel. As I was saving my work, I heard what sounded like someone fussing. I went to the door, and, to my surprise, I saw Principal Strudel and Mr. Boots in what seemed like a heated conversation. I couldn't hear what was being said, but I could see Principal Strudel flailing his arms around and speaking in his high-pitched voice.

Mr. Boots, looking around, placed his finger over his mouth, giving the signal to be quiet, trying to calm him down. He grabbed the principal's arm and was coming straight toward my room. Not knowing what to do, I had to think quickly. I spotted the studio equipment in the room and slid behind it. Large studio lights with umbrellas, green screens, and tripods — a good place to hide, I concluded. I was hidden but also had a good look at what was happening.

As soon as I jumped behind the equipment, the door came swinging open, and then there was a forceful slam as the door shut.

"Get it together, Ritchie," the steaming Mr. Boots said. I thought that this may have been the first time I'd ever heard Mr. Boots speak.

"I'm sorry, Bo Bo," the principal replied.

"Do you want the whole school to know?"

It was taking every ounce of energy I had to restrain myself from bursting out with laughter. *Ritchie? Bo Bo?* What kind of names were they? "Ritchie, I assumed, was short for Richard, Principal Richard Strudel's first name. But "Bo Bo" — I had no idea.

"Is this room secure?" Mr. Boots asked.

"Yes, it is. All the students are gone."

Not all of them, I thought to myself.

"Okay. How are you doing with the staff? Are all of them on board with their support of the senator?"

"Mr. Donovan and Ms. Rand are being difficult, but don't worry. I have ways of convincing them," Principal Strudel said in a slithery voice, sounding as though he had some evil plan.

"I like it," Mr. Boots replied with approval.

Principal Strudel and Mr. Boots were definitely a strange couple, gay or straight. They were total opposites. Principal Strudel was high-strung, spoke in a high-pitched voice, and was an older man — in his fifties. He had a small frame, was very controlling, wore coke-bottle glasses, and swayed like a woman when he walked. One hand was always glued to his hip.

His partner, Mr. Boots, on the other hand, was a man who appeared to be in his thirties, with a full head of hair, a well-built, clean-cut, military-looking man. From his looks, no one would guess that he preferred to be with men over women. I'm sure many women would've loved to be with him. I would hear the whispers of the women teachers, swooning over him, determined to make him a straight man.

"How can anyone support that independent silver-haired coon? Ooh, she just angers me with all that religious talk!" The outraged Principal Strudel was letting out his frustration, speaking about the President.

"You don't worry about that," Mr. Boots calmly answered.

"I know you can't talk about your work, honey, but what is going to be done about this? She's rising in the polls."

"All I can say is we also have ways of convincing the public who to vote for. Don't worry. The senator will win."

Who is this man? And what did he mean, "We have ways of convincing the public"? Does he work for Senator Wright?

Principal Strudel seemed to be pleased with his answer. He placed his hand on Mr. Boots' shoulder and said, "Oh, my Bo Bo." All these pet names and signs of affection toward one another were starting to make my stomach queasy. Mr. Boots placed his hand back on Mr. Strudel's face and smiled, looking into his eyes.

The sight of that and the sudden thought of what was about to happen cause a taste of vomit to rise to my lips. I swung my hand over my mouth to prevent the projectile of vomit. In the process, I clipped the tripod stands near me, causing them to make a noise and tumble.

"What was that?" Mr. Boots frantically said.

I had to think quickly. The table near me held Mr. Spring's class pet Slow-mo, a little box turtle. I scooped up Slow-mo out from his aquarium and placed him onto the floor. Then I quickly slid underneath the table. Mr. Boots came rushing over to the area where the noise had come from.

"What is it, Bo Bo?" Principal Strudel worriedly asked.

"Turtle."

"What?"

"A turtle must have rattled this equipment." Mr. Boot said with a chuckle of relief.

"How did that turtle get loose?"

"Maybe one of the students forgot to put him back in his box."

"Possibly. I wouldn't put it past one of those irresponsible rascals."

Mr. Boots came walking toward the table I was under. He put the turtle back into his glass aquarium. *Lord, please don't let him look down*, I silently prayed. He was about to take another step forward when Principal Strudel spoke.

"Let's get out of this room. I don't like being in a room with all these cameras around," he said, stopping Mr. Boots in his tracks.

After they left, I waited at least another fifteen minutes, catching my breath, before I decided to move. I gathered my backpack that I'd left on my work desk and cautiously peeked out the door. *The coast is clear.* I decided to bypass going to the faculty room to let Mr. Spring know I was done. I just wanted to get out of the building. As I rounded the corner to head for the exit, I was suddenly confronted by Principal Strudel, standing inches from me.

* * * * *

Dear God, I am on my knees praying for my girlfriend Jazzy. Please, Lord, open her eyes so that she may see you like I see you. Touch her heart so...

"John, are you ready?" Philip yelled across into my room.

"Give me a second. I'm coming," I replied. *Lord, be with me.* I grabbed my jacket and tablet. "I'm coming." We met in the garage.

"Am I still picking up Jazzy?" Philip asked.

"Yeah. She said she needs a ride."

"Alright."

That day was Wednesday, and, for the first time in a long time, I was looking forward to going to church. Jazzy's mom wasn't able to drop her off at church, and her step brother wasn't willing to take her, so Philip volunteered to pick her up. I loved Jazzy, but I was definitely sensing a distance growing between us ever since I'd said that I was a believer. I managed to convince her to come to church with us that day, even though her mom was not going.

We arrived at Jazzy's, and I went to get her. "Hey, beautiful."

"Hey, handsome."

"Oh, please. Get in the car," Philip said to us.

"Hey, you guys won't believe what happened to me yesterday after school. I forgot to tell you."

"What happened?" Jazzy perked up like she was ready for some juicy gossip.

"OK. You know yesterday I stayed after school to work on my video project in Mr. Spring's class. So when I finished my work, I was about to leave the classroom when I saw Principal Strudel and Mr. Boots outside the door in what looked like a heated argument.

"Next thing I knew Mr. Boots was trying to get out of the hallway and pulled Principal Strudel into my room. I managed to hide just before they burst through the doors.

"Now, here is where things get interesting." I proceeded to relate the details about what was said between them and how their actions nearly made me puke, causing me to make a loud ruckus.

"So, after they left the room, I waited awhile, and then I headed for the exit doors. It felt like I was in on an evil plot. I was listening to something I wasn't supposed to hear. When I rounded the corner and was going to the exit, I ran into Principal Strudel. Standing with his hand on his hip and his thick glasses on the brim of his nose, he said, 'Oh, Mr. Mann. What are you still doing here so late at school?' I explained that I was catching up on my schoolwork from my absences.

"'A student working hard. I like to see that,'" he said. I was praying that he wouldn't ask me what classroom I'd come from. Thank God, he didn't.

"'So how are you recovering?' he said."

"'I'm doing just fine,' I said. 'Thanks.'

"'Good to hear,' he replied. Now this is the strange part. When I was walking past him and was about to open the door, he said to me 'Nice backpack.'"

"So, he complimented you on your backpack. What's strange about that?" Philip said, like 'What's the big deal?'

"It wouldn't be, but he said it in a creepy way, which got me thinking. While they were talking in the room, my backpack was still lying on my desk in plain sight. Mr. Boots was coming close to my table, just about to see me, before Principal Strudel turned him around to leave. Do you think — ?"

"I think that you're overthinking this. Making more of it than it should be," Jazzy said, blowing off the notion that the two of them were in on a wicked plot and that they knew I was in the room.

"Maybe so, but I have a bad feeling about this," I said.

As we finished our conversation, we were pulling into the church. I was ready to hear from God today, expecting something to happen. We headed to our young adult/teenage class, where Pastor Joel was getting things ready to begin.

He approached the front of the class. "Hello, everyone. I want to ask you a question today. How old do you have to be before God can use you to change the world?"

One teen raised her hand and answered, "Once you become an adult, that's when God can use you to reach people."

Some kids in class were laughing at her reply. Another student proudly stood and answered, "God can use you at any age."

"You're right — he can," said Pastor Joel. "When David was only a youth, God used him to save Israel by defeating the giant Goliath. His brothers told him to go back home, and King Saul said, 'Who is this youth?' But God used a teenager to save his people."

Pastor Joel went on to give another example.

"Daniel and his three friends were ripped from their families as teenagers and brought to a foreign land to serve King Nebuchadnezzar. When the king ordered them to worship him, they refused, showing that they would rather burn than bow their knee to him. As a result, God came and delivered them.

"Mary, the mother of Jesus, was probably somewhere between the ages of 12 and 15 when an angel came to her, giving her the news that she was going to give birth to the savior. God called her 'highly favored,' and this young teen girl was given the task of raising the savior of the world.

"I'm saying all of this as a way of telling you, 'You're right. God can use anyone at any age.' So, my question is, why are we waiting to be an adult before we decide to commit to him? I just want to challenge each of you to go after God. He is not a respecter of person. Don't let anyone look down on you because you are young, but set an example. Jesus is coming soon, and he wants young soldiers who are ready for battle. Will you be one?"

CHAPTER

11

"Hey, there, sexy mama," a dark-skinned boy said as he leaned against his locker sucking his teeth with an evil grimace. Grins and looks of lust were in his eyes. His comment was directed to my girlfriend. I tried to keep walking and let his remark slide, but that wasn't going to happen. I turned to speak to the dark, square-faced boy.

"Who are you talking to?" I said, angrily.

"Not to you — but to the pretty girl next to you, though."

Raging with anger, I walked up to him and looked straight into his lustful eyes. "Well, she's my girl. Back off."

An awkward silence descended over those nearby, questioning my decision to challenge the boy. Tension was building, and students were stopping and starting to gather around to see the spectacle. Jazzy jumped in between us.

"Guys, stop it. Please — John, Triston."

"What are you going to do, church boy?" Triston said pushing off his locker and standing tall.

Church boy? I thought. The realization hit me: He's right. I can't be getting into fights. I am a Christian, and this is not Christ-like. I began to relax my balled fist, unwound my arm, and took a step back.

"You're not worth it," I said, backing off to leave the scene, when, all of a sudden, I saw a flash of light and a hard slap to the left side of my cheek. Triston had sucker-punched me. The punch caused me to fall to the ground, scattering my belongings. Jazzy came to my aid and pushed him away.

"Leave him alone, you jerk" she snapped at him.

"Aren't you supposed to turn the other cheek?" Triston said turning and playing to the crowd, summoning up laughter. All eyes were on me, and all I saw was red. I had to do something. I couldn't let this slide. I wiped the blood from my lip, and, with a surge of anger, I lunged forward, ready to rip his head off. My attempt to demolish Triston was met by my brother's arms stopping me in midair.

"You're right, John — he's not worth it. Let it go," Philip said restraining me and giving Triston a fiery look. His words must have shook Triston a bit as he and his friends saw teachers approaching and backed off to retreat. Before leaving, Triston made one last remark to Jazzy.

"Let me know when you are ready to leave this loser and hook up with a real man," he said, blowing her a kiss, causing giggles among his friends. Disgusted by the thought, Jazzy gave him a middle-finger salute.

Triston Stewart was a junior at our school. Your typical jock, a 6'4" athlete, star quarterback, who happened to also be a major jerk and school bully. Ever since our freshman year, he had been trying to get with Jazzy. He was jealous at the idea that she had fallen in love with a guy like me. Whenever he could, he tried to make my life difficult.

The crowd managed to disperse before any teachers could arrive at the commotion. We were also able to get away before any teachers arrived.

"Sorry, guys, for losing my cool," I said to Jazzy and Philip.

"You have nothing to be sorry about," Jazzy said, dabbing my face with a tissue. "He's such a jerk," she added.

"Yeah. If he would have laid one more hand on you, John, I would have been *turning*

both of his cheeks," Philip said.

Jazzy and I just stared at Philip, surprised at what he was saying.

Sensing that we were looking at him bizarrely, he replied, "What? God is still working on me, too," causing all of us to burst out laughing.

* * * * *

I stood staring at the shell of a familiar face. His motionless body just lay there. One would have thought that he was just in a deep, peaceful sleep, if not for all the tubes flowing through his body, keeping him alive. My once-vibrant friend was now confined to a bed, trapped in his body. Pete, however, had made *some* progress. That day, they'd removed his ventilator. Thank God — he was able to breathe on his own now, but he was still unresponsive.

"I don't know if you can hear me, buddy, but I'm praying for you. I need you to wake up. I need you… "

As I was praying for Pete, I got a text from Stephen.

To all the on-fire youth who are believers in Christ: Are you tired of the hypocrisy in the church and want to see God manifested? If so, let's meet at my parents' place to chop up this word and discuss. This Saturday @ 6 pm, 1153 Grand Ave., Kansas City. See ya there, and spread the word. God Bless, Bro. Stephen.

Minutes later, I got a call from Philip.

"Did you get the text from Stephen?" he asked.

"Yeah. I just got it. I guess Stephen is taking Pastor Joel's words seriously," I said.

"Yeah, I guess so. Are you down for this weekend?"

"You know it."

"By the way, how is Pete doing?" Philip asked.

"He is breathing on his own now."

"Praise God."

"Yeah. Keep praying for him."

"Alright, bro. Talk to you later," said Philip as he ended the conversation.

After the week I'd had, I needed the prayers and strength from my brothers and sisters in Christ.

* * * * *

The once-azure skies suddenly turned dark and gloomy. The charcoal clouds rolled in, swallowing up the sun's rays and causing the frightened sun to flee into hiding. Flashes of lightning and rumbles of thunder fill the sky. The scent of rain lingered in the air before the heavens finally opened, with the knob to the shower turned on, full blast, soaking the entire Kansas City metro area.

This wet, drowsy Saturday made it very difficult to find motivation to leave the house for anything. The couch was calling my name, the television was seducing me with programs, and laziness was whispering sweet nothings in my ear. "Stay home and relax," I could hear them saying.

I was ready to give into their lure. That's when a message from

Stephen snapped me out of the spell. Stephen was sending out a reminder: *Are you still on for tonight? My place. Don't miss out on what God wants to do, bro.*

I hesitantly respond, *See you there.*

We had to go now. So Philip and I decided to brave the elements. We hopped in the Camaro and headed towards Stephen's place. While on the drive to his place, we were bobbing our heads to a song called *Are You Ready?* By an up-and-coming Christian artist named "New Wine." The hook was *"Are you ready for the rapture? Ready to be captured? Gonna see the Master?"*

After the song ended I had to ask Philip what was going on with him and Tameka.

"Is Tameka coming to the meeting?" I asked.

"I don't know. Why?"

"Yeah, right — you don't know. What's up with you and her anyway?"

"We're just cool like that. Don't worry about it, little bro," he responded.

"Just cool, huh?" I didn't press it any further. I just sat back, relaxed, closing my eyes, tapping my fingers on my leg to the music.

As we arrived at the Ortega's household, the rain finally decided to go for a lunch break from its hard work. We were one of the first to arrive. There were two other cars parked in front of the house. We were curious as to whom those cars belonged to. As we parked, Stephen's older sister Anita was leaving the house with her son Rudy. Now there was one other car in front of the house besides ours.

Stephen greeted us. "Glad you could make it. Come on in," he said. When we entered, I was watching my brother scan the room. I knew who he was looking for. I was also hoping that Jazzy would show, like she'd said she would. Philip had offered to bring her, but she assured me that her brother would take her to this meeting. I had a sinking feeling that she was just saying that to get me off her back about God.

Carl Green came from the kitchen with a soda and cookie in his hand. Now we knew who the other car belonged to, and, to Philip's dismay, it wasn't Tameka's.

"Man, where's everybody at?" Philip said, anxiously.

"They're coming. The weather may be causing some delays," Stephen replied.

Stephen's family lived in the revamped area of the inner city. The once-desolate downtown of Kansas City had returned to its glory; many were flocking back to the city. The Ortega's had a gorgeous home. Stephen's dad was a district manager at Burner Corporation Campus, the biggest business in the city.

Stephen was waiting patiently for the guests to arrive and decided to give them another ten minutes before starting the meeting. It was 6:45 pm, forty-five minutes past the scheduled start time, so we decided to go ahead and get started. Carl was about to start in his prayer to open the meeting, but he was interrupted by the sound of the doorbell. Rachel Matthews was at the door.

"Hey, Rachel," Philip and Carl said.

"I would have been here sooner, but there was a wicked accident on 71 highway" she said. I could see the concern on Philip's face.

"Did you see who it was?" Philip asked.

"No, I just saw the paramedics putting a black girl who looked around our age on a stretcher. It looked pretty serious though," she replied.

My brother got panicky when he heard Rachel say "a black girl who looked around our age was on a stretcher."

"I guess that explains why people aren't showing up yet," Carl interjected.

Stephen, being sensitive to the matter, said a short prayer: "Lord, please watch over that girl."

Slowly, others started to arrive, trickling into Stephen's house.

Finally Carl was able to open up the meeting with prayer. Philip was unusually quiet, looking anxious and disappointed. Outside the rain had decided to return from its lunch break, with increased activity. The thunder was so loud my grandfather would say that "the angels were bowling in heaven."

As we were connecting our devices to view the Bible, there was another ring at the door. Stephen left to answer the door. As he opened the door, Hannah came in, dripping wet, and then another girl, and finally Tameka. I was observing my brother. When Tameka entered the room, he looked relieved and struggled to contain his smile.

"Wow! It's pouring out there! I had trouble finding Hannah's house. Then, on the way here, we got caught in traffic. Must have been an accident or something," Tameka explained.

Stephen and Carl took their raincoats and umbrellas. As Hannah was handing Stephen her raincoat, she slipped on the entrance tile. Stephen quickly responded, preventing Hannah from hitting the ground. The already-shy Hannah had a sheepish grin as Stephen held her in his arms. Looking into her eyes, Stephen said, "Sorry about that. I'll get that cleaned up. Are you okay?" Hannah, smiling back, nodded her head "Yes." I could see the look in her eyes, wishing he would have held her a little while longer, but Stephen was clueless, as usual.

At last, the meeting started at around 7:15 pm, a whole hour and fifteen minutes late. Surprisingly, around thirty or so young people showed up, even with the downpour of rain outside. It was bitter and sweet. Sweet to see all these young people here to seek out God. Bitter that Jazzy didn't make it. *Jazzy, what is going on?* I texted.

Stephen stood to address everyone. "First of all I would like to thank all of you for showing up today. You could have easily decided to stay home, especially on a day like this, but you are here, and I believe God will reward you for this.

"Well, you know the reason why I called this meeting.

"Pastor Joel gave us a challenge as young people to be God seekers. A few days ago, while I was pondering the pastor's words, I just happened to be reading a biography of Dwight L. Moody. He was a powerful evangelist in the nineteenth century who later started a church and school. I was moved by his passion, and these two quotes stuck with me."

Stephen reached into his pants pocket and pulled out a crumpled piece of paper. Why he had written it on a piece of paper and not his digital notebook, I didn't know. Anyway, he began to read. *"The Bible was not given for our information but for our transformation."* Stephen paused a beat, letting those words sink in. Then he continued, *"'The world has yet to see what God will do with and for and through and in and by the man who is fully consecrated to Him.'* These are the words of the great evangelist Dwight L. Moody. These words inspired me. I know that I have not given God my all, with no reservation, but I am ready. How many of you are ready to see what God can do with a man or woman who has sold out for him?"

There was a silence throughout the group as people meditated on what was said. Then someone from the back said "I'm ready." It was Carl. Then another voice said "I am," and then another and another. Before I knew it, just about everyone had pledged their commitment.

Finally, I stood and said, "I'm ready," not fully knowing what I was committing myself to, but I did know that I wanted God to use me for his glory. Philip spoke and said what many of us were thinking.

"So what does this mean? How do we become fully consecrated?"

Stephen gave a broad smile like he'd been expecting this question.

"Well, I suggest that we fast," he says.

We all looked at him like he had just said a curse word.

"Fast?" Carl said in disbelief, as he took another bite of his cookie.

"Yes, fast. The Bible tells us that there are some things that will be broken only during prayer and fasting. Did you know that times of fasting is expected for believers? Jesus says in Matthew 6:16, 'when you fast...' Then he goes on and gives instruction for fasting. Did you notice that he said 'when you fast,' like he expected that this be something we should do?"

"I don't know, man. I don't think that I have gone a day without eating, at least not on purpose," a glooming-looking Carl said.

"Come on, man. This can be an adventure," Philip excitedly said.

"How long are you talking about, Stephen?" Rachel asked.

"Well, today I was also reading about Daniel and his friends not wanting to eat the king's food. So, for ten days, they ate nothing but vegetables and drank water. I suggest that we fast for ten days. Meaning that we abstain from any secular media, social media, and either eat vegetables, fruits, and nuts or eat no food at all for ten days. Depending on your level of commitment. I personally, by God's grace, want to take the challenge of only water for five days and then, the other five days, eat vegetables and fruits.

"Each of you must follow your own conviction."

"I don't think I can do the no-food thing just yet. I am going to eat just vegetables and drink water," Carl said.

"It's a start," Tameka said.

Stephen suggested that all who were committing join every morning for prayer. Carl helped him set up on his social media page a login to join in on a video-conference call. Carl also created a message board for prayer requests and praise reports. We all shook our heads in approval.

"So, it's settled then?" Stephen asked.

About twenty-five of us out of the thirty committed to taking this journey to seek God. Our scripture theme was Jeremiah 29:13: **"You will seek me and find me when you seek me with all your heart."**

The time had flown by, and it was around 10 pm. Stephen and Philip decided to walk the girls out to their cars even though the rain had all but stopped. Stephen was so clueless to Hannah's flirtatious vibes, and Philip was diffident when it came to Tameka.

I checked my messages, hoping to get some reply from Jazzy, some message explaining why she didn't make it. But, as I looked at my phone, all I saw was a blank screen.

What is going on, Jazzy?

CHAPTER

12

Weakness was invading my body, and my energy was slowly draining. Simple, routine tasks like lifting my backpack were becoming very difficult to do. It was day two of our youth-group fast. Day one wasn't as arduous as I thought it would be, but this day was a totally different story. Hunger and fatigue were starting to win the battle. Mentally, I was having second thoughts about this whole fasting thing.

To get my mind off of physical food, I decided to delve into some spiritual food. Sitting at the kitchen table with my Bible pulled up, scrolling through scriptures, I pushed the "Random" button on my Bible app, asking for it to give me a scripture to read.

I landed on the book of Matthew, chapter four. Ironically, this chapter was talking about Jesus fasting. Wow! Even Jesus fasted. While Jesus was fasting, Satan tried to tempt him into turning a stone into bread. Verse four was the verse that stood out for me today. It said, *Jesus answered, "It is written: 'Man shall not live on bread alone, but on every word that comes from the mouth of God.'"* I felt as though God was saying to me that he wanted to give me something more than what natural food could provide.

In the background, I heard a news commentary on yesterday's presidential debate. My dad was reclined on the sofa, soaking in all the information. Early polls were showing that the race between President Copperfield and Senator Wright was very tight. Independent President

Sandra Copperfield had a slight lead, with 55% of the votes. The Republican candidate had 5% of voters. Undecided voters were at 3%, and Democratic Senator Cordell Wright currently had 38% of the votes.

My dad was beaming from ear to ear as he listened, cheering on President Copperfield. Philip was sleeping, trying to pass the time away, and my mom was upstairs reading another one of her mystery novels. In just these two days of fasting, it made me realize that I had more time on my hands than I thought. I used to just waste it on frivolous things.

When I finished my reading in the book of Matthew, I began to wonder what Jazzy was doing and how she was doing. Saturday, when she didn't show up to the meeting, I was concerned. Then, on Sunday, she wasn't at church, either, causing me even more anxiety. It wasn't like Jazzy not to reply to me. Yesterday, I'd finally been able to get in contact with her. I found out that her grandmother had been rushed to the hospital on Saturday and that they'd spent the night at the hospital until the next day.

I was able to explain to her what had gone on during Saturday's meeting, and she agreed to fast with me. I was pleasantly surprised at her decision to join me. However, yesterday had been a rough day for her. Like many of us, Jazzy had never fasted before, and that first day wasn't kind to her. She was complaining of headaches and fatigue. So I gave her a call to see what her status was with the fast.

"Hey, beautiful," I said.

I heard a groggy response: "Hey, John."

"So, how are you doing, babe?"

"Not good. Not good at all," she said.

"Hang in there. God will give you strength."

"Look, I can't do this anymore."

"What? Are you talking about fasting?"

"Yes, silly. This is not natural. I can't even function."

"Well, you can switch to eating only vegetables and fruit, if that will help," I suggested.

"It's too late for that. My mom cooked some fajitas today, and I couldn't resist them. Boy, did that hit the spot." I could hear her smacking her lips as she spoke.

Disappointed, I tried to convince her that she should start the fast again.

"*No!* I am *not* doing this!" she said emphatically.

I began to hear the frustration in her voice.

"Why are you doing this? It doesn't take all of this to be Christian." She paused and then continued, "Lately, I have been worrying about you, John. Especially since you had your so-called conversion."

"What do you mean, 'so called' conversion?" I retorted.

"Look, I'm sorry. I just don't want you to veer off into some cult with all your Jesus-dedication stuff. That's all I'm saying," Jazzy calmly expressed, trying to retract her words.

It was too late though. Her comments had hurt me. I didn't know that she felt this way. Was I going off the deep end? I didn't think so. As a matter of fact, I knew that wasn't true. Why was she discrediting my commitment to Christ?

"Jazzy, I want all that God has to offer me — don't you?"

"To be honest, John, if it takes all of this fasting and prayer, then I'm not sure I do," she bluntly said. Before I could respond, she interrupted, "Hey, John. My mom is calling me. I'll talk to you later. See you tomorrow at school, OK?"

"Alright. Love you, Jaz," I said feeling dejected after her words.

I could hear the hesitation in her voice before she finally said, "Me, too."

* * * * *

Day three, and I could feel a little strength coming back to my body after being on the prayer call this morning. After just three days, the twenty-five youth who were committed to the fast had now dwindled down to seventeen. Many of them had posted negative comments on Stephen's message board saying that this movement was not of God and that they were unnecessarily starving themselves.

Stephen, however, was resolute in his decision to continue and sent out encouraging messages and scriptures to back up his position. We finished our prayer call, and I was preparing for school when I saw my brother still kneeling by his bed — something that he had been doing before school lately.

"Do you mind if I join you?" I said to Philip.

"Not at all, bro," he replied.

"What's up? Why the downcast face? What's weighing on your heart?"

"My friends — Jazzy, Pete," I said, solemnly.

"Well, let's take it to the Lord. The Bible tells us to cast our cares on him. So are you ready to do that?" he said.

I nodded, and then we began in our prayer.

Philip's prayer did bring me some peace about my friends. The drive to school was a smooth, peaceful ride; the presence of God was in our Camaro. There was no music playing — just peace and quiet. Every now and again, we could hear the growls from our stomachs, reminding us that we still hadn't eaten anything.

We arrived at school, and I met with Jazzy to walk her to her first class.

"Hey, Jaz" I said.

"What's up, Johnny?"

"So how is your grandmother doing?"

"My grandmother?" she questioned.

"Yeah, your grandmother."

"Oh, oh yeah — she is doing fine. Just fine," she replied. I thought her answer was kind of odd, but I didn't think much more of it. As we were walking to class, I could see my nemesis, Triston in the distance. He was leaning against his locker, like always, with that same twisted smile painted on his face.

The only thing that I was thinking of was that if something was to go down today, I didn't know how much strength I would have to defend myself. My body was weak. I was determined to just let whatever comment Triston was going to say roll off of me. "God, help me with this," I said, sending up a short prayer.

"Hey, Jazzy. Nice shoes you have there. What are they — Pristoes?" Triston politely asked. Jazzy nodded her head "Yes."

"My mom has some like those. They look good on you," he said. Triston was being unusually nice today — or at least acting as though he was. Normally Jazzy wouldn't have even acknowledged Triston's comments, or, if she did, she would reply with a hostile comeback. This time was different. She surprised me and, I think, Triston too.

She smiled and turned to look at him and said, "Thank you for noticing." Then she gave me a look like I should have been the one saying those things.

"You spoke to that clown," I said, conveying shock and trying to process this but also trying not to expend the little energy I still had on arguing.

"Well, at least he noticed. I guess he's not always the jerk you make him out to be," she answered, with her head held high.

I was in disbelief at what I'd just heard. I looked back at Triston with his joker smile, gloating over a victory won. Was Triston starting to become a threat to me?

* * * * *

Day five finally arrived. This was the last day of the full fast — water only. Tomorrow I will be able to eat vegetables, fruits, and nuts. I remembered that, on the first day of the fast, out of habit, I went to the fridge, like I normally did, and was about to bite into a leftover pizza. My mouth was ready to chomp down on the cold, flavorful, pepperoni pizza before Philip stopped me and reminded me that the fast had begun.

I finally managed to break my habit of constantly opening the refrigerator doors every morning. On day five, I had been dreaming of what food I was going to eat the next day. Even though I was going to eat only vegetables and fruits, the thought of food energized me. Never thought I would be looking forward to eating grapes and cabbage.

I was sitting alone at the cafeteria table; my lunch buddies Gary and Eugene had abandoned me. I guess I was turning out to be too much of a super saint, according to them. Jazzy and Philip ate lunch on the shift before me, so I couldn't even confide in them now.

Ever since I had committed myself to Christ, it seemed as though my so-called "friends" didn't want to have anything to do with me — especially since they'd found out that I was doing a ten-day fast. They said that I was too extreme for them. Kids at school used to call me

Johnzmine. Now the names I was hearing were "super saint," holy broth-ers" (referring to me and Philip), and "Jesus freak." Even though Jazzy was sticking by my side, I could sense the shame that she had for me. The peer pressure was starting to get to her.

I was at a huge table alone, feeling like a bag of bones. I was be-ginning to look like a walking skeleton. My once one-hundred-and-seventy-pound frame had been reduced to one hundred and fifty-eight. I'd lost twelve pounds, and I barely had enough strength to lift my tablet to read my Bible. I couldn't laugh too hard, or I might get my rib caught. Even walking was laborious. Headaches and fatigue were overpowering me. It was taking every ounce of mental strength not to quit this fast.

If it had not been for the prayers of the youth and the support of my brother, I don't know if I would have even made it that far. Out-wardly I was fading away, but, inwardly, I was being renewed. I felt a closeness to God that I had never felt before. While I was going over our scripture theme in Jeremiah 29:13, I saw Principal Strudel approaching me.

"Well, there Mr. Mann. Is everything alright?"

"Yes, sir. I'm doing well."

"Too me, you are looking quite famished, I must say. You have no food to eat? I hear rumors saying that you and a few other students are starving yourselves."

"No, sir. We are fasting for religious reasons."

"Nonsense. I can't have that at my school. Let's see what I have to eat. Hey, what about this scrumptious cookie? Homemade chocolate chip, just for you — my treat," he said, waving the cookie back and forth. The aroma of the cookie was enticing, and the thought of a cookie was mouth watering. The scripture flashed in my mind: *Man shall not live on bread alone, but on every word that comes from the mouth of God.*

"No thank you, sir. I'm OK."

"Well, I am going to leave it here, just in case you change your mind," he said, placing the cookie right next to my tablet. Then he spoke again.

"Ah, studying, I see. May I see what you are reading?"

"Sure." I handed him my tablet. The text on the tablet read: *You will seek me and find me when you seek me with all your heart.*

A loud scream startled everyone in the cafeteria. Principal Strudel had let out a high-pitched squeal, tossing my tablet straight into the air.

"Ew, I just touched a Bible!" he shouted again and again as he went dashing off, sashaying to the restroom. "I must clean my hands," he said, frightened, in a state of shock. I just managed to dive and catch my tablet before it shattered to the ground.

The sight of Principal Strudel hysterically running off caused the whole cafeteria to erupt in a thunderous uproar of laughter. I could see Mr. Boots, in the distance, glaring at me as the students were laughing.

Rachel Matthews approached me.

"Hey, John," she said.

"How's it going, Rachel?"

"What was that all about?" she said, trying to contain her laughter.

"I guess the principal doesn't like the Bible," I said as we both chuckled.

"Why is Mr. Boots looking at you like that? Creepy," she whispered.

"Yeah, I'm telling you: Something evil is going on in this school between those two," I commented.

"Can I sit down?" she asked.

"Sure, pick any seat you like," I said, waving my hand across all the empty chairs at the table.

"How is your fasting going?" she asked.

"I'm hanging in there," I said as my stomach growled. "What about you?"

"By God's grace, I'm still hanging in there," she said as she plopped down in the seat across from me.

"I see your lunch friends have left. Are you okay?"

"I guess I'm doing okay. I never knew that this was going to be this hard. Not just the not eating part but also the onslaught of name calling and mockery I'm getting."

"Tell me about it. I totally understand. People are starting to call me 'Psychic Rachel.' It's weird. Since I've been fasting, God has been giving me words about people's futures."

"Wow! That sounds cool."

"Hey, I can tell you more about it later if you like. I am starting a Bible study and prayer meeting before and after school. Do you want to come?"

"Sure. Don't you work at Manny's Deli after school, though?"

"Not anymore. I just quit. It was requiring too much time and was starting to interfere with my schoolwork. The Bible study is tomorrow at the church across the street. I know a few people who go to that church. I'm sure Principal Strudel wouldn't allow any religious meetings on school property."

"You mean any *Christian* meetings," I said.

"Exactly. Well, it was nice talking to you, but I have to go. I'm going to let you continue your reading. Let your brother know about the Bible meeting, and stop harassing our principal." She laughed and smiled as she got up to leave. Then she turned to say, "Keep the faith, John. God will reward us. We must remain faithful because I just know God is going to use this group for something special. Some time ago, I had questions about your Christian faith, but look at you now. I have no doubt about your sincere commitment to our Lord."

"Thanks, Rachel — that means a lot," I replied.

After our talk, I went to Stephen's social page to check the group's prayer message board to see if there were any new prayer requests. I also checked to see what the participation status was. Out of our seventeen members, only twelve remained online and active in participating. Five had messaged that they were dropping out of the fast.

CHAPTER

13

Philip and I cruised in the Camaro down a windy neighborhood road. Looking out into the cloudless indigo sky, most people were still sound asleep at that time of day, but not us. The roosters were not even stirring yet. It was a little over an hour before the start of school, and we were headed to a Bible study.

We'd accepted Rachel's invitation and were on our way to a church called Manna House. Rachel had a friend, Cassandra Clayton, whose dad was a pastor at that church. He willingly opened the doors of his church for Rachel to have her Bible study and prayer meeting before and after school.

This was day six of our fast, and, for me and Philip, our first day of eating just vegetables and fruit. Before we left, I'd packed my lunch full of chopped apples, nuts, cantaloupes, and a salad. I had a cup of orange juice before getting into the car and a bunch of grapes. I must admit my eyes were bigger than my stomach. Due to the shrinkage of my stomach from not eating for five days, I was able to finish only a few grapes before my stomach was full.

We approached the church, but Philip decided to park in the school parking lot and walk over to the church to ensure a good parking spot at school. We parked close to the building, a premium spot that was normally hard to get. As Philip turned off the car, we saw in the distance a silhouette of a boy coming out of a side door near the football field. The embers from his cigarette were glowing as he took a few puffs.

"Is that Triston Stewart?" Philip asked.

"Yeah that's Triston. Triston Stewart. What is he doing at school so early?" I said with displeasure.

"Beats me." Philip said as he was about to exit the car.

"Wait."

"What?"

"Don't open the door yet. Look!" I said.

"Mr. Boots — Principal Strudel?" Philip said. The principal and Mr. Boots were coming out of the same door as Triston. They all seemed to be having a casual conversation. Not only was Triston smoking in front of them, but Mr. Boots took a puff from Triston's cigarette.

"What is going on with them?" I said, perplexed. Probably not a minute, later an attractive girl came out of the door, too.

"Tiffany Storm. What is she doing there?" Things were becoming weird. Tiffany was a junior and captain of the cheerleading team, kind of conceited, selfish, and concerned only about her image. The question was, why was she with them?

"It looks like they were having a secret meeting or something," I said. We both just sat in the car, not wanting to be seen. A jock, a cheerleader, a principal, and his partner meeting together. Sounded like a beginning of a joke, but their meeting would be no joke.

We waited for them to go back into the building before we exited the car. It was still dark and it would be hard for them to see us from where they were.

Finally, after their smoke break ended, Principal Strudel, looking concerned, hurried them back into the building. Taking a look to his right and left and then squinting his eyes through his thick glasses, he looked in our direction before he finally went back inside.

"Man, I hope he didn't see us," Philip said, slumping down in his seat.

"I told y'all that something evil was going on in this school with our principal," I reiterated.

"I'll agree something strange is happening. Why were those four meeting? I want to know."

Once the coast was clear, we exited the vehicle and arrived a little late to the Bible study. When we got there, only Rachel and Cassandra were there. We connected and attended our fasting prayer call. Afterward Rachel, Cassandra — or "Cassie," as we called her — Philip and I held hands to pray for our school. Rachel sent forth a powerful prayer for our school and afterwards came up with the idea of passing out flyers to spread the word about the Bible study.

* * * * *

It felt as though a dark cloud was blanketing over Grand Lake High School that day. As I and Philip entered the school, there were Senator Wright campaign paraphernalia everywhere. It seemed as though we were at his campaign site.

Just about all the teachers had his "Vote the Wright Way" buttons pinned to their clothing, except for Mrs. Rand, my freshman Spanish teacher, and Mr. Donovan, my World History teacher. There was a hazy look in most of the teachers' eyes. I saw Mrs. Rand outside her room and decided to ask her what was going on. She was one of my favorite teachers and one of the sweetest, too.

"Hola, señora Rand."

"Hola, cómo estás, John?" she replied with a bright smile.

"I'm doing fine," I answered. "Why aren't you wearing the senator's pin?" I asked. Mrs. Rand's bright smile suddenly transformed into a grim countenance. All she said to me was,

"John, pray for your school." It looked as though she wanted to say more, but Mr. Boots walked by, causing her to end the conversation early. Weird.

I spotted Jazzy at her locker and was happy to see her as she pulled back the bangs from her caramel face.

"What up, Jazzy?"

"Hey, Johnny."

"Missed you this morning at prayer."

"Come on, John. Don't go there. You know I don't get up that early," she replied. Sensing the tension mounting, I switched subject matters.

"Hey, I guess you were right about the principal wanting to have all the teachers wear those buttons, huh?"

"Yeah, it looks like campaign central up in here," she said as we both laughed. It felt good to laugh with her, something that we hadn't done in a while. Jazzy turned and rubbed my hands and then touched my ring — the silver "J&J" paper ring she'd made for me.

"Hey, Johnny. I know things have been strained between us. I miss laughing with you, being with you. It seems as though you're spending more time in church. How about you coming over to my place in a few days? I'll cook."

"You, cook?" I said, surprised to hear her say that.

"I know you're eating only vegetables and stuff. So I will make you up something special, with my specialty drink, lemon water."

I chuckled as she jokingly tried to make the meal sound appealing.

"That sounds good."

"OK. Well, it's a date. I will call when the time comes. I'm running late," she said as she kissed me on the cheek and hurried off to her class.

Later that day, after devouring my fruit-and-veggie lunch, I was sluggish and full, not ready for my history class. When I arrived at Mr. Donovan's class, I could see that Mr. Donovan also wasn't supporting Senator Wright — no campaign buttons for him.

That day, our grades from our Thirty Year War essay were posted to our student accounts. Checking my account, I was somewhat surprise that I'd actually done very well on my assignment, receiving an A.

After class, Mr. Donovan asked to talk with me. Immediately, my mind went rushing to figure out what I'd done wrong. *Does he think I cheated on my work? Did he mistakenly give me the wrong grade?*

"Mr. Mann."

"Yes, sir," I answered.

"Just wanted to tell you that you're doing a great job. Over the past week, your school work has vastly improved. Why the change?"

"I guess I have a new perspective on life, sir."

"Well, keep up the good work."

"Thank you. I will." When I thought that the conversation had ended, Mr. Donovan went to the door, surveyed the halls, and then closed the door.

"John, there is something else I want to tell you. I have seen your brother and Rachel passing out Bible study flyers and just wanted to warn you to be careful around here. What you guys are doing is great, but Principal Strudel can be — "

Before he could finish, a voice over the intercom spoke, "Mr. Donovan, could you please report to the office? Mr. Donovan, please report. Thank you."

His last words to me were "John, be careful." I could see the seriousness on his face with a hint of panic as he left.

* * * * *

The room was like I expected it to be — organized, sterile, and clean enough to eat off the floors. There were no family pictures, at least none with people. He had pictures of his two Persian cats and many academic awards adorning his walls.

Rocco and Matty. Rocco, the ugly male cat, with long gray hair, and Matty, the feisty female, with cream-and-white-colored fur. Obviously, he loved his cats and achievements. I was in Principal Strudel's office — as well as Philip, Cassie, and Rachel. Not because we'd been in a fight or cheated on an exam but simply for passing out flyers. I was in the office for saying "Bless you" to a classmate. Can you believe that? I sure couldn't.

According to Principal Strudel, "student policy states that there should be no distribution of any religious material before, during, or after school, on school property." Also my teacher Mrs. Tolle claimed that I was being disruptive during class when I told my classmate, "May God bless you" for helping me out with my lab assignment.

After we sat in his office for a long period of time, wondering what was happening, Principal Strudel finally swayed through the doors holding one of his cats, the ugly one.

"Students, your intolerable actions have been brought to my attention today. I will not allow such blatant disregard for the rules in this school. This is a serious offense, and I am recommending in-school suspensions for each of you, for violating school policy. Disrupting the classroom?" he said, looking at me. "Distributing and pushing religious beliefs on students is just not acceptable. Your suspension will begin tomorrow."

Why our principal hated God so much was a mystery to me, but he had no qualms about expressing his dislike for any religion — but especially Christianity. Rachel must have been thinking the same thing that I was.

She boldly asked, "Why do you hate Christians so much?"

"Oh, young lady, the question should be, 'Why do you guys hate me so much?' I just don't like how you people can be so intolerant, judgmental, self-righteous, and hypocritical. That look that you have in your eyes, young man, is the same look that my parents had toward me when they found out that I had a boyfriend," he said, looking into Philip's eyes. "That look of disappointment and disgust — I see it so often from you Christians. You act as if you're better than us. Just because you are not attracted to the same sex, but what about all those other sins you guys commit?

"You say that God is love, but you don't show his love to me. Even though the law says I can marry who I want, you people are still opposing the ruling. Why don't you Christians understand that we can't help who we fall in love with? Why can't you accept that? Love is love, God is love, right?"

I looked at Philip and saw what Mr. Strudel was talking about. Philip did have that look of disgust in his eyes. I wondered if I looked like that, too.

Rachel took a moment. I could see the wheels turning in her head on how to respond to Principal Strudel.

"Mr. Strudel, I will agree with you that many of us Christians need to do a better job of showing love to everyone, but we as Christians must also uphold the word of God. These are God's rules, not mine. Homosexuality is not our fight, but sin is. We have all sinned, and we all fall short of God's requirements, including me. Like David in the Bible said, he was born a sinner. We are all born sinners, wanting to do things that God doesn't approve of.

"That is why we must all be born again. God wants to give us a new nature — one that desires to please him and not ourselves. I don't hate you. I accept you as a person, but I don't approve of your lifestyle because God doesn't. Just like I wouldn't of an adulteress, a thief, or a liar," Rachel graciously answered him.

I think that Cassie, Philip, and I were shocked at how Rachel had answered our principal with love. I think God was using her to show us that we needed to be a little more gracious toward others with different views.

Rachel's words caused a fleeting moment of tenderness in our principal's eyes before he returned back to his normal self.

"I didn't ask for a sermon, young lady, and I will not allow your preaching at my school. Your suspensions will start tomorrow," he adamantly stated again.

"Mr. Strudel, can I call my parents?" Cassie asked.

"Your parents will be informed, young lady," he smugly says as he stroked his cat. His cat was just staring at us with his beady eyes, purring with each stroke from his master. Principal Strudel was stroking his cat and typing in an exaggerated report for the reason for our discipline.

I was in shock as to why our actions would warrant an in-school suspension. I had never been suspended before. Sure I had gotten in a little trouble with Pete in the past but nothing that required a suspension, especially for saying, "May God bless you" to someone.

Rachel looked terrified. She had never even been near a principal's office. I imagined what was going on in her head. She was an honor student, the perfect example of what a student should be, and, now, she might have this on her record — at least, that's how she was looking.

Philip just sat there, not saying a word, consumed with anger, with his scrunched face and brown skin slowly turning deep red.

Mr. Strudel had a devilish smile, just pecking away at his keyboard. Meanwhile, Cassie secretly messaged her dad, explaining our predicament at school. Finally, after about an hour of us being trapped in his sterile prison with his guard cat, Principal Strudel began to pass out discipline forms to be signed by each of us.

While he was passing out the forms, Mr. Boots entered the room with the principal's other cat, Matty the feisty, mean one, hissing as she walked toward us.

"Now, now Matty," says Principal Strudel, bidding her to come to him. "She must sense the hatred from their kind" he mumbled, looking at Mr. Boots.

"How much longer?" Mr. Boots said waiting impatiently for the principal to finish.

"Not much longer. I just need for them to sign this paper admitting to their wrong," he said.

"I am not signing anything," Philip said, angrily.

"Yeah — you can't do this," Rachel said, looking furious.

"Oh, yes, I can. Miss Rachel Matthews, you are a bright girl, an honor student, a woman of supposed integrity. You are in your senior year, getting ready for college, I would hope. Now it would be a shame if for some reason colleges would not accept your application. You know I get a lot of calls from schools asking about my students, wanting to know if they would be a good fit for their program. How will I answer them if I get a call for you?" he said, looking at her with a sinister smile like he had her trapped.

"You wouldn't!" Rachel said, looking as though she was about to cry.

Principal Strudel slid the piece of paper in front of Rachel, extending his hand, holding a pen.

"Now what are you going to do — "

While Mr. Strudel was trying to blackmail us, Ms. Drew, the school secretary, called Principal Strudel, notifying him that someone was there to meet him.

"Send them away. I'm busy," he answered and hung up. Principal Strudel turned his attention back to Rachel. "I'm waiting, young lady — "

The phone rang again. Ms. Drew's ID appeared on the phone. Mr. Strudel was now visibly angry. He grabbed the phone and answered harshly.

"I said that I was busy. Send them away."

"But —" Ms. Drew tried to explain, but, before she could warn him, the door swung open. Two men were standing at the door.

"What is the meaning of this?" Principal Strudel questioned. Mr. Boots and the principal both looked befuddled.

"My question, exactly. What is the meaning of you holding these kids hostage?" one of the men asked.

"Dad — uncle, you made it." Cassie joyfully said.

"Mr. Strudel, this is my brother, our lawyer. My daughter has informed us of you trying to suspend them for passing out flyers," Cassie's dad said.

"Yes, your daughter has informed you correctly. They were just about to sign their admission of guilt, before you so rudely interrupted," he said.

"Don't sign anything," the lawyer, Cassie's uncle, jumped in and said. "You have no right, Mister…Mister—" he said, trying to remember his name.

"Strudel" the principal firmly said. By now both of the cats were hissing, arching their backs, ready for an attack. Mr. Boots was trying to restrain them and making an effort to calm them down. Principal Strudel walked to one of his filing cabinets and pulled out a long sheet of paper, adjusting his glasses to read.

"Here it is, Grand Lake High School policies." He handed the lawyer the long sheet of paper and recited a portion of the rules verbatim. "If you will look at section two, number three, you will see what it states. 'There should be no distribution of any religious material before, during, or after school, on school grounds or property.' Read further down, and you will also see that it says that students are not allowed to disrupt their class by forcing their religious beliefs on anyone. What do you have to say about that?" the principal said, snapping his fingers and placing his hand on his hip.

The lawyer, Cassie's uncle, straightens his suit and tie out and calmly answered, "If that's your school policy, then you need to revise it. Your policy may say this, but let me tell you what the law says. First of all, students have the same constitutional rights as all of us, which includes freedom of speech and freedom to exercise their religion. Schools can restrain speech only when the speech is disruptive. You can't prove that their actions are interfering with the mission of this school and that their speech was causing a disruption."

Principal Strudel's resolve was starting to crack, but he was still not willing to concede. "This is my school, I am the principal, and what I say goes. Don't test me."

"Mr. Strudel, you live in America, and these students are granted a right to exercise their beliefs in a civil manner. You, sir, are the one who is in violation. As my brother and I walked into your school, we could see who you are favoring as a presidential candidate. You are in violation by clearly showing support for a candidate on school grounds. I also noticed on your message board several flyers from other students' invitations to parties, concerts, and other outside social events. There is even a full-sized poster of a rapper holding a gun on one of your bathroom doors. I'm sure the courts would like to hear about all of this."

The lawyer stood erect as the principal was starting to look defeated.

"Now if you don't let these kids go, I will be forced to pursue legal action against you and your school. Now, do *you* want to test *me*?" the lawyer said with a slight smile.

Steaming, Principal Strudel turned to Mr. Boots and said, "Do something, Bo Bo." Mr. Boots didn't say a word. He just shook his head, signaling to the principal to yield to this battle. In frustration, Mr. Strudel grabbed all the discipline forms and began frantically ripping them up. He looked like a toddler throwing a temper tantrum because he couldn't have his way.

"Just leave. Get out of my office — all of you."

"Let's go, kids." Cassie's dad, Pastor Clayton, said to us.

"This isn't over. Wait until the Senator becomes President. Things are going to change." Principal Strudel said in exasperation.

"Well he is not President now, and you must abide by these current laws," the lawyer remarked.

We all gathered our things and headed for the exit. As we were leaving, Mr. Boots let go of Matty the cat. She dashed toward us and swiped at Cassie's uncle, barely missing his face.

"Matty," Principal Strudel called, causing the cat to retreat back to him. Both Mr. Boots and Principal Strudel chuckle at Matty's actions.

This day had definitely been a strange one. I couldn't help but think about our principal's words as we left: "Wait until the Senator becomes President. Things are going to change." For some reason, I had a weird feeling that his prediction might come true.

CHAPTER

14

Sunday, day eight of the fast. The end was near, and I believed something great was about to happen. It felt good to be sitting next to my girl again, looking at her necklace dangle with the ring I gave her, symbolizing our love for each other.

Lately, Jazzy had been missing church a lot, and she seemed to be somewhat distant from me. It has been hard on Jazzy, still trying to stand by me even when she couldn't quite understand my conviction for Christ. I noticed how she shrank away from being labeled a so-called "super saint" like me. The constant harassment was starting to wear on her.

That day, I was just happy to be with her again. She had invited me over to her house for a delicious dinner. The next day, I was looking forward to seeing what kind of vegetable meal she had planned. I must admit that it had been hard trying to be creative with eating fruits, vegetables, and nuts. Sometimes I'd rather not eat anything at all than eat another piece of lettuce. My body had been craving for some meat, and I was tired of seeing the color green on my plate.

Praise and worship had just ended, and our weekly announcements and offering were about to happen. While all this was going on, my mind drifted, wandering back to Friday's school day. The strange early-morning meeting with the Principal, Triston, Tiffany, and Mr. Boots. The campaign-littered school. Mrs. Rand's and Mr. Donovan's horrid looks and the meeting in Principal Strudel's office were just plain eerie. The dark side of Mr. Strudel was on full display.

The day before, in our morning prayer meeting, Philip, Rachel, and I told of our encounter that day. The once-strong twenty-five participants in the fast had now shrunk to only nine of us, but the prayer that went forth the day before was powerful. We all prayed for God's strength and that he would move in Grand Lake High School.

Later that day, it was on my heart to check on Pete to see how he was doing. Mrs. Woods said I could come visit, and Jazzy agreed to go with me. Unfortunately, not much had changed with Pete. He was still clinging to life, alive but not responsive. Jazzy and I watched the withering Mrs. Woods hover over her only child. She had aged just in the few weeks since the accident. The grays in her hair had significantly multiplied, while the bags under her dark, sunken eyes grew more prominent. Her daily routine consisted of going to work and then coming to the hospital, forgetting, sometimes, to even eat.

If only I could — .

"John… John," Jazzy said tapping me on my shoulder and snapping me out of my daydream.

"Huh… What?"

"The offering."

I could see the offering bucket being passed down our aisle, and I emptied whatever loose change I had out of my pockets.

"Is everything OK?" Jazzy asked.

"Yeah."

"What were you thinking about?"

"About school on Friday and our visit with Pete," I said, soberly.

"Poor Mrs. Woods. She's not looking well," Jazzy said softly.

"Tell me about it."

Jazzy grabbed my hand and then suddenly spoke as though something had just come to her mind. "Did you hear about Mrs. Rand?"

"No. What happened?"

"She just quit Friday."

"Quit? I just spoke to her that morning."

"Well later that day, she got called to the office, and my girlfriends told me that she came storming out of Principal Strudel's office upset and put in her resignation that day."

"What?" I said loudly, in disbelief, causing a few church members to look back at us and my mom to give me the evil eye from the choir stands.

By now the announcements had been viewed and the offering given, and it was time for Pastor Bruce to appear.

The salt-and-pepper-headed Pastor Bruce Marino came jogging up the stairs to the podium, with a broad, radiant smile.

"Good afternoon, saints. If this is your first visit, welcome to Life Changers, where lives are changed," he cheerfully said as the congregation applauded. The two back screens had the word "Welcome" projected on them, and then it faded into his title message, entitled "Don't Be out of Season."

He began with giving examples of what happened when someone dressed out of the winter and summer seasons. "If you are wearing a winter coat in the middle of a hot summer day, you could risk putting yourself in danger of heat exhaustion. If you are wearing shorts and a tank top in a below-freezing winter, then you risk the chance of getting frostbite. In other words, when we are out of season and don't dress appropriately, we could put ourselves in danger," he said.

Pastor Bruce signaled to the media booth to show his sermon scriptures on the screen. The book of Second Samuel chapter eleven appeared on the two screens. He read the text about David and Bathsheba. The pastor explained how it was the season for war and that David should have been at war with his men, fighting, but, instead, he took a break and stayed home. He was out of season. The pastor went on and asked the question, "How many of us are out of season or out of God's will?

"When we are out of God's will, we are more susceptible to our adversaries' attacks, just like David," the pastor said, pausing a moment as he looked out into the audience.

Pastor Bruce was preaching with a seriousness that I had seen only a few times before — or maybe I hadn't paid much attention to him before now. He continued on and talked about how when David went to the roof of his house, he saw a naked woman named Bathsheba bathing. David could have turned away when he realized what he was looking at but instead he stayed and continued looking lustfully at her — a woman who was another man's wife.

This was David's downfalls — lusting after another man's wife, getting her pregnant, and then having her husband killed. All of this was a result of David being out of season or will of God. He was in the wrong place at the wrong time. "Don't Be Out of Season," the pastor emphasized.

Man, was this a powerful message! After Pastor Bruce concluded and the altar was flooded, a reminder was announced.

That day was the day that our church and many other churches were going to protest Haven Abortion Clinic in Kansas City, Kansas. L3C had rented a few buses to make the trip to the protest. My parents decided to drive to the area, while Philip and I took the bus with some of the youth from our prayer group.

* * * * *

Dr. Benjamin Macbeth, also known as "Macbeth — Doctor of Death" was a doctor who specialized in late-term abortions. He had one of the largest abortion clinics in the nation, right in the heart of inner-city Kansas City, Kansas.

Dr. Macbeth claimed that his clinic was a safe haven for women who wanted to safely terminate their pregnancy. However, there would be one blemish on his record that would outrage the Christian community. He was already a controversial doctor who frequently performed abortions on women who were well into their second trimester. He teetered on the edge of defining what was abortion or murder in the eyes of the law.

He had one incident that occurred that would unite the church and cause this protest to take place. Anna Rose, a young teen, only thirteen years old, found herself pregnant by an older boy, who was fifteen. Anna, a vulnerable, scared little girl, for a while was able to successfully hide her pregnancy from everyone, including her strict mother. Anna wore oversized clothes and attributed her weight gain and depression to the breakup with her ex-boyfriend and father of her growing child, which was somewhat true. No one suspected that she was pregnant.

No one, that is, until one day when Anna was in her room changing clothes, her mother barged into the unlocked door of her daughter's room to tell her something. What she saw was a thirteen-year-old standing, looking in the mirror, with an oversized belly. There was no mistaking her child was pregnant with child.

The heartbroken mother demanded an explanation from her daughter. After a long period of disbelief, sobbing, and seeing her hopes and dreams for her daughter vanish before her eyes, she came to the conclusion that it was best for her to have an abortion. Anna, on the other hand, wanted to keep the child.

Her mother at least convinced her to tell her ex-boyfriend that she was pregnant. When he heard the news, he begged her to have an abortion also, stating he wasn't ready to be a father. The boy's family didn't even believe that it was his child, but he knew he was the only one she'd ever been with.

After a week of arguing with her mother and ex-boyfriend, her mother gave her an ultimatum that if she didn't get rid of the child, Anna would have to find somewhere else to live. Anna finally conceded. Her mother was determined not to raise another child in her house. She was too young to be a grandmother.

By this time, Anna was twenty-two weeks into the pregnancy, and every clinic in her area turned her down, saying that she was too far along into the pregnancy for an abortion — but her mother wasn't giving up that easily. She searched and searched online and found Haven Abortion Clinic. She was happy to find out that Dr. Macbeth was willing to perform the termination.

However, due to his busy schedule, he wouldn't be able to schedule an appointment with her until three weeks later. Three weeks passed, and Anna was now twenty-five weeks along. It is said at this stage that the baby is able to hear the mother's voice. Anna's mother didn't know, but, two weeks prior, Anna decided to get an ultrasound and discovered that she was carrying a baby girl. She was hopeful and thought that maybe if her mom could see the pictures of the baby girl, she would change her mind. Instead, this only hardened her mother's heart even more. Her mother stubbornly went ahead and booked a flight from Arizona to Kansas City, Kansas, to have her daughter's abortion done.

Anna reluctantly arrived at Haven Abortion Clinic and was assured by Dr. Macbeth that he had done hundreds of procedures like hers. The process would be quick, and she would have her life back in no time. The quivering, bloodshot-eyed Anna put her trust in him and spoke to her baby one last time, asking for forgiveness for what was about to take place.

Anna lay on the clinic's bed, closed her eyes, and woke up to Dr. Macbeth telling her that the procedure was over. When she awoke, she awoke to the feeling of emptiness and had pain in her abdominal region, which caused some trickles of blood.

The clinic was overbooked, and the doctor and nurses didn't check Anna as thoroughly as they normally would. Some bleeding and pain was expected, the nurses told her. They sent her on her way, and Anna and her mother caught the next flight back home.

After her surgery, Anna was like a zombie, not talking much, only complaining about the pain in her stomach. Her mother didn't think much of her statement — after all, she did just have an abortion, and the doctor said cramping and some bleeding was expected.

When she returned home, she only wanted to go to bed and try to sleep away the physical and emotional pain. Her mother didn't bother her, only occasionally peeking through the door. She thought it was best to leave her daughter alone to grieve. Seeing the sadness on her daughter's face made her question and have regrets about the duress she'd placed on her.

Anna slept the day away. The next morning, her mother went to check on her daughter only to find that Anna was unresponsive and dripping wet with sweat. When she pulled the blanket off her daughter's cold, limp body, she was confronted with a terrifying, horrific sight of a blood-soaked torso and crimson-stained sheets. Anna Rose was dead.

After Anna's medical examination, her cause of death was determined to be a perforated uterus from her abortion, causing her to bleed to death. Dr. Macbeth, the highly skilled surgeon, had been sloppy with his work, puncturing her uterus with his instruments. Post-surgery, he and his staff also failed to thoroughly check their patient and discharged her early due to an overbooked clinic.

After Anna's death, Dr. Macbeth was still allowed to practice. He stated that this death was an unfortunate event but a very rare one, and nothing further was mentioned in the media about this, but Christians everywhere were not going to let this be forgotten.

Meanwhile, the L3C bus finally arrived at the scene after a long ride filled with multiple traffic stops. On the bus, my brother managed to muster up enough courage to sit next to Tameka, while I sat in the back and talked with Carl. Carl was in his second year at CC Tech University, a university that specialized in computer technology and business. He went on about how he was designing an application that would improve facial-recognition detection — it would be better than any of the other programs that existed.

Jazzy couldn't come again. I forgot what excuse she used this time, but it was starting to be a common thing with her. I brought my camera to record this event, hoping to catch some great footage for my next project in Mr. Spring's class.

We exited the vehicle to a sea of people, and the bitter cold hit us. I tightened the scarf around my mouth, as I could see the vapor from my breath. I quickly grabbed my camera to scan the site. Churches from all over the metro descended on the area. Protestants, Catholics, and just about every Christian affiliation was represented. I had never seen the church so united before in all my life. All were there to peacefully protest this clinic and bring awareness to the nation of the murder of millions of unborn babies and how things were getting worse. Anna's case had awakened the church.

With my camera, I panned the crowd and saw numerous people with signs, some saying "Macbeth — Doctor of Death," or "Dr. Death, Macbeth." Other people were chanting "No more deaths — lives matter." Fearful workers from the clinic rushed inside the building, hiding their faces as they went to work. By this time, police also had arrived to make sure that this protest didn't get out of hand and that we were not prohibiting people from entering Haven Abortion Clinic.

While I was filming, there was a group of signs that caught my eye — bright-color rainbow like signs that looked odd. This group of people stood out like a sore thumb. They were standing near the clinic with signs that said, "God Hates Jews" and "God Hates American Soldiers." I saw a little snot-nosed boy with a crooked stocking hat holding a sign saying, "Go to Hell." I was sure this boy wasn't even old enough to read the sign that he was holding.

The boy and group of people he was with were from Hardline Church. Many churches in the Christian community didn't agree with this church's ideologies and had denounced any affiliation with them. Hardline Church was located in Eureka, Kansas, and was founded by Henry Joseph. He and his members had extremist views and hatred for gays, Jews, Catholics, and the military. They spent most of their time and money traveling to protest different sites like this.

I thought it was strange that their signs were directed at Dr. Benjamin Macbeth's race; his mother was Jewish, and his father was Scottish. They were speaking against his Jewish heritage and not the fact the he was killing babies. They were also mocking the fact that his son, who'd served in the army died in the line of duty, which had nothing to do with why we were there. These people definitely did not represent our church or any other church here.

Besides the Hardline Church, most of the people were calm while they picketed. Local television station's vans were positioned throughout the area trying to cover the rally. Police enforcement had increased, and helicopters swarmed the skies. On this cold, frosty day, everyone was waiting on Dr. Benjamin Macbeth to exit the clinic.

Twilight was approaching, and the amber sun was about to set. Some protesters were starting to leave. Finally Dr. Macbeth decided to come out of his clinic cave and address the people. I had my camera on a tripod, trained on the crowd, while all eyes and cameras were on the doctor. He had no entourage or escorts, just himself, vulnerable to everyone.

A flock of reporters were rushing to him, and, somehow, the attractive Gracie Mitchell from GSTH network managed to be the first to question him. Before the doctor could speak, there was a loud sound, a crackle that echoed in the air. No one knew where this sound had come from. As I whipped my camera around toward the doctor, I zoomed in and saw a drooping body hitting the pavement, with blood splattering everywhere.

CHAPTER

15

Chaos ensued as the thunderous sounds of the helicopters draw nearer to the ground. The police radio chatter was ubiquitous. The policemen put on their masks and raised their plastic shields. They begin forcing the crowds back. Most of the people weren't even aware of what had just happened and were confused as to why the police were telling them to leave.

Not everyone came to the rally intending to be peaceful. There were thugs, hoodlums, and just curious people who showed up at the protest — a perfect situation for a crime.

I could see the police officers becoming more and more aggravated at the disobedience of the people. The officers were imploring to the people to leave the area, pushing them back, a little too aggressively. I was sure the officers didn't envision spending their Sunday evening babysitting an abortion rally. And now tension was growing, as officers were frustrated that people weren't leaving, and the people were on edge, not knowing why they were being told to leave.

I thought it best if I moved to higher ground to record what I predicted was about to unfold. Everyone was on pins and needles as confusion swarmed the area. All it would take was one mishap to spark this peaceful rally into a full-fledged riot.

Ministers from different congregations were trying to calm their people down, but one teenage thug was tired of being pushed by the officers. He swung his fist wildly and connected squarely with one officer's face, giving him a bloody nose.

That was it: The pin had dropped, and the spark was lit. I could hear the hum from the cops' electric nightsticks being turned on. They were zapping anyone who was near them, going through the crowd like a sickle in a wheat field. Men of the cloth were being handcuffed. Pastors and priests, deacons and nuns were all being arrested. I zoomed closer to the clinic and saw the same little snot-nosed boy standing in place, balling his eyes out, as tears mixed with snot smeared his face. His mother was being handcuffed, and his sign that said "Go to Hell" was lying by his side. Hell had come, and it was taking place at that moment. A riot had broken out.

Everything had gone to pieces about the time that Dr. Macbeth was being questioned. A loud, crackling sound had rung through the air. It took everyone a moment to finally figure out what had happened. Dr. Macbeth had been shot in the head. A bullet had gone through his right temple, sending his body immediately collapsing on the ground. News cameras zoomed in on the body of Dr. Macbeth as his blood began to flow down the concrete. Young reporter Gracie Mitchell was standing next to him, paralyzed, as her microphone and new, white blouse were covered with his blood splatter.

Seconds later everyone turns to see the police wrestling a man to the ground. That man was Henry Joseph the pastor of Hardline Church. He was cuffed by several officers and as they patted him down they found a black 9mm gun in his coat pocket. That's when the police started forcing the crowds away, and, soon after, the riot was in full force.

I tried to stay out of harm's way but still capture some good footage. People who were not even a part of this protest were starting to get involved now, burning buildings and looting stores. I could hear the booming speakers from the helicopter shouting to everyone to leave or face the release of tear gas. Police officers were pulling down and securing their gas masks. That was my sign. I knew it was time to shut down and leave.

I packed my camera and spotted the bus labeled L3C. My bus was starting — *Oh, no, they're leaving!* I was about fifty feet away from the bus and knew I had to make a dash for it. I weaved in and out of the labyrinth of people. Running in an all-out sprint, I desperately tried to flag down the bus. As I was running, I heard the hum of an electric nightstick whiz by my head and suddenly saw an overweight cop appearing out of nowhere, trying to keep pace with me.

On the bus, Philip spotted me and yelled to the bus driver to stop. After several calls to him, the bus finally halted, and I just barely escaped the grasp of the beer-bellied officer. Once I jumped on the bus, I could see the first round of tear gas being dispersed. People were gagging and fleeing like cockroaches in the light. As the bus drove away, looking back I could see the overweight officer bent over and panting heavily.

"Glad you could join us, young man. After all, there was no need to rush, now, son. You see, we were just enjoying the sights," the bus driver said sarcastically, laughing to himself, making a lame attempt at humor.

The looks on everyone's face said it all — no one saw this coming. I looked out the window and saw smoke rising from what I thought was the clinic. More reinforcements were being brought in. We just made it out before the area was starting to be locked down.

"What just happened?" Tameka said, in shock.

"I think we all want to know," Philip replied.

Not everyone on the bus knew that Dr. Macbeth had been shot. We all started pulling out our mobile devices and saw that just about every newscast was covering the story. Headlines begin to surface that Christian radicals had killed the doctor. Aerial shots were showing people, still in their Sunday clothes, fighting law enforcement. Nuns were being loaded into police vans, and a massive black cloud was coming from the Haven Abortion Clinic.

No one could have imagined that this rally would have escalated into a riot. This riot would leave a doctor dead, hundreds injured, five civilians dead, one police officer dead, and incur millions of dollars in damages to the community.

That night, we finally made it home, after hours of being stuck in traffic. All I wanted to do was go to bed and wake up from this nightmare that was happening. However, I didn't get much sleep. Mom told us that my dad was in jail for protesting. It wasn't until about two-thirty in the morning that he was finally released. With a stitched eyed, he walked through the doors.

My dad had a weary look to him, and all he could say to me and Philip was, "It has begun. The persecution of the church has begun."

* * * * *

It was day nine of the fast. I awoke from a few hours of sleep, exhausted and sleep deprived but still determined to attend Morning Prayer. There wasn't a morning Bible study today because Cassie's dad was still locked up from the riots and couldn't open up the church. So, from home, I logged into the prayer session and could see that six others were still as devoted as I was to the group. It's amazing how our group had gone from twenty-five members all the way down to only a faithful seven. The seven members were: Philip, Stephen, Rachel, Tameka, Carl, Hannah, and myself.

There is much to pray for today, especially with the recent events that had just unfolded. Tameka invited all of us over to her place the next day to end our fast together, face to face, in fellowship and prayer.

Once our meeting was over, I finished getting dressed and turned on the TV to check the news. The news outlets were really placing the blame on the church for "their irresponsible actions to the community," one anchor said. On the TV screen was the reporter who had been inches away from the doctor when he was shot. Gracie Mitchell, the blonde, blue-eyed reporter from GSTH Network spoke:

"The Christian community should be ashamed for stirring up such violence. All those so-called peacemakers claim that abortion is killing babies. So what is their answer — killing doctors? They say God is love? Which part of the Bible are they following? The passage about an eye for an eye or the passage that says turn the other cheek?" she concluded. It wasn't only her — it seemed that most of the media felt the same as she did.

GSTH was a liberal network that stands for Global Solutions Television Home, but, as my dad liked to call them "the Going Straight to Hell network." In the midst of all this turmoil, a new name had emerged for Christians everywhere — a name that would quickly take hold and become a label for us. The name that was on every blog, every social site, and every television channel was "Zealots."

A zealot (**zél-ut**) is a person who is fanatical and uncompromising in pursuit of their religious, political, or other ideals. That's what anyone who said that they were a Christian was being called.

With all the chaos of the day before, I hadn't even bothered to check my messages. When I did, I saw that Jazzy had messaged me several times the day before, checking to see if I was okay. Boy, was I really looking forward to hanging out with her that evening.

After our prayer meeting and watching the morning news, Philip and I headed out for school. As we were approaching the high school, we could see red and blue lights flashing in the school parking lot. Several police vehicles were in front, and a local news team was also there.

"Man, what's going on now?" Philip questioned aloud. As we came closer, we could see a crowd. Students were gathering outside of the building, and teachers were not allowing us to go in. Philip parked the car, and we began searching for answers as to why the police were there. No one seemed to know, but, after a while, it became clear as two police officers came out the front school doors, with Mr. Donovan trailing. He was handcuffed.

There was a genuine display of shock on the students' faces. Not Mr. Donovan! He, out of all the teachers, probably was the most honest and fair person I knew. The odd thing was the expression on his face. It was not one of shame or guilt but one of anger. He was furious that he was being arrested and was pleading his innocence.

Another strange thing I saw in the distance was Principal Strudel. The look on his face — that smirk. I could tell that he was trying his hardest to contain his satisfaction.

"I smell a fish," I said to Philip.

"Yeah, something is really fishy. Look over there," Philip said, pointing in the direction of the news crew. Tiffany Storm was weeping, distraught, and visibly shaking as local news reporters spoke with her. To me, she seemed a little too over-dramatic and willing to speak to the cameras.

I wonder what's going on. Philip nudged me to look at his phone. I couldn't believe what I was hearing. Philip had a live feed on his phone of the news station airing this event just a few feet away from us.

Tiffany storm was accusing Mr. Donovan of rape.

Rape?

She claimed that her relationship with Mr. Donovan started off innocently, staying after school to complete assignments. He was nice, and she felt safe around him. Then he gradually became more flirtatious, and she admitted that she liked it. Each time that they were together, he seemed to be more and more forward with her.

One day, when they were alone, he leaned over and kissed her. She said she knew it was wrong to kiss a married man, but she didn't resist. One thing led to another, and, before she knew it, he had taken advantage of her. Tiffany went on to claim that she felt so guilty that she asked to meet Mr. Donovan the next morning to tell him that their relationship had to stop.

That's when Mr. Donovan told her that it was too late. They had gone too far. She said that he grabbed her, placed her on the wall, and pressed himself against her. Principal Strudel came into the classroom and witnessed a rape in progress. That was Tiffany's story, but anybody who knew Mr. Donovan found that story hard to believe.

After the circus outside the school cleared, we were allowed in. In the hallways, I could hear the chatter about Mr. Donovan. Everyone knew that Mr. Donovan was a Christian, and people were starting to call him a Zealot — a Zealot who'd raped a teenager. More fuel for the media to eat up. More blame to be placed on Christians.

I walked past Ms. Rand's classroom and hoped to see her, but Jazzy was right: She wasn't there, and another Spanish teacher had taken her place. Mr. Donovan and Ms. Rand were gone. Seeing that odd smirk on the principal's face made me think of the words he'd said to Mr. Boots in the video room. *Mr. Donovan and Ms. Rand are being difficult, but don't worry: I have ways of convincing them.*

Was this part of Principal Strudel's plan? Was this why Tiffany was meeting with them in the morning? If so, then what were Mr. Boots and Triston's roles? What did all this mean? While my mind was racing, I felt a warm hand on my back. Jazzy kissed me on the cheek.

"Hey, stranger."

"Hey, Jazzy. You scared me."

"I see. What were you daydreaming about this time?"

"About you," I said, lying. Lord forgive me, but she would have thought I was crazy if I had told her what I was really thinking.

"Whatever. Why didn't you answer my texts yesterday? You had me worried."

I was about to reply to her question when I saw Triston coming with his crew toward us. "Hey, Zealot," Triston said.

"You talkin' to me?" I answered.

"Yeah. You one of those Zealots — right?"

"If you mean I'm a believer in Christ, then, yes — I am"

"Well, I don't believe in him. Are you and your kind going to kill me, too, like that doctor?" Triston said with a hearty laugh, trying to get a rise out of me. Then he turned to Jazzy and said, staring her down, "You're not one of those Zealots, are you?" Jazzy paused for a long time, looking at me, and then at Triston, and then at me again.

"I'll see you tonight, John. Don't want to be late for class," she said after kissing me on the cheek before leaving. I was stuck feeling a bit disturbed because she didn't confirm or deny her allegiance to Christ.

CHAPTER

16

"Looking good, bro," Philip said, sneaking up behind me, startling me, and nearly causing me to slice my throat. This was my second attempt at shaving. I had just recently begun to sprout some hair nubs around my chin.

"I do look good, don't I?" I replied, looking at my reflection in the mirror. Philip chuckled as I burn my face from applying too much aftershave.

"Alright, don't get too cocky now," he said, laughing at my attempt at shaving.

"So what's the occasion, bro? I could smell your cologne from all the way down the hall," he says fanning his hand across his nose.

"I've got a date with Jazzy tonight."

"So, what's the big deal? It's not like this is your first date."

"I know, but it almost feels like it. I haven't really spent that much time with her lately. Seems like we've been going in two different directions ever since I— ."

I stopped myself mid-sentence.

"Ever since you gave your life to Christ," Philip said, finishing my thought.

"Yeah."

"Well, you know what the Bible says: 'We shouldn't be un-equally yoked.'"

"I know...I know. This is Jazzy we're talking about though. I pray almost every day that she will surrender her life to him."

"But what if she doesn't, John?"

"She will. She has to," I said more to myself than to Philip, trying to convince myself that everything would be alright.

"Look, I'm not saying that she won't. I pray that she will also, but what if it's not now but later in her life, when she realizes her need for him. Are you just going to hang on to something that wasn't meant to be?"

"I have to go," I said, more harshly than I'd intended to my brother. I knew that he was right, but I didn't want to hear that at that moment. Jazzy's relationship with God seemed to be fizzling, not grow-ing, but I still had hope and couldn't fathom not being with her. So I had to make it work.

I finished getting dressed, feeling fresh and clean, with a perfectly trimmed afro and new gear. I was ready to meet my girl.

"You need a ride?" Philip asked.

"Nah, I'll be okay" I stubbornly said, still upset at him for being right.

I went to the garage, pulled out the old bike, and pedaled my way in the dark, looking out into the clear, starry night. After the long week-end that I'd had dealing with a scheming Principal Strudel, nearly being electrocuted by a police officer at the riot, and earlier that day finding out that Ms. Rand had quit and Mr. Donovan was being accused of rape, I needed a break. There was someone I could talk to about all this. In the past, Jazzy had always been that person, the one I could talk to about se-rious matters.

I looked at my watch to find that I had arrived at her house a little early. As I rolled into her driveway, I noticed that there were no vehicles there, and it looked like nobody was home. Randall's car wasn't there — or her parents' either. Maybe she wasn't home yet. After all, I was a little early. So I decided to sit on the front step until they arrived.

I had my back to the front door when I heard someone say, "Do you want to come in?" When I turned around, I wasn't expecting to see what I saw. I was in awe. The only word I could say was, "Wow."

Jazzy had opened the door, looking drop-dead gorgeous. I had seen Jazzy dress up before, but that day, she was just mesmerizing. She looked like a Greek goddess, wearing a flowing, sleeveless, forest-green dress that came down to her knees. One side of her hair was behind her ear while the other was flowing across her face.

"Are you just going to stand there?" Jazzy said with a slight smile, acknowledging my reaction to her.

"Wow," I said again.

"You like?"

"Me like." After I finally picked up my jaw from the ground, I began to speak again. "Sorry — I didn't think anybody was home. Didn't see any cars here."

"They're all gone. Just me and you, Johnny."

I suddenly remembered what had happened the last time it had just been the two of us. *Trouble* was the only thought I could think. After all, I thought we'd agreed not to put ourselves in compromising positions again. It was as though she could read my thoughts and sense my hesitation.

She replied, "Come on, John. I won't bite. Besides I slaved in the kitchen all day just for you. You have to at least let me know if you like my meal."

I *was* hungry and curious as to what kind of creative vegetable concoction we would have. So I agreed to come in, and I was pleasantly greeted with aromas of spices and appetizing food when I entered her house.

"Let me take your jacket," she said.

"Why, thank you."

As she grabbed my jacket and passed by, I got a whiff of her refreshing, signature ocean-breeze perfume.

"Are you ready to eat?"

"I sure am!" I excitedly said, rubbing my hands together.

We sat at the table. The table was lit with candles and laid out with fancy silverware and quality dishes. Soft music was playing in the background — the perfect romantic ambiance. Jazzy brought me a veggie chili with corn salsa, tortilla chips, and lemon water. It looked and smelled delicious. I was curious as to why she had gone through all this trouble for me.

The candlelight was reflecting off her eyes, making them sparkle, just like the day at the lake.

"I must say, Jazzy, you look stunning."

"Why, thank you, Mr. Mann," she said playfully.

"But why all this? Fancy clothes...food...candles?"

"I just want to treat my man," she said looking at me with her warm, alluring smile, enticing me with her deep dimple and almond eyes. "Aren't you going to eat?"

"Oh, yeah" I said, snapping out of my trance.

There was only one day left in the fast — one more day of eating vegetables and fruits. But if I'd had what Jazzy had prepared for me that day earlier in my fast, I think I could have fasted even longer. I didn't know vegetables, spices, and beans could taste so good.

We sat closely by each other, having a good time catching up on things. I went into a rant about how chaotic it had been at the rally, and she discussed her difficulties with her stepdad.

"I miss this," Jazzy said.

"Miss what?" I inquired.

"You know — just talking, you and me."

"Yeah, me too," I agreed.

I think we both realized that our relationship was not like it used to be. The days of spending hours on live chat talking, not wanting to be the first to disconnect, or when we were looking forward to sitting next to each other every Sunday — those days were slowly fading away.

After my car accident, when I'd made a decision to dedicate my life to Christ and seek after him, things between us had started to change. Jazzy and I used to be the same — attending church only because our parents made us. We didn't give much thought to God and religion. But now I was trying to get Jazzy to see what I was experiencing with God. I was aware that this was causing a strain between the two of us. Even though I knew this, I still felt compelled to share with Jazzy in hopes that one day she would see the light.

"Hey, Jazzy. There is something that I'd really like to talk to you about," I said with uncertainty.

"What's that, handsome?" she said with a smile.

"Where do you stand with Jesus?"

This question wiped the smile off her face. "Come on, John. Don't do this. Don't ruin this evening talking about God and church again. OK?"

Sensing the tension starting to develop, I unwillingly decided to back off.

"I'm just not ready to think about that now," she continued. I wanted to reply with a barrage of questions, but I decided it best to hold my tongue.

"OK," I conceded.

"Hey, I have something I want to ask you," she said nervously, rubbing the ring I'd given her and changing the course of our conversation.

"OK. Ask away."

"John, do you really love me?"

I thought, *What kind of question was that? Of course, I do — at least to the measure I knew how.* I carefully responded, "Of course, I do. I have loved you for a while. It wasn't until this year that I gained enough courage to let you know." I thought that was a good answer. Jazzy smiled and breathed a sigh of relief.

"Good, because I knew that you were the one I would be with ever since you gave me that pencil in the fourth grade. I thought you would never pick up on all the signs that I had been giving you over the years."

Honestly, I hadn't picked up on any signals, but now it made sense why she liked to fight me when we were younger. Jazzy leaned over and gave me a big smooch on the lips. At that moment, I felt my flesh reviving. For the past nine days, I had disciplined and denied my flesh food and made it submit to the things of God. I had been killing it and putting it under submission, but then I could feel life coming back to my old desires. Everything in me started to rise, and my appetite for Jazzy sexually was awaking. If Jazzy didn't stop, I wasn't sure I would be able to.

Finally, she did, and I was glad. A second longer, and I was about to go there. The animal was rising in me, and I wanted my prey.

"Have you seen my house?" she said as she stood up.

"No. I've only been in the living room," I replied, still tasting the grape-flavored gloss from her lips.

"Come on. Let me show you around."

"I don't know. When are your parents coming home?" *This could lead to trouble*, I thought.

"Don't worry about them. Let me take you on a tour of my home."

I reluctantly agreed, "Alright."

Jazzy had a cozy place — pretty simple, just a few family photos on the wall. A picture of her as a snaggletooth girl, wearing one of those yellow berets, hung over their fireplace. As we roamed through the house, I noticed that even her cat Bailey wasn't home. She showed me her brother's Randall's messy room. It looked like a tornado had come through there, and the smell was horrendous. We just made a pass at her parents' room, not daring to open that door. Finally, she took me upstairs, and we arrived at her chamber.

My girl definitely loved cats. She had all kind of ornaments of them placed around her room. I had gotten only a glance of her room be-fore, the day when I visited her on the roof. Now I was standing in it. I noticed Jazzy was starting to act a little strangely while we were in her room. That's when the unexpected happened. Jazzy nervously turned to me and said,

"John, I always knew that I wanted you to be my first." I was clueless — not knowing what she meant.

"Your first what?" I curiously asked.

"Well... well," she repeated, acting even more skittish. "Let me just show you. I will be right back," she said, as she rushed to her bathroom, nearly tripping over a rug.

I was puzzled by the way she was weirding out. I didn't think long about it. I just brushed it off as Jazzy being Jazzy. While she was in the bathroom, I inspected, her room, seeing photos of the two of us making funny faces near her bed. Bailey's little cat bed was near hers, and stuffed animals, mainly cats, covered her bed. *Why was she taking so long in the bathroom?* I wondered.

"Is everything OK?" I yelled to her.

"Yes. I'll be out in a minute."

So I just continued to examine her bed. Her pillows were nice and firm, but her mattress was soft and fluffy. I took off my "J&J" ring to examine it a bit more. As I sat down on her bed. I noticed a small, silver-looking package reflecting from the lamp. The item was on her night dresser beside her bed. Curious as to what it was, I picked it up and was shocked when I read the label. It read, "Pleasure Condom." *What? Why does she have this?* No sooner than the thought ran through my mind, Jazzy appeared out of the restroom, wearing a silk robe and the necklace with my ring on it.

Deja vu. It was like I had been in the place before. It was my dream, after the night on the roof. It was coming true.

Jazzy approached me and said in a sultry voice, "I want you to be my first," winking her eye and pointing at me.

Now I got it. A lump formed in my throat as I tried to swallow. I was starting to sweat profusely. The animal in me was rattling the cage, wanting to break free, but the God in me was saying, *Flee youthful lust.*

It was at this moment that I was stuck with the decision again of which path I was going to take.

Joseph or David? a small voice rang in my head. The sermons of Pastor Joel and Pastor Bruce came to my mind. Joseph and David were in similar situations but had two different outcomes. Joseph was tempted by Potiphar's wife but fled temptation. David, on the other hand, was on the rooftop and wandered upon his soldier's wife bathing. Instead of turning away, he gazed upon her, asked for her, laid with her, got her pregnant, and then tried to cover his sin by sending the word to murder her husband, his faithful servant.

All this was flashing through my mind as Jazzy stood in front of me. A part of me was saying that this was the moment that I had dreamed about. No one was in the house — just me and her. Even the cat was gone. How could I turn away a beauty like this? Her sweet smile and her alluring scent were calling me, and I wanted to answer.

A faint small voice from within was also speaking, urging me to flee. How could I do this sin before God? How could I throw away these past nine days of putting my flesh under submission, fasting and praying every day, being made fun of because I'm a so-called "Zealot"?

That night, I chose to be Joseph and flee. Jazzy was beginning to approach me, and I knew that, if I didn't get out of here before she touched me, I wouldn't be able to resist. With the little strength I had, I sprang to my feet, telling Jazzy, "I can't do this." I bolted for the door, determined not to look back, leaving my silver "J&J" ring still on her bed. I ran out the door, faintly hearing Jazzy yelling something at me. Her yell turned into a cry. A painful, uncontrollable weeping belted out from her, but I couldn't look back. I couldn't give in to her, as much as I wanted to. If I looked back, I would return to comfort her. I grabbed my bike and pedaled fast as I could home.

I know it was the right thing to flee, but I felt so horrible leaving Jazzy in such a vulnerable state. *Was this Jazzy's plan? Was this her desperate attempt to mend a relationship that was growing part? The candles, the food, no parents, her makeover, and a condom near her bed. This all seemed like a strategic enticement to hold on to what was crumbling. Jazzy? Why...Why?*

CHAPTER

17

The drive to school was a quiet one. My brother tried to engage in conversation, but I was in no mood to talk. My thoughts were somewhere else. My mind kept replaying Jazzy's painful look when I said, *I can't do this.* The feeling that I had was a sick one, a feeling of guilt. Lord knows I was trying to do the right thing, but, in the process, I was hurting someone — not just anyone, but the one I loved — .

"John...John?" Philip said, shaking me from my thoughts.

"Huh...what?" I replied. I guess Philip finally noticed that I hadn't been paying attention to him talking. All I heard him say were a few words about "...last day of fast and tonight's meeting...." Everything else sounded muffled like the adults on Charlie Brown.

"Man, what's going on with you?" he said with a look of concern.

"I don't know. I just don't feel like talking." That, of course, wasn't a good-enough answer for him, so he kept pushing me until I said something.

"I know that look, bro. You look hurt. What happened last night?" Philip was seeing right through my phony façade.

We were nearing the school. Not wanting to answer, I tried to stall until we got there, but when we arrived, Philip turned off the car and just stared me down until I gave him an answer.

I finally broke and spilled my heart out to him.

"I think it's over," I said, with my voice beginning to crack. I could feel my eyes welling up.

"Are you talking about you and Jazzy?"

"Yeah," I said, closing my eyes, not wanting to open them because I knew that, if I did tears would fall.

Philip realized that I was not joking and showed some sympathy. I don't think that I had ever cried like this with Philip before. After all, men didn't do this — right? Philip looked surprise. I don't think he had seen me like this before. The only time I'd cried in front of him was when we were little kids and he had just hit me too hard.

"What happened? You seemed excited when you left yesterday," he said.

"I was. Our date started off great, she looked stunning, and we had a great time talking — " I paused a moment, not wanting to continue.

"But, what?" he questioned.

"But things turned when she took me to her room and surprised me with her confession of wanting to be with me."

"'Wanting to be with you'?" he asked, not getting what I was trying to say.

"You know she wanted to *do the do*. She even changed into something sexy, and, boy, was she tempting."

"John, did you — you and Jazzy — you know?" Philip said, fumbling trying to hint at what he wanted to say.

"No, we didn't have sex." I said, plainly.

Philip breathed a sigh of relief. "So why the long face then, bro?"

"I just left her there. I ran out of the house, leaving her crying." Realizing what I had done, the faucet of my tears began to flow even more.

Philip placed his hand on my shoulder in an attempt to comfort me.

"You did the right thing, bro," he said, trying to cheer me up.

"Funny, because it doesn't feel like it."

* * * * *

The final bell rang at school. The day was finally over, and life at school didn't seem to be getting any better — only worse. More name calling of "Zealot" from students and dirty looks by Principal Strudel as I passed through the hallways. I was beginning to hate high school. The year had begun so brightly, but now it was quickly fading to black. The darkness was only increasing.

Triston detested me and boldly bullied other students, especially his favorite target, Trevor Jacobs. Head cheerleader Tiffany Storm's popularity had only grown since her accusation of Mr. Donovan raping her. And creepy Mr. Boots still quietly lurked in the shadows of the school.

However, one bright spot was Rachel's Bible study. The attendance was slowly increasing as other hidden Christians were starting to come out of the closet and join the group — even with Principal Strudel's blatant hatred for "Zealots."

Rachel had decided to only have her Bible study after school so that everyone could meet at one time. That day, I decided not to attend. I just wanted to go home and try to sleep away my pain. Jazzy hadn't been at school that day, and I tried calling her several times, only to get her voicemail. I texted her several times but got no reply.

It was the last day of our ten-day fast, and I hadn't eaten anything. I had no desire for food, vegetables, or fruit — my appetite was gone. My heart was sick, and I longed to talk to Jazzy.

Since Philip had stayed for the Bible study, I had to take the bus home, something I hadn't done in a while. It was a long ride home. When I arrived at home, I went straight to my room and checked my phone. My message box was still empty. I sent out another text to Jazzy.

Hey, Jazzy. It's me again. Please reply. We need to talk. OK?

I tossed the phone on my glass desk and plopped down onto my bed, looking at the ceiling. I tried to close my eyes to sleep, but I couldn't. My phone began to vibrate on my desk, clattering against the glass, which caused me to sit up on the bed. I rushed to the phone, hoping it was Jazzy replying. But, instead, I got a message from Stephen.

Remember meeting @ Tameka's, 7pm. Let's end in a bang. See you there!

Our meeting was that night, but I didn't think that I was going. I didn't want to see anybody, and I didn't feel like praying right then. While I was still holding my phone and reading Stephen's text, I received another text. Jazzy's name appeared in the message box. She had finally replied. My heart stopped as I got a sinking feeling in the pit of my stomach, nervous and anxious about what was on the other side of my click. After a few seconds, I clicked to open her reply.

HOW COULD YOU, JOHN? HOW COULD YOU LEAVE ME LIKE THAT? YOU HURT ME...MORE THAN WORDS CAN SAY.

I don't think I can do this anymore, I'm tired. Ever since your so-called conversion, things have changed. I am a second thought to you. I tried. I tried to look past this and still love you. I was willing to give you my precious body in hopes that things would change between us, but you, in return, you hurt me!! You leaving me there is unforgivable. I have been crying and thinking about us all day. And maybe it is best if we break this relationship off. I will always love you, but I can't continue this way. Sorry if I don't view God like you do. I'm not sure if we can still be friends. Looking at you will only hurt too much. Like you said in your own words, "I can't do this."

There it was. She'd just thrust a dagger in my heart and turned the blade. I couldn't believe what I was reading. I read her painful, angry message over and over again, several times. It confirmed what I knew — she was breaking up with me. I fell to the side of my bed on my knees and directed my anger and hurt up to God.

"God, how can you let this happen? I have been faithful to you. I have been starving myself and talking to you every morning. I was trying to do the right thing by following Joseph's example, and now this is what I get. Maybe I should have been like David."

I leaned back onto my bed and began crying like a baby. Not only my best friend Pete, but now Jazzy, too. Both had left me. Heartsick and overwhelmed with emotion, I buried my head in my pillow, and I just let the tears flow.

A couple of hours passed, and I still hadn't moved, still lying in the same position, looking at the ceiling and wondering what was going on in my life. I heard a knock at my door. Philip was outside.

"Are you ready, John? I'm leaving in ten minutes."

"I'm not going." I answered. Praying was the last thing I wanted to do. I just wanted to lie on my bed and sulk.

"Let me in, bro"

Before I could speak, Philip swung the door open. "You alright?"

"She broke up with me," I muttered, showing him the text message that was burned in my mind.

"Whoa! Sorry to hear that, man."

"I don't understand. Why is God punishing me?" I said.

"What do you mean?" he questioned.

"I mean, ever since I got serious about serving him, everything seems to have gotten worse for me. Pete's still in the hospital, my friends at school have abandoned me, and now the only person who matters to me is leaving me, too. I was trying to follow the scriptures. I was fleeing fornication, and this is the result I get. I think I'm just going to stay home tonight."

Philip approached me and sat down next to me. He looked me straight in the eyes and said, "Accepting Christ is simple, but that doesn't mean it will be easy. We have this promise that his commandments are not burdensome. We can come to him when we are weary." Philip paused a beat and then continued. "Let me ask you this. What happened to Joseph after he fled his master's wife?"

Where is he going with this? I wondered. "He was accused of rape and went to jail."

"That's right. He followed God's commandment, but things seem to have gotten worse, not better, for him. He went to jail for something he didn't even do, but the one thing that the scriptures says over and over about Joseph is that God was with him. God favored him. And at the end, all the things that Satan meant for evil, God made good out of them.

"Don't give up this fight. God sees your effort, John, and he is with you."

I'd never heard my brother speak like this before, and I knew that the words that he was speaking were coming straight from God. Feeling convicted, I had to ask God for forgiveness. Philip made me realize that

God was in control of my life. Things may be dark now, but they could change in an instant.

Needless to say, he convinced me to attend our final meeting. After wiping away the snot and tears, I cleaned up and got ready to meet my fellow believers in Christ.

We hopped into the Camaro and headed to Tameka's place. The peace of God was resting on me, and I was in a little better mood. Philip was in a great mood, ecstatic, actually. I think it was because we were going over to Tameka's house. As a matter of fact, I *knew* it was because we were going there.

Tameka was a freshman in college, while Philip was just a junior in high school. But I must say that was not stopping him from pursuing her. He finally confessed that he liked her even though everybody already knew. You should see the transformation in my brother when she appeared. He'd go from confident to unsure of himself. It was hard to gauge if she liked him back or not. One minute, it looked like she was flirting with him, and, then, in the same instant, she acted like he was her little brother.

While Philip was beaming, I turned on the radio to get my mind off of Jazzy. As I scanned through the channels, just about all of them were still talking about "The Zealots," as they put it. I finally landed on GSTH radio station and heard Mr. Donovan's name mentioned. The broadcaster spoke: "More news to report about the Zealot movement. In Grand Lake, Missouri, a history teacher is accused of luring a teenage girl into his classroom after school. He promised that her grade would improve if she took private Bible history lessons with him. His Bible lessons were from King David's book on how to take advantage of a young, impressionable girl."

The tone in the speaker's voice was sarcastic, making jokes about the Bible. They played an audio clip of Tiffany Storm speaking.

"If it wasn't for my brave principal, Mr. Strudel, God only knows what would've happened to me" she said in a quavering voice.

"Oh, please — that's baloney," Philip blurted out. "Turn that mess off." The tone in Philip's voice sounded just like my dad's.

So I scanned for another station and stopped on a channel when I heard our President's voice. President Copperfield was on her final campaign tour before the election. She just so happened to be in Saint Louis, Missouri, that day, about a four-hour drive from Kansas City. A sound bite was playing of the President giving answers to reporters earlier in the day.

"Mrs. President, what do you think about the Zealot movement that is taking place?" one reporter asked.

"I don't know about a movement happening. What happened at the abortion clinic in Kansas City was an unfortunate event, and it looks as though law enforcement has the suspect in custody."

Another reporter jumped in and asked, "Mrs. President, are you a Zealot? After all, you are a Christian. Right?"

"Yes. I am a believer in Christ. I am a Christian."

"So you agree with Zealots Henry Joseph and school teacher Ray Donovan," another one questioned her.

"I agree with the Bible. What these gentlemen have allegedly done does not line up with the teachings of the Bible or with our laws."

"So what about all the preachers who are refusing to marry same-sex couples even though the law says these couples have a right to get married?"

"Like I said, I agree with the Bible."

"So you are a Zealot!" Someone yelled in the background to the president.

I flipped to another station and heard another sound bite. This time, it was from Senator Wright. He was also rounding out his last campaign tour before the election and was in the neighboring state of Kansas.

The press brought to the senator's attention the remarks President Copperfield had made earlier in the day.

"Senator, what do you think about the recent Zealot movement that is taking place?" someone questioned.

"Radical Christians are a threat to the world, just like radical Muslims are. I have been addressing this for a long time, and now it is being manifested. If you vote for me, I assure you that I will make some revisions to our current hate-crime bill. It will be unacceptable not only to assault individuals because of their sexual orientation or identity but also to speak hatefully against them."

"Senator, what do you think about the President's remarks on preachers refusing to abide by the law?"

"Well that's another reason why you should vote for me. Any clergyman who refuses to give couples what they are entitled to have should have their license revoked, and repeat offenders should do time."

Finally, I just turned off the radio, and Philip and I looked at one another in disbelief.

"I can't believe that the Senator is comparing Christianity to a jihadist group like the Islamic State," I said.

"Have you checked any of your social media pages?" Philip asked. Since we'd been fasting, I hadn't really been on any of my pages — kind of out of touch with what had been transpiring over the last ten days. Sure enough, like Philip said, when I opened my page, I saw what was trending. *Zealots, hateful Christian group, history teacher, doctor death, President's answer* were the leading topics. A huge debate had broken out in cyberspace about the difference between Zealots and Christians — if any.

We were nearing Tameka's house. My brother and I could definitely sense a shift in our nation. The latest poll now showed that Senator Wright was edging out President Copperfield. Fifty-two percent of the votes were going to the Senator, and forty-five percent were going to the President. The other three percent were undecided.

"We have a lot to pray for," Philip said, somberly.

"Yes, we do" I replied.

CHAPTER

18

Low-hanging clouds descended upon the night. As heavy fog began to fill the air, visibility was difficult as we navigated to Tameka's home. After a few wrong turns, we finally managed to find her place. We exited the Camaro, and, immediately, we were met by the cold, howling winds and misty drizzle pushing against our faces. I had an eerie sense that it felt like something was brewing in the atmosphere.

Tameka lives in an old neighborhood that once was a thriving area but then was only a remnant of what it used to be. Her part of town was a diverse area, with many cultures and ethnic groups.

Naked trees surrounded her house, with just a few leaves still hanging on to limbs. Leaves are scattered everywhere on her unkempt lawn. The concrete steps leading to her door were cracking and crumbling away, and the handrails were wobbly and ready to fall at any moment. Mr. Wilson's presence was definitely missed at their household.

After a few knocks on the door, it opened, and we were greeted by Tameka's bright-eyed little brother, eight-year-old Derek, a.k.a "Little Man." Little Man seemed to have taken a liking to Philip.

"What up, Philly?" Little Man said to him, trying to impress him by acting cool and older than he was.

"Hey, what's up with you. Little Man?" Philip had also taken a liking to him. "Where's everybody at?"

"They're all upstairs. Tameka asked about you," he said, laughing while pointing to the stairs. His statement made Philip display one of the biggest grins I had ever seen. Before we could head toward the stairs, Mrs. Wilson, Tameka's mom, came from the back room and stopped us.

"Hello, boys."

"Hello, Mrs. Wilson," we both replied.

"Hey, I have something for your mother. Remind me before you guys leave. Don't forget." My mom and Mrs. Wilson talked almost every day. They were very close friends.

"Yes, ma'am."

"Well, you boys can go upstairs. They've been waiting on you," she told us.

Waiting on us? I guess my apprehension about coming to the meeting and Philip making a few wrong turns had caused us to be a little late.

Climbing the squeaking stairs, we made it to the top, and, unsurprisingly, we were the last ones to arrive. After ten days of prayer chats online, we all arrived in one place, face to face. Everyone's face seemed to be downcast, with heavy hearts. All of us had had a tough week of school, not to mention hearing the news media slaughter anyone who was a Christian, calling us a group of terrorist zealots. On top of that, I myself was still battling thoughts of Jazzy running rampant in my mind. Distracted, I tried to push away those thoughts and focus on Christ.

When we first began this journey, there were twenty-five committed young people participating, but now it had dwindle down to only seven of us. The faithful remaining seven were Hannah, Tameka, Stephen, Philip, Rachel, Carl, and myself. At this meeting, there was a seriousness in all of us — we all had a business-like attitude. There wasn't much joking in this meeting. Carl wasn't his usual humorous self. Tameka wasn't her sassy self. Hannah was even quieter than usual. Rachel wasn't upbeat, and Stephen looked like he had aged from the ten days of fasting. I could see the weight that was on him. The pressure of trying to keep a group of young people focused on God among all the turmoil that was going on in our nation was getting to him. His normally perfect, dark, wavy hair had a few strands that were out of place. And I thought I was the only one going through some issues. I guess not.

Stephen stepped forward and declared in a loud voice, "Like Jacob, Lord, I will not quit until you bless me. Lord, we have committed ourselves to you. Many of us are facing insults and laughter from our peers. We have given up our desires to seek you, Lord. You said, Lord, 'If we seek you with all our hearts, we will find you.' Please, Lord — manifest yourself to us. We are pleading! Let what we are doing not be in vain."

I could feel the anguish bleeding from his heart. We all felt the same and were crying out to God. Our hearts were aching for a revelation from him. We wanted God, and we wanted all that he had for us. That day was, by far, the most I had ever cried in my life. At first, it was over Jazzy, but now I was crying and praying so hard that my voice was gone. I was speaking to God, but no words were coming out. Hours passed in that tiny room upstairs, and we were well late into the night.

We were praying, faces to the ground and lying prostrate on the floor. Suddenly, I felt a rushing mighty wind blow through the room, swinging the windows wide open with such force it got all of our attention. I thought that it was a tornado coming. The wind was so powerful that it sounded like a train was coming through the room. Fear was upon all of us. I faintly saw an ember that was glowing and steadily getting brighter. It looked like a ball of fire forming. Then the large fireball divided into seven little fireballs and started moving toward us.

Suddenly the fear that we had turned into an unexplainable peace, even though everything seemed chaotic. I was overcome with a sense of peace. The presence was so strong that I didn't want it to leave. One by one, the fireballs started to rest on our tongues, causing us to speak in an unknown language. We were all speaking in *different* languages. One of the fireballs came toward me. I looked up as the fire rested on my tongue.

Fire began to tingle up and down my body, and it felt like an inner vessel had broken inside me, causing water to gush out of my mouth. I was speaking, but the words I was saying were not in English. All seven of us were producing a thunderous sound, which could be heard throughout the neighborhood.

All the commotion in the room must have awakened Tameka's neighbors. A couple of her neighbors came to the house, knocking at the door. Her next-door neighbor, Mr. Abram, who was Russian, strode over to see what the disturbance was and what was happening at the Wilsons' house. He told us that he'd heard a loud boom, and, that, when he went outside to investigate the sound, he could hear someone speaking in Russian. Not only were they speaking in Russian but were praising God in a loud voice.

Jin and Farooq were two foreign-exchange students staying at Tameka's neighbor's house behind her. They were from China and India; they also came over to investigate. Like Mr. Abram, they'd also heard a loud boom, but, when they went outside, they heard someone from our group speaking — in their languages — about God.

That certainly was strange. Even Mrs. Wilson told us that, while she was downstairs, she heard one of us speaking in her native language, French. Tameka's mother had been born in Togo and had moved to the United States for a better education when she was a teen.

The noise from Tameka's house seemed to have caused a crowd to gather outside her home. Many of her neighbors were dressed in night robes and pajamas, with coats on, standing outside. There was so much turmoil going on that one of her neighbors called the police.

Flashing red and blue lights pierced through the dense fog — the police had arrived. A veteran African-American police officer came ambling up the crumbled stairs. Mrs. Wilson gingerly opened the door.

"Good evening, ma'am," he said in a southern voice, tipping his hat, smiling and showing a pleasant demeanor. "We received a call of a disturbance at this location and possibly underage drinking."

While the officer was speaking, the neighbor who had made the call — a round, pudgy, balding man — came rushing over, walking briskly in his night robe, raising his voice, making accusations against us.

"Officers, those teenagers in that house are having a rowdy party, making a bunch of ruckus, waking every one of us up," he said, waving his hand across the crowd to show how many were outside. "And to think the parents of this home are letting them drink alcohol," the round, pudgy man said, looking at Mrs. Wilson with a look of disgust. He continued, "Officer, I heard them speaking gibberish so loudly they woke me out of my bed, and I am a heavy sleeper. Look at them: They have no respect for others. You need to arrest these drunken teenagers and their mother for waking up half the neighborhood."

The seasoned officer didn't respond quickly but assessed the situation. He gestured to calm down the angry neighbor and a few others who were starting to take his side. The officer said to Mrs. Wilson, "Do you mind if I search your home for any alcohol?"

"Not at all, sir," Mrs. Wilson complied. Going from room to room, surveying the house and looking at our appearance, he finally concluded that there was no foul play involved here. No evidence that there was ever a party at this place. The officer inserted a few notes into his tablet and then displayed his pearly white smile and just requested that we keep it down.

This, of course, angered the pudgy neighbor, and he went storming off, swearing under his breath. Then he stopped, speaking loudly so everyone could hear.

"I have an important business meeting tomorrow. They should be arrested. Taking away my precious sleep. What the h — "

"Sir, are you speaking to me?" the officer interrupted him, silencing the belligerent man.

"No, I'm just thinking out loud. Can I do that?" the neighbor said, with a snarky tone. With a haughty attitude and head held high, he walked toward his home.

The officer gave us a grin and a wink and said calmly, "Just keep quiet, folks." He then directed his attention to Mrs. Wilson. "I don't want to have to arrest anyone," he said, winking again at Mrs. Wilson.

"Yes sir, officer," Mrs. Wilson replied.

I wasn't sure if the officer was flirting with Mrs. Wilson or if he was just being nice, but the exchange seemed a little awkward. Mrs. Wilson, still blushing from the officer's gesture, turned and suddenly remembered the gift she wanted to give our mother.

None of us knew what had just transpired that night. This would change each one of our lives. God answered our prayers in a mighty way, and we were about to go on a spiritual adventure that you would not believe. A new world was about to be unleashed.

At least for the rest of the night, my mind was clear. No thoughts of Jazzy invaded my mind. I was on a high — not a high from a drug like *Blue* — but this high I was experiencing had no bad side effects. This powerful presence of peace rested on me and I didn't want it to ever leave.

CHAPTER

19

Tuesday would be a turning point in America, with two opposing views battling it out. The nation is split, divided right down the middle. The Christian community is showing strong support for President Copperfield, while Hollywood and the majority of media networks seem to favor Senator Wright.

Electricity, excitement, and anxiety filled the air that Tuesday morning. News cameras showed hundreds of people waiting outside in long lines just to vote. The atmosphere in Grand Lake was the same as everywhere else in the nation. A change was coming to America. People who normally wouldn't vote were wanting to make their voice heard. My dad had been campaigning tirelessly for President Copperfield ever since the riots in Kansas City, Kansas.

Pastor Bruce had opened the church door that day for everyone to come and pray for the future of America. I hadn't seen Pastor Bruce this involve in political matters before. Normally he avoided talking about politics in the church. But, in this election, he, like my father, would not apologize for his support of President Copperfield. They felt that the winner of this election would determine the fate of America.

It was uncharacteristic, but clergymen everywhere were voicing their support for the President, while many celebrities, sports figures, movie stars, and news networks were unabashedly praising Senator Wright as the one who would bring reform to the United States of America. He was the one who had the right plan for progress, so they said.

All the news networks and social media outlets were covering every nuance of this Election Day. Reporters were on the grounds interviewing voters in lines. Polling-place monitors were discussing how they were prepared for the largest voter turnout in history. Radio stations were taking calls from callers happy to express their opinions about the day. This was a historic day, one that would be remembered in this country.

All of this was happening while Philip and I were getting ready for school. I ate a hearty breakfast and gathered my things as Philip was in the garage, honking the horn, trying to hurry me along. We got into the old trusty Camaro and continued listening to the news coverage of the election as we drove to school.

Looking out the window, I faded into one of my daydreams. It had been a week since that night at Tameka's house and a week since the breakup text from Jazzy. I must admit that it had been tough and awkward seeing Jazzy at school. Students once use to call us "Johnzmine" because we were so close. Now she couldn't even look me in the eye when we crossed paths. I missed waiting on her to exit her Algebra II class. I loved seeing her eyes brighten when she saw me. Now there wasn't a light in her eyes when she saw me, just a look of pain. She had even taken off the necklace that had the ring that I gave her attached to it. She used to always wear that necklace, but now her neck was bare, her face hidden, and her mouth silent toward me. I really missed her company. *Boy, have I messed things up between us!* I thought.

On the bright side of things, since our meeting at Tameka's, the group had become stronger. I wouldn't have imagined being friends with Stephen, Carl, Rachel, Hannah, and Tameka. I used to laugh and make jokes about these guys. Now we are closer than ever, and I am one of them. The "super saints" or "Zealots" was what people in school — and, surprisingly, some at church — called us. Since that night when we'd been overcome by the Holy Spirit, we all seemed to have gained a boldness and a stronger awareness of the Holy Spirit. I was no longer timid when speaking to strangers about the love of Christ — something that I would have never imagined. If only Pete could have seen me. He wouldn't believe what I had become.

At school, Rachel's Bible study was continually expanding. In these tough times at Grand Lake, Principal Strudel was starting to threaten — with discipline — anyone who shared their faith on school grounds. He claimed that we are part of the Zealot movement and that he might even report us to the authorities. Even with all his threats, those students who were Christians in our school pledged their allegiance all the more to Christ. This infuriated Principal Strudel, and Rachel seemed to be his primary target. Her Bible study was empowering the believers, and he was just waiting for her to slip up in some way so that he could unleash his wrath.

After my time of reflection during what seemed like a longer ride than usual to school, we finally arrived. The school was looking like Senator Wright's campaign center with red, white, and blue everywhere. At the main doors, every student was being greeted by Principal Strudel and Mr. Boots. Principal Strudel was wearing two noticeable buttons on his newly pressed suit. One button said, "I Voted Today" while the other one, right underneath it, said, "I Voted the Wright Way."

The Principal was taking aside those seniors who were eligible to vote and encouraging them to "vote the Wright way," he said. He was even offering a day off from school if they voted for Senator Cordell Wright. The only other person I had seen who is so diehard about their support for a candidate is my dad. Two people with the same passion but with different views.

We spotted Rachel and Cassie lingering outside the school, chatting, and I decided to meet up with them. After our conversation about the great anticipation of the day's final results and Cassie telling us about how Principal Strudel fought against her dad having the voting polls at his church and not the school, we finally decided to enter the school.

When Principal Strudel saw us approaching, his phony smile quickly turned devilish. He didn't even extend his hand to pretend that he wanted to greet us. He just looked at us and said, "Today the senator will become President, and things are about to change for you Zealots." His expression was cold, giving us a look that sent shivers down our spines.

Once we passed, he went back to putting on his plastic smile to greet the next student.

Once again, I had to enter into this dark place called "school." I attended class after class looking at the same thing — teachers with buttons like Principal Strudel's saying, "I Voted the Wright Way." It was weird how our teachers at Grand Lake were like mindless drones under the control of the Principal. They are afraid to challenge him, especially since the arrest of Mr. Donovan.

The bell rang, and the time had finally come for me to pass Jazzy's Algebra II class. I used to look forward to this moment, but now I dreaded being ignored by the one I still loved. I even waited awhile before heading that way, hoping to miss her exiting the class. When I arrived at her class, I was shocked by what I saw. Her classroom was empty, but she was outside the door in the hallway, talking and smiling with another boy — not just any boy but my nemesis, Triston "Square Face" Stewart.

For a moment Jazzy's and my eyes met as I passed. That second seemed like a minute. She finally looked away and went back to talking to Triston as though she'd never seen me. I tried to hide my emotions, but I think she could see the hurt, anger, and jealousy burning in my eyes.

How could she? Of all people, *Triston.* Was she doing this just to hurt me? I couldn't stay there another second, so I hurried off to my class. But before I could leave, Triston looked at me and winked with his perverted, crooked smile.

I knew that I would have to repent for the thoughts I was having at that moment. I had nothing but hatred for him right then. Ungodly thoughts flooded my mind about what I wanted to do to Triston. I was upset at him, but, really, the overpowering feeling that I had was being hurt by Jazzy. We were no longer a couple, but I still had love for her. It had only been a week, and she was already moving on.

I couldn't even pay attention to the teacher in my class. All I could see is flashes of Triston winking as I walked by. Hatred was boiling in me, and my fist tightened as my mind went to a dark place. I hated the way I was feeling. I asked my teacher if I could be excused to the restroom, so that I could sort through my feelings. While I was behind the closed doors of the stall, I poured my heart out to God and asked that he would take away my hatred. I didn't receive an answer, but I felt a comfort from above, a burden being lifted and strength to go on. I flushed the toilet, cleaned my face, and returned to class.

* * * * *

I wasn't sure if I'd ever seen that many people there in the church on a day that wasn't a Sunday. The night had come, and most of the polls were starting to close. My family was at L3C. Pastor Bruce had opened the doors for prayer and to watch the coverage of this Presidential election. Everyone from our group was here. The seven of us sat in the foyer area of the church. Carl believed that the senator would win, but Stephen was almost certain that the President would be re-elected.

Some saints were in rooms designated just for prayer, while others were glued to the television, watching the outcome of the polls. Both projectors in the sanctuary were displaying a huge map of the United States, with blue representing Democratic nominee Senator Wright, while green was the color for Independent President, Sandra Copperfield.

The map was traditionally red and blue, but our President is anything but traditional. Four years before, the state of America was very bleak. We were on the verge of a depression. Our debt to China had increased dramatically, and many were unemployed. Most Americans were growing sick of the political games that the Republicans and Democrats were playing. They were more concerned about pushing their agendas than the well-being of the United States.

In Arkansas, there was an independent governor, Governor Sandra Copperfield, who would rise to prominence. She took the state of Arkansas and made it a model of what the United States could be. Arkansas was thriving, and many flocked there for employment. Many of her peers had pressured the governor to run for the presidency. At first she was unwilling, but, after a while, she finally conceded and ran. She easily won the election, setting all kinds of records. She was the first African-American woman President and first Independent President.

During her presidency, she had turned America around, increasing jobs, producing alternatives to oil, reforming the healthcare system, and making the United States relevant again. All that might have changed that day if the smooth-talking Senator found himself being elected. Even though our President had done a great job of turning America around, many seem to have forgotten the state that we were in.

If our president had any downside, it was that she was not very personable. She didn't have the charisma of Senator Wright. She was somewhat stoic, focused, and all about business. Senator Wright came across like he was everybody's friend, very charming, and a great orator. Many of the young voters were starting to show support for him. With the recent events and the media and famous stars crucifying Christians, labeling us "Zealots" and an intolerant hate group. President Sandra Copperfield had lost some support because she was not ashamed to say that she was a Christian.

We all sat in a group, looking at the screen. Philip managed to sit next to Tameka again, while Hannah and Rachel were conversing. I was sitting next to Carl and Stephen, listening to them argue over who was going to win. "Breaking News" flashed across the television. The news anchor spoke as the first projections were in. Senator Wright was projected to win the state of Vermont.

"Told you so," Carl said to Stephen.

"We have a long way to go," Stephen reminded him.

President Copperfield's face appeared on the screen as she won the state of Kentucky.

So far, there were no surprises in the projections. They both were winning the states they were projected to win. Our state, the state of Missouri, was a swing state. No one knew who would win this state. While we sat outside the sanctuary in the foyer, I could see my dad pacing back and forth, praying after every victory the President achieved.

I never did quite understand the whole electoral thing. Why can't we elect a President based simply on just the popular votes? The smiling face of the Senator and the serious face of the President were side by side, with the electoral count 53 to 62 in favor of President Copperfield — even though the President had won more states: Texas, Louisiana, Oklahoma, North Dakota, and her home state, Arkansas. The Senator had won the high electoral-vote states, New York and Pennsylvania, along with the small state of Vermont. Two hundred and seventy votes were needed to win the election.

We were out in the foyer. Stephen, Carl, and I were sipping on bottled water and snacking on popcorn that had been provided. We watched the states on the map slowly turning blue and green.

"You know that this election wouldn't even be close if it weren't for the riot at the abortion clinic," Stephen said.

"Yeah — it's amazing how quick everyone turned on us Christians," I said.

"It was that Henry Joseph and his Hardline church that was giving us believers a bad name — 'Zealots,'" Carl interjected.

"Something was strange about his arrest, don't you think?" Stephen said.

"It didn't surprise me. That guy is a nut," said Carl.

"I know, but if he actually *did* kill the doctor, do you think that he would be so vehemently denying it?"

Stephen's statement caused Carl and me to pause and ponder on it.

"Henry Joseph is fanatical, and I don't agree with his beliefs, but he is the type of person who, if he killed the doctor, he would be boasting, taking all the credit, saying that God told him to do it — something like that. Don't you think?"

"So, what are you saying? *Somebody* shot the doctor," Carl said.

"Yes, but who?" Stephen replied, resting his chin on his hand.

This got me thinking: *My camera was recording when the doctor was speaking. Maybe I can find something on it.*

While we were speaking, more announcements rolled in about the race. Senator Wright had won California, a big electoral state, along with Oregon, Washington, and Nevada. The counter was now showing 133 to 62. The Senator seemed to have taken a sizeable lead.

"Told you so," Carl said again.

"The President still has a lot of states left that are projected for her to win," Stephen responded.

No sooner did he finish his statement, another announcement came in. The President's face appeared on screen with the states, Tennessee, Ohio, Iowa, Florida, New Mexico, and Indiana. Florida, Iowa and New Mexico had been in the "tossup" category for the President. The race was now becoming tight: The President was ahead 142 to 133.

Poor dad. He was exhausted from the roller-coaster results. Many children of the people at the church were getting restless as the night grew late. Anxiety was growing. Most of the results were in, and the tally was showing Senator Wright with 260 votes and President Copperfield with 267 votes. Two hundred and seventy votes were needed to win. There was one state left, one state that would determine who the president would be. Like many had predicted, it had come down to the state of Missouri.

The vote count was too tight to call. Many headlines were showing that President Copperfield was winning the popular vote, but, of course, what counted was the electoral vote. Finally the news anchor spoke:

"This just in. We have finally tallied all the votes in the state of Missouri, and the projections are saying that the winner is — "

The nation was holding its collective breath. It was silent in the church, as those who were praying stopped, those who were socializing stopped, and even the kids were quiet at that moment. All eyes were glued to the television, to see what the future of America would look like.

* * * * *

Caves of Palestine

John was about to continue on with his story, but he and the sergeant heard the sounds of light-weight footsteps approaching them quickly. The crushing sounds of the gravel were getting louder. They both prepared themselves for what may have been coming through the door, and they were surprised when they were confronted by a little boy.

A smudged-face boy was carrying one bowl of rice in one hand and one tin cup of water in the other. The young boy gazed upon Sergeant Jake and John. This was the first time that he had seen any Americans.

The wide-eyed boy cautiously placed the rice bowl and water cup on the ground, still looking at the two like they were animals on display at a zoo. Sergeant Jake grabbed the bowl of rice and said to the boy, "Shukran," which means "Thank you" in Arabic. The boy's reply was a total shock to John and Sergeant Jake. The little boy hocked a loogie, spat on the sergeant, and quickly ran off.

"What was that about? Why did that boy look so hateful?" John curiously asked.

"It's a shame that many radical Muslims teach their kids to hate Americans and Jews at such an early age. I see it all the time down here."

Sergeant Jake said sadly as he wiped away the spit from his cheek. Quickly changing the subject, the sergeant asked, "So what happened next in your story?"

Dumbfounded, John couldn't understand how a little kid could have so much hate toward people he didn't even know. John took note of this and then continued with his story.

Part Three

Remaining Faithful

"Where the battle rages, there the loyalty of the soldier is proved."

— *Martin Luther*

CHAPTER

20

Four years before

My heart was pounding and my hands were trembling as I sat on the edge of my bed, gasping for air. My bed was saturated with sweat, and I heard the blaring sound of a song called "Today Is a Good Day" playing on my alarm.

It didn't seem to be starting off as a good day, though. I awoke from a dream — or should I say, a nightmare, a terrible nightmare. I was trying to make sense of what had just taken place. I'd had realistic dreams before, like the time I was a spectator to a robbery taking place involving Pete, or the time I had a vision or dream of Jesus telling me about the gates. This, however, was different: I was dreaming of something that was *about to take place* — something bad.

Just moments before, I'd been deep in sleep. In my dream, I was in my school library with a magazine in my hand, going to sit down at a table. Rachel Matthews was a few tables away, reading what looked like her Bible. My phone buzzed, and I reached for it. But before I could pull it out, I heard what sounded like fireworks. Outside of the library, fireworks were going off and screams soon followed. The sounds were getting louder and closer. Someone burst through the doors yelling, "Run! Run!" but there was no place to run. I ducked under my table and saw that Rachel was also under hers. The boy who was yelling, "Run! Run!" became silent as another sound went off. He fell next to me. That's when I realized that the sound of fireworks were really sounds of gunshots.

His lifeless body was lying just a few feet away from me. His blank stare of death was looking right at me. The realization that there was a shooter in our school sank in, and fear gripped my heart. What was going on? Who was shooting and why? The shooter let off another round of gunfire, and I could hear the thud of bodies hitting the carpet. I peeked through the chairs from under my table and saw black boots — black, bloody boots — coming in my direction. Blood was splattered across these boots — boots that, oddly, I had seen before: Army boots.

The shooter came to my table and stopped. At this moment, through the cacophony all around me, everything slowed down, and I could hear the killer's breath and the reloading of his gun, as water from the sprinkler system poured from the table onto the floor. I closed my eyes tightly, listening to the sounds of loud whimpering and alarms going off, pulsating in the air. Then something even stranger happened: I heard music playing. It was "Today Is a Good Day." That's when I opened my eyes, gasping for air, trying to make sense of things.

* * * * *

Three months had passed since the election, three months since my breakup with Jazzy, and three months since that night at Tameka's house. A lot had happened since then. The seven of us who were there at Tameka's were now starting to experience strange, supernatural phenomena. Just the other day in church, a church member was in danger of losing her job because someone had falsely accused her of stealing products from the store she worked at and had found some of the merchandise in her car. Even though the evidence made her look guilty, she wasn't.

My brother was moved by her story and stood in front of the whole congregation, proclaiming to the lady that, by next week, not only would she get her job back but she would also be promoted. Of course, everyone in the church thought my brother was crazy — including myself. After my brother spoke, Pastor Bruce took the microphone to do damage control and smooth things over, stating, "This will happen if it is God's will," just in case Philip had been wrong.

My brother knew something that we all didn't, even if he didn't know how — he just knew it was going to happen.

The next week in our Sunday service, that same lady stood before the congregation and gave her testimony. Her accuser, who was her manager, had been caught on camera stealing items from the store and placing some of the smaller ones in the lady's back seat when they went to lunch. The manager had it out for this lady, even though she was a great employee. The manager seemed not to like so-called "Zealots."

When the store owner saw the footage of the store manager creating this elaborate scheme, she immediately fired the manager. The owner pressed charges and had the manager arrested, and then she made the accused lady in our church the new store manager.

All of the saints were in awe and rejoiced at the turn of events. Somehow Philip knew all of this was going to happen. My brother couldn't hide his wide grin of satisfaction that said, "I told you so." He had faith that God was going to bless this woman, and this was just one instance of what was happening to us as a group.

Carl suggested that we all meet together to talk about some of our experiences, over some food, of course.

* * * * *

We all stood in front of the highly talked about Mexican restaurant, Burrito Perfecto. It had been open for several months then. Carl loved Mexican food and suggested we meet there. He was eager to try this place out. Several months before, just across the street from this restaurant, was where I'd met trouble. Outside that abandoned building was where Pete introduced me to his gang and where I saw firsthand the effects of the highly addictive drug called *Blue*.

"Slash," the scarred-face boy who took the drug, had passed away last week. Randall, Jazzy's step-brother, took it hard. On his social page, he had all kinds of memorial montages dedicated to him and pictures of the funeral and burial site.

Ever since that day when Slash was on the floor, foaming at the mouth, his life had changed. Even after he'd recovered from his near-death experience, only one thing had been on his mind — *Blue*. Two weeks before, Slash had taken the drug and was found dead. He was on his high and thought that he could fly, jumping off a four-story building to his death. Unfortunately this was the same story of many who had fallen prey to this potent drug that had overtaken the city.

The city was finally planning on tearing down that wretched building across the street from this restaurant, because it was a hub for criminal activity. I can only thank God, because I could have easily been in Slash's shoes, if I had taken the drug that day.

"Earth to John," Philip said, snapping me out of yet another one of my daydreams.

"This restaurant has been open for months, but the wait is still crazy," he complained.

When we exited our vehicle, we could see that all the group had managed to arrive at the restaurant around the same time. The place was crowded. With the line outside the building, there is about a fifteen-minute wait in line before we even got into the building. We finally made it to the hostess, and she told us that there would be an additional thirty-minute wait to be seated because of our party's size.

"Ah, man," Carl sighed as he rubbed his belly.

"I guess we'll have to wait," I commented.

While we were waiting, I was checking out the decor. The restaurant had a spacious, open floor plan with beautiful Aztec art mounted along the walls. The smells of Mexican spices and the sounds of mariachi music playing and people chattering filled the atmosphere. This was a welcoming place, with huge TVs lined across the walls and bar area.

The moment finally came. Our buzzer lit up and vibrated, indicating that our table was ready. We walked through a maze of Mexican art and rowdy customers at the bar who'd probably had a little too much to drink. The restaurant seemed to be a lot bigger on the inside than one would imagine, with a tall ceiling and huge ceiling fans. A young, sophisticated man with slicked-back hair, wearing a black tie and white shirt, led us to our seats in the spacious party-room area.

There was no need for a waiter or waitress at Burrito Perfecto. At each table, they had a computerized menu system in place, where you input your order and it went directly to the cooks.

We were scrolling through our menu options, when news of the presidential inauguration appeared on many of the television screens. The inauguration was being replayed on the GSTH network. This caught our attention. We all plugged in our earpieces and set the channel to GSTH to hear the news. On the screen was Gracie Mitchell, the reporter who was next to the slain abortion doctor. She had now quickly graduated to top news anchor at the network. Gracie showed a full, bright smile as she began to replay video clips of the inauguration.

In Washington, DC, it was a cold, blistering day, with light snow starting to fall. Flags blew in the bitter winds as thousands of people braved the weather just to get a glimpse of the President. The boys' and girls' chorus opened the event, followed by a poem and then another musical selection from a legendary opera singer. This inauguration was noticeably missing a person of the cloth. There was no preacher, priest, or spiritual guide who would open in prayer to bless the President and the nation. They elected to exclude any religious participation at the inaugural because of the whole "Zealot" situation, probably the first time this had ever happened.

The honorable Judge William Mathis took the podium. He stood and looked at the President-elect and said, "Would you repeat after me."

Judge: "I, Cordell Sylvester Wright, do solemnly swear."

Senator: "I, Cordell Sylvester Wright, do solemnly swear."

Judge: "That I will execute the office of the President of the United States faithfully."

Senator: "That I will execute the office of the President of the United States faithfully."

Judge: "And will to the best of my ability."

Senator: "And will to the best of my ability."

Judge: "Preserve, protect, and defend the constitution of the United States."

Senator: "Preserve, protect, and defend the constitution of the United States."

Judge: "So help me God."

Senator Wright took a long pause before answering. You could tell that it was killing him just to have his hand on a Bible. You would think that his hand was burning, the way he was looking.

The judge repeated himself, "So help me God."

Senator: "So help me."

Judge Mathis looked at him strangely but didn't bother to challenge him anymore and just accepted his statement.

"Congratulations, Mr. President," he said to now-President Cordell Wright.

The sea of people sent up a thunderous roar, as cannons shot and trumpets played in the background.

Senator Cordell Wright was President now. The night of the presidential election had been a stressful one, especially for my dad. When the anchor announced that the projected winner was Senator Wright, the whole church sighed, and some began to weep. My dad was frozen, shocked, in disbelief. He'd been so certain that President Copperfield would be re-elected. Everyone was demanding a recount. I think the thing that made it hurt even more was knowing that the state that had determined the next President was *our* state. Pastor Bruce, who was visibly shaken, tried to encourage and reassure the congregation that the heart of the king was in the hands of God.

President Copperfield conceded. She didn't challenge or demand a recount but called the Senator to congratulate him on his victory. The always-gracious President Copperfield took the stage to address her supporters. Her husband, General Copperfield, stood by her side with her two sons. The dark-skinned, silver-headed woman thanked the crowd and gave a stirring speech, asking all to pray for this nation, the nation she'd tirelessly given herself to. She asked everyone to humble themselves before God and trust in him.

My mom turned to my dad and said, "You know, the last I checked, God is still in control, no matter what events may happen."

This brought a slight grin to my dad's grim face.

"You're right honey — God is in control," he said as mom kissed his cheek.

Now three months later, I was in a restaurant watching the inauguration. GSTH showed clips of the President's speech. The tall, regal President stood and waved to the audience, showing all of his dental work. The camera panned to his wife, first lady Susan Wright, and their two young children, Larissa and Judy.

Once the applause ceased, President Wright began his speech.

"My fellow citizens, I stand here today humbled by the task before us. I thank President Copperfield for her service to our nation as well as the generosity and hospitality she has shown throughout this transition. That we are in the midst of a crisis is now well understood. Our nation is at war from within, against violence and hatred. Our economy is weaker, and we must seek alternatives."

The immense crowd was silent, with everyone intently listening to every word that came from his mouth. Cameras were surveying the sea of people, as the President spoke with a serious demeanor. He grabbed the podium with both hands, smiled, and said with a loud voice, "But today is a new day for America. Today, we put things back in order. To-day, we will be united as one."

This excited the crowd. Yells and whistles of approval went up as many began to celebrate. All were on their feet, with some recording the event and taking pictures with their mobile devices. Others wept tears of joy, clapping their hands.

While we were glued to the TVs, the server came out with our food. She was a pretty Hispanic teenager around our age. Her English seemed to be very limited, though. She was having a hard time trying to decipher which order belonged to who. While we were watching her passing out the dishes, Carl spoke up:

"Tengo los burritos, el número cinco con guacamole adicional."

"Número cinco?" the server asked.

"¡Si, gracias!" he replied. *"¿Cuál es su nombre?"*

"Maria."

"Gusto en conocerlo."

The server nodded her head and left.

"What did you say to her?" Rachel asked.

"Whatcha mean, what did I say?" Carl replied.

"Dude, you were speaking in Spanish to her," I said.

"What are y'all talking about? I just told her that I had the burri-tos, the number-five combo with extra guacamole, and then I asked her what her name was. She said 'Maria,' and then I said, 'Nice to meet you.' Everyone heard me say that, right?"

"Nah, man. You were speaking in Spanish," Philip said.

"Stephen, you know I don't know any Spanish," Carl said.

"I know, but you were speaking Spanish — and pretty well, too, I might add," Stephen said.

Stephen's parents' native language was Spanish, and he knew a little himself. Tameka recalled an earlier incident.

"Carl, remember when you told us the story of you speaking French to foreigners at the charging station last week? Well, it sounds like the same thing is happening."

"Now that you say that, the night when everyone was speaking in different languages at your house, I could understand what everyone was saying in English," Carl confessed.

"Strange things are beginning to happen to us," Rachel stated.

"Strange things, indeed," I agreed.

"Tell us what strange thing happened to you, John," Stephen inquired.

I was debating if I should tell the group of my horrific nightmare or not. I guess if anybody could understand it, it would be these guys. So I nervously prepared to go back into that dark place in my memory.

"Well, something strange and scary happened to me just this morning, or I should say last night, when I was sleeping. I'm not sure what to make of it, though. I'm not sure if it was a warning from God or the Chinese food I ate late in the night talking."

"Well, tell us what happened, man," Carl said eagerly awaiting.

"Yeah, why haven't you told me about this?" Philip asked.

"I don't know. Like I said, I'm still trying to process this."

"It's okay, John. You can tell us," Hannah said, encouraging me to go on. Hannah normally didn't say much in the group, but when she did speak, it had weight to it.

"Alright, well, in my dream, I was in our school library about to look at a book when…"

I proceeded to tell them the gruesome details of what happened in the library. When I got to the point in the story where I was explaining to the group about a boy running into the library to warn us, something I didn't expect happened. Rachel simultaneously said the same words as I was about to say. "Run! Run!" we both said.

All of us were surprised at how Rachel knew what I was about to say.

"I had a dream like yours last night, too," she said. "I was sitting at the library table reading my Bible. My Bible was opened to Isaiah 41:10. It read,

'Fear not, for I *am* with you; Be not dismayed, for I *am* your God. I will strengthen you, Yes, I will help you, I will uphold you with My righteous right hand.' As soon as I finished reading that scripture, I heard people outside the library screaming, screeching screams, followed by loud noises — like fireworks. Then that's when the boy came into the library yelling 'Run! Run!'"

Rachel's dream differed a little from mine, but we'd both heard gunshots, people were crying, and we both saw bloody boots. Neither one of us saw the killer's face — only the military boots covered in blood.

Philip looked at both of us and said, "There is only one person I know who wears Army boots to school all the time — "

"Mr. Boots," Rachel and I said, together with Philip, finishing his thought.

CHAPTER

21

Several months had passed since the night of the police chase that caused Pete and me to have a life-altering experience. After the accident, I'd been able to recover in just a few days, but Pete was still in the same state. Not much had change these past three months. He is still being fed through tubes, breathing but motionless. He is just a living shell, not the vibrant Pete I once knew. I tried to visit Mrs. Woods, Pete's mom, every so often, just to keep her spirits up. She always looked like she was worn out, just getting by, and carrying a heavy burden. I prayed daily for the both of them, my childhood friend Pete and his mom.

My relationship with my other childhood friend — and ex-girlfriend — hadn't gotten any better, either. I thought at first Jazzy was with Triston only to make me jealous, but now I wasn't so sure. She had been regularly hanging out with this loser, showing the same affection toward him that she'd once shown me.

It was a daily struggle seeing the one I love with someone else, and, this day, that struggle would probably replay again. Philip and I had arrived at school a little early. Since we were early, I decided to take the scenic route to my home room, so that I could mentally prepare for the day.

As I rounded the corner, I saw the dark, square-faced jerk, Triston Stewart, grabbing Trevor Jacobs and shoving him against the lockers. Few people were at the school this early, and those who were there just walked by like nothing was happening. I hate to say it, but, normally, I would have, too. It shames me to say that I was one of the many who would make fun of Trevor on different social sites, laughing at his funny speech. Whenever someone in our school would stutter or fumble over their words, we would say that they were "Trevoring."

Trevor was always being picked on by Triston for some reason, even though Trevor was a senior and Triston a junior. Trevor never defended himself, allowing Triston to harass him whenever he wanted. The pimple-faced, scrawny boy had always been a prime target for bullying.

When Trevor was younger, it was discovered that he had a tumor in his mouth and throat that caused his tongue to swell and for him to drool a lot. The tumor was benign and the doctors were able to remove it; however, it affected how he talked. His speech was slurred, and he produced uncontrollable saliva, dribbling from his mouth.

Trevor didn't say much because people would always make fun of his speech. I was standing there, watching Triston intimidate Trevor. An anger toward Triston began to rise in me. Compassion for Trevor flooded over me. I couldn't watch this same scene replay countless times anymore. Somebody had to step in. Not even thinking, I was compelled to do something. I rushed over toward Triston, pushing him away, knocking him to the ground, and causing the few who were around to point and laugh at him.

"Leave him alone," I said, angrily.

This enraged Triston and he quickly bounced up to his feet, ready to strike me. By this time, the halls were beginning to fill as students poured in for school. Teachers also had started roaming the halls. And even though Triston was boiling with anger, he was smart enough not to strike back with all the teachers present. He showed unusual restraint and brushed himself off, displaying his twisted grin at me.

With his deadly glare, he said, "Look at you — a Zealot wimp trying to defend a pimple wimp."

"Leave him alone, Triston." I repeated.

"Or what?"

Honestly, I didn't have an answer. I just knew I couldn't continue letting Triston pummel Trevor and have no one do anything about it.

"Like I thought," he said. Then, laughing at me, he continued. "You know what Jazzy told me? She says that now she knows what it's like to be with a real man. She also told me that she was tired of being with a religious Zealot." Triston laughed.

I knew he was just trying to get a rise out of me. I knew Jazzy didn't think that this chump was a real man, but the part about me being a Zealot might have been true. Before Triston turned to go away, he said something odd.

"If it was up to me, I would take all of you Zealots out. One by one. Then reload and do it again."

The way that he said it was creepy. It was like he really meant it. I couldn't help but feel that I was looking into the eyes of a demon in a letterman jacket.

He finally left, but I knew it wasn't over between the two of us. I turned my attention to Trevor, who was still on the ground with his belongings scattered everywhere. I helped him gather everything and place them in his backpack. The fragile, scrawny kid kept his eyes to the ground, not knowing how to react to someone helping him.

As I reached out to give Trevor his backpack, something strange happened. When I touched him, I suddenly saw a flash of his life. Trevor was in his bedroom, sitting on the floor with his back to the door. I could hear yelling between a man and a woman outside his door. Trevor had his hands over his ears, trying to muffle the sound. The argument outside his room intensified. The man continued to yell. Then I heard a scream from the woman. It sounded like she had been hit. I couldn't see behind the door, but I could see Trevor beginning to cry as the woman continued to be beaten by this angry man. Were these his parents?

Suddenly, I was sucked back to reality, with Trevor looking at me holding his backpack. It felt like time had slowed down. Those few seconds seemed like a few minutes. I had never experienced anything like this before. God had shown me dreams, but I hadn't seen anything like this while I was awake. I felt a prompting from God to speak to Trevor, to let him know that God loved him.

"God loves you," I said sincerely as I gave him his backpack.

"Does he?" he said in a mumble, a barely audible whisper.

"Yes, he does." I replied compassionately.

Then Trevor did something that I hadn't seen him do before. He stopped looking at the floor, looked me right in the eye, and spoke.

"Then why does he keep letting my stepdad beat my mom?" Trevor's eyes begin to water, and he snatched his backpack and rushed off, not waiting for a reply.

I could feel the hurt behind his words. As Trevor hurried off, I saw a few post-it notes float to the ground. I scooped them up and tried to catch up with him, but he'd vanished into the crowd like a ninja.

When I looked at the notes that he left behind, one read, *Looking at you makes my day better*. Another note read, *You are so beautiful. One day, I will tell you that.* Trevor had several love notes written — but to whom? Who was he talking about?

* * * * *

My project for Mr. Spring's video-editing class was coming due soon; there were just two weeks left. I'd gathered all my footage and done all my interviews. Now I just had to edit everything. For my video project, I'd decided to tell the real story behind the abortion-clinic riots and the results of this on our nation. I gathered the rally footage, and I did interviews with those who were there, including pastors, priests and even some police officers.

Looking at the news media outlets, one would think that Christians started this hate movement at the abortion rally. I was determined to tell the truth — our side of the story. I was at home in my computer lab, which was my bedroom, scrubbing through the videos of the protest. I was now at the point where the shooting occurred. I scrubbed through to find footage of the doctor speaking in front of the crowd but quickly realized I hadn't had my camera on the doctor when he was about to speak, Rather, it had been on the people in the crowd.

I let the video play and saw Pastor Henry Joseph in the crowd, yelling while the doctor was about to speak. That's when the loud sound rang in the air. I was looking at Pastor Henry, but I didn't see him holding a weapon — only a sign in both of his hands that said, "Go to Hell." I rewound the video and zoomed in on the footage at the exact moment when the sound went off.

To my surprise, I saw a man behind the Hardline Church pastor. The man's hand was holding a gun, pointing in the direction of the doctor. The suspect had on a long trench coat, with gloves, hat, and a scarf covering his mouth. I played the video in slow motion to try to capture every frame. This man moved quickly after the loud sound rang out. He slipped the gun into Henry Joseph's coat pocket and vanished into the crowd. Pastor Henry noticed something in his pocket, and he looked surprised when he pulled a gun out. That's when nearby police officers tackled him and accused him of the murder of Doctor Macbeth.

I couldn't believe what I was seeing. I replayed that clip over and over, zooming in and out, trying to figure out who the sketchy man was. There wasn't any clear picture of the man's face — only his eyes and nose were exposed. He'd covered himself well, not leaving much to look at, but I was sure one thing he hadn't counted on was me catching him on video.

Carl immediately came to my mind. I remember on the bus, him talking about some kind of facial-recognition software he was working on. I couldn't believe that I was sitting on some life-changing information. Someone had framed Pastor Henry Joseph.

I called my brother into my room, and we both watched the video again, trying to decipher who this man was. Why had he shot the doctor and then framed the pastor? Flabbergasted, we decided to call Carl. Maybe, with his technology, he could tell us who this guy was.

* * * * *

Freezing drizzle hit the windshield as Philip and I cautiously drove through the slushy, muddy roads. Our radio broadcast was interrupted with the daily news updates. President Wright was in the process of proposing a new bill, redefining hate laws and religious expression. The clear, assertive voice of our new Commander-in-Chief pierced the airwaves.

"Fellow Americans, today I am proposing a new bill that will allow all to live as one, with no judging or harassment from those whose beliefs are different. This is the age of tolerance, and we should be united as one. Those who try to oppose this will be dealt with harshly. We will not tolerate the intolerant," the president said.

"So, in other words, any Christian who doesn't agree with this law will face criminal action," Philip sharply blurted out at the radio.

I could see my dad all over Philip. He was sounding more and more like him.

"Yeah, us 'Zealots' — we're his real target," I concurred.

"Looking at your video makes me think that this whole movement against Christianity was planned," Philip stated.

"Yeah. I hope Carl will be able to give us some answers."

While we were driving, I could see a few cars off to the side of the road. The weather was getting worse, and the roads were getting slicker. We were determined that the weather wouldn't prevent us from getting to Carl's house. When we talked to Carl on the phone, he said that we could come anytime we like. The information I was holding was hot, and I had to know who this killer was. So Philip and I had decided to take our chances on the icy roads. Looking outside at all the vehicles piling up on the side of the road, we were beginning to second-guess our decision to leave. It was too late — we were already in the trenches, so we thought it best to keep going.

Carl lived about twenty miles from our place. He resided in the south Kansas City area, not far from his school CC Tech University. He and his dad had just moved to the new apartment complexes built about a year before.

When it came to tech stuff, Carl was a genius. He'd received a scholarship to attend this elite school and now was into his second year, pursuing a software-engineering degree.

Normally the ride would have taken about fifteen minutes, but with the roads like they were, we were taking twice as long to get there.

"When we make it to his house, do you think mom and dad will let us stay the night?" I asked.

"If this keeps up, we might not have a choice," Philip said with the defrost blasting and the wipers working overtime trying to clear the freezing rain.

Finally, after about an hour of inching our way through traffic, we arrived at Carl's place. With a copy of the shooting footage in my coat pocket, we made our way through the icy parking lot. After avoiding several near falls, we came to his door. To our surprise, Stephen answered the door.

"What's up Mann," Stephen said, in a horrible attempt at humor. How many times had I heard that line before?

"What are you doing here?" Philip asked.

"Carl told me that you guys had some information that could change things. So I wanted to check it out," Stephen replied.

"This footage will change everything," I said agreeing with Stephen's assessment.

"Well, let's see it," Carl said, coming from the back room with his tight undershirt on, showcasing his portly belly.

I handed Carl my copy, and he led us to his room. It was like a control center, with all his monitors and computer parts everywhere.

"I was just checking out the weather report. It looks like schools are already cancelling tomorrow. If you guys want to stay the night, you're more than welcome. My dad is okay with it."

"Maybe, it's starting to really coming down now," Philip said, peeking out the window.

"Well, make yourselves comfortable. You may be here awhile."

Carl powered up his PC and pulled up the video of the doctor's shooting. When the footage was played, the look on Carl and Stephen's face was one of shock. Carl quickly dialed up his facial-recognition software to try to identify the culprit. His fingers were dutifully typing away as he froze every frame and then ran his software.

I could see the frustration on Carl's face, as he was not getting the results that he'd hoped for. After about an hour of Carl freezing every frame and sipping on his 44-ounce Coke, he finally spoke.

"Guys, this is not turning out like I expected it to. Whoever this guy is, he is a professional."

"Why do you say that?" Stephen curiously asked.

"He had to know that facial recognition is based on the matching of distances between fixed points on your face. For instance, the distance between your eye and ears, eye and nose, shape of your head, etc. He was clever enough to hide his mouth and distort the shape of his head with the hat and scarf. I don't have much to go on. Nevertheless, here are the results of possible suspects," Carl said, agonized.

Carl pulled up a list of possible suspects from a database matching the data from the mysterious killer's face. There were more than two hundred possible matches.

"It looks like we're not going to find out who this guy is," Philip said, with disappointment.

"Well I'm not giving up just yet," Carl said. "I've been working on an advanced feature with my software, called 'retina recognition.' It looks like there are a few frames that clearly show a front view of this man's eyes. Some flaws with facial-recognition programs are what we are experiencing now. If a person changes their face with plastic surgery, it can change the data needed to detect who a person is, but, with my new feature, things are a bit more reliable."

"How is that?" I asked.

"You see, it is very rare that a person would risk changing their eyes, especially their pupils. What my new feature does is match the unique points in the pupil. Everyone has unique eyes, just like they have unique faces. And I think I might have enough information here to scan his eyes, checking the database for possible suspects."

"Those eyes look oddly familiar," I stated.

"Yeah. I've seen this person before somewhere," Philip added.

"Well, let's see who this guy is," said Stephen.

"Well, I'm not quite finished with my updates. I still have to do a few more tests."

"How much time are you talking about?" I asked.

"If I focus, it should be ready in a few days," Carl said, confidently. "Until then, why don't you guys relax? It looks like no one's going anywhere tonight."

He was right. An ice storm was barreling through the city. My mom sent a text telling us to stay put for the night and asked us to thank Mr. Green, Carl's dad, for letting us stay the night.

CHAPTER

22

"Run! Run!" the boy said. Ducking under the table, I looked and saw the boy's body drop. I stared into his dead, blank eyes. Again, I saw the relentless killer coming toward me, with blood-splattered Army boots. He reloaded his gun, and, like before, I awoke, shaking, looking at the pale popcorn ceiling.

The same nightmare as before had invaded my sleep. It was Friday, and school had reopened. We were returning from having the day off Thursday, due to the ice storm. The night of the storm, Philip, Stephen, Carl, and I had a great time watching movies, talking about our strange supernatural experiences, and trying to figure out what to do with the information on the shooting.

Stephen thought that we should turn the video into the authorities, but Carl thought it was a part of a conspiracy being formed to eliminate the strength of Christianity in America. I didn't know what to think, so I agreed to wait and let Carl first identify who this guy was before getting anyone else involved. This also had the potential to be a big boost for my school project. I needed this footage to complete my project and couldn't risk the cops confiscating it.

Philip came into my room. He must have heard me tussling in my bed this morning.

"You alright, bro?"

"I had the dream again."

"The bloody-boot dream?" he asked.

"Yeah. Why am I having this?"

"Maybe it's a warning?"

"I don't know. Maybe you're right. But of who or what?"

"Come on. We need to get ready for school," Philip said looking at the clock.

"Why are we having school anyway? They could have at least let us finish the week off with no school. It doesn't make any sense for us to return to school on a Friday," I complained, but my complaint fell on deaf ears.

"Well if we don't go now, we'll have to make it up at the end of the year. Let's go, lazy bones," Philip urged me.

* * * * *

The salt trucks had been working overtime the past few days. They finally would get a break today, with rising temperatures and a forecast calling for a sunny day. The sun was starting to peek above the horizon in Grand Lake, with icy roads slowly melting away. Philip and I barely made it to school on time. Principal Strudel was at the doors, looking at his watch, waiting for us to slip up and be tardy, but we made it in enough time.

It was uniform day for the Army Junior Reserve Officer Training Corps — or JROTC. When I entered the school, I saw a sight that I thought I would never see. Triston Stewart was leading a march in the hallways in full Army gear and his shoes were... shiny, army — . *Nah, it can't be!* I thought. *Boots...shiny boots.* Triston saw me watching him and gave me a salute with his middle finger.

How and why is he a part of the JROTC? I thought this program was supposed to be about building a student's character and leadership.

224

They are supposed to be about integrity, honor, and all that stuff. All the things that Triston is not. How is he leading this group? Another surprising thing I saw was Trevor in the back of the group, trying to keep up with his oversized uniform on. *What is going on here? I would think that Trevor would want to get away from being in the same space as Triston. Strange!*

* * * * *

First, second, and third period at school seemed to fly by. Now I was at the point in the day where Jazzy's and my paths usually met. Fourth period is when, in the past, I would meet Jazzy and walk with her to her next class. But things were different now. This was the time of the day I used to look forward to, but now I dreaded this hour. I never really had time to talk things out with Jazzy ever since our relationship had ended so abruptly.

I missed her being my friend more than I missed her being my girlfriend. I missed those times we spent at the lake, the messaging at church, and how she always knew what I was feeling before I even said a word. Where had we gone wrong?

On this day, in the fourth period, would be the day I would finally realize that Jazzy's feelings for me were no more. I came to her classroom, only to make a heartbreaking discovery. Jazzy was kissing Triston — not just a peck, but a full-blown, lip-locking, saliva-exchanging kiss.

My heart sank with sadness. Then anger engulfed me. Jealousy and hatred toward Triston was what I was feeling. I felt hurt and betrayed by Jazzy, and my heart was shattering. Frozen in place, I stared at the two of them. I must have caught Jazzy's eye. She saw me and pushed Triston away, looking at me with a sense of shame. Then she quickly bounced her eyes away from me, fastening them onto the floor. I gazed at her with painful eyes and a wounded heart, but she couldn't seem to bring her eyes to meet mine.

Triston noticed the exchange between us and positioned himself closer to her. He wrapped his arm around her.

"Hey! Why you looking at my girl like that?" Triston said.

His girl? My eyes were still glaring at Jazzy, but she wasn't moving, only taking quick peeks at me and then shifting her eyes back to the floor. She just stood there, not denying his statement about her being "his girl," which angered me even more. My eyes began to well up, and I must admit that, at that moment, I was not thinking about Jesus and turning the other cheek. The only cheeks I wanted to turn are Triston's. I wanted to smack that smile off his face.

How ironic! Just months ago, I was telling him to back away from *my* girl, Jazzy. Now things had turned, and he was telling me the same.

I stepped toward Triston, ready to finish this feud between us once and for all.

"What are you going to do, church boy?" he said. Daring me to swing.

I took another step toward him, looking him in the eye, and smelling his tobacco-laced breath. Triston pushed me away, and I reared back, ready to swing. But, out of nowhere, I felt someone holding my hand back.

I turned and saw Rachel.

"Don't do it, John," she said. Her soft-spoken words seemed to calm the jealous rage in me. I relaxed my hands and stepped away from Triston.

"Yeah — you betta listen to what your girlfriend says," Triston remarked.

"Girlfriend?" a soft voice said. That voice was Jazzy's. She'd finally spoken, and in her voice was the sound of surprise and disappointment. Was she disappointed that I might be with someone else?

Rachel quickly answered Jazzy's question by laughing and saying, "'Girlfriend' — oh, no. I'm not his girlfriend. We're just friends."

What Rachel said was true, but she didn't have to say it like that. She laughed at the thought of being with me. "'Girlfriend' — please," she repeated with laughter.

"OK. I think they get it. You're not my girlfriend," I said, trying to stop the laughter.

Rachel's presence had defused the potential explosion between Triston and me. Jazzy managed to convince Triston to leave, while Rachel persuaded me to back off.

"Wow, Rachel — do I look that bad? I know we're not an item, but laughing at me? Come on," I said, playfully, to her.

"I'm sorry, John. I guess you look okay, for a sophomore," she replied. "Anyway, what's going on between you and Triston? You seemed like you and he have been really going at it lately. Is this because of Jazzy?" Rachel asked, turning her tone from playful to concern.

"Well, Jazzy is a big part of it. That chump's been after her since last year. He knew that we were together, but he didn't care. And Jazzy — Jazzy couldn't stand him then, but now that we've broken up, all of a sudden, she wants to be with him. I just don't buy it."

"Look, John. I know you still have feelings for her. I can tell. Maybe you guys need to talk out your feelings, but, eventually, you're going to have to let her go" Rachel stated plainly.

'Let her go'? I'm not sure that I'm ready to do that. I thought to myself.

"John, remember who we are. We are ambassadors of Christ. The Bible tells us to love our enemies and pray for those who persecute us. It's easy to love those who love you, but it takes God to love those who hate you. But this is what we are called to do," Rachel reminded and encouraged me.

She sounded a lot like my brother — giving me advice that I needed but didn't want to hear at the moment.

"Yeah. I guess you're right," I admitted.

"Stay strong. You coming to Bible study today?"

"Yeah, I'll be there," I said, solemnly.

Before Rachel left, I noticed on her tablet a post-it note with the same handwriting as Trevor's. The note read, *You look so beautiful today.*

Curious, I asked, "So what you got there?" I said, pointing at the note on her tablet.

"This? I don't know. Someone has been putting notes on my locker every morning this week."

"It looks like somebody has a secret admirer," I said, smiling at her.

"It's not you, is it?" she laughed.

"Please — you wish you had this sophomore."

"Whatever — so not true," she said with a face of disgust. "See you at the Bible study, John."

"Alright, see you there."

Seeing that classes were about to start, we both hurried off. Principal Strudel and Mr. Boots were lurking in the halls, waiting for the right moment to catch us breaking any rules. So we had to make sure we arrived at class on time. Ever since our dream, Rachel had grown terrified of Mr. Boots — and I couldn't blame her.

Imagine that: Rachel Matthews had a secret admirer. It wasn't me, but I thought I knew who it was.

* * * * *

Sitting at my desk, I was putting the final touches on my video project of the abortion-clinic riot. There had been no news from Carl yet about who our mystery man was. Unfortunately, I couldn't wait any longer on this project. Mr. Spring had already extended my due date. So I didn't have any more time to wait. I didn't have a choice. I had to submit what I had. Hopefully Carl would be able to find out who this guy was. I opened my school account, scrolled to Mr. Spring's class, and uploaded my project.

While I was at my desk, my mind began to wander about the week's events: Waking up from a repeated nightmare, seeing a vision of Trevor's life, discovering that Pastor Henry Joseph didn't kill the doctor, losing my temper and almost fighting with Triston twice, and finally seeing the one I love falling for someone else.

This week had definitely been weird. Rachel and my brother were certain that Mr. Boots was the killer in my recurring school-shooting nightmare. I also was sure that he was the one, but, lately, I had not been so sure. This week, my encounter with Triston made me think that he may have been the one who was planning a shooting at Grand Lake High. Seeing him in that uniform with those boots sent a chill down my spine. I also recalled him saying, *"If it was up to me, I would take all of you zealots out. One by one. Then reload and do it again."* I wouldn't put it past his twisted mind to have something like this planned. If it was Mr. Boots or Triston — either one — they both seemed creepy to me, and I knew that Rachel's and my dream was a warning of something to come. The question now was, "How do we stop this from happening?"

This past week at school had also made me look at Trevor differently. Now I knew why he was always so withdrawn. I couldn't imagine enduring constant abuse from my peers and parents. If it was me I would have snapped, but Trevor seemed to go into his shell, internalizing everything. I actually felt sorry for him — and to think that all these years I'd been like everyone else, making jokes about his appearance and speech. Lord, forgive me!

It seemed that Trevor might have had a thing for Rachel. All those notes on her locker were in his handwriting. I thought that maybe I should confront him about it.

These random thoughts zipped through my mind as I sat at my desk staring at a black screen that had just gone into sleep mode. Yesterday at school, Rachel had got me thinking about my actions toward Triston and Jazzy. I was ashamed that I'd let my emotions overtake me. I had so much hatred toward. Triston. I knew it was wrong, but it was hard not to feel that way. God was going to have to help me to love my enemy.

After school on Friday, during our Bible study, God was really dealing with me. The words that Rachel had spoken to me about being an ambassador for Christ and loving Triston really stuck in my head and pricked my heart. What if God was using me to be a light to Triston? If so, then I needed to replace my bulb because my light was burnt out.

Philip, Cassie, and Rachel really prayed for me at the Bible study, and I could feel the peace of God rest on me. I really wanted to be that light in my school, but loving Triston was going to be my hardest challenge.

When I thought about Jazzy, and her kissing... kissing him, it made my heart sink and my jaws clench. I knew that we were not together anymore and that she had every right to see someone else — but that didn't change my feelings for her. I thought that she still felt the same way about me. The way she pushed Triston away when she saw me, how she couldn't look me in the eyes, and how I saw a tinge of jealousy rising when she thought that Rachel was my girlfriend. I thought that something might still be there. I needed to talk to her. Maybe Rachel had been right in saying that I should talk things out with her.

The day before, I'd left multiple messages and voicemails on her phone, but she had not replied. So I was going to call her home phone. I knew someone would answer. I had to get some kind of closure between us. My heart had been sick for a while, and I needed to know where we stood.

I grabbed my phone, taking deep breaths, psyching myself up to make the call to her house. I nervously rubbed the smooth exterior of my phone, searching for her home phone number. I found it and paused for a moment, rethinking if this was a good idea. *I had to know.* My shaking thumb pressed the green call button.

The phone rang three time before Mrs. Smith, Jazzy's mom, answered.

"Hello" she said.

"Hello, Mrs. Reed. I mean, Mrs. Smith. This is John." I was still not used to calling her by her new married name.

"Yes, I know who this is. How have you been, Johnny? I haven't heard from you in a while."

"Yes. It has been a while."

"So, what can I do for you, honey?" she said, knowing that I didn't call to chat with her.

"Well, I was wondering if Jazzy was home."

"Okay, let me go get her — hold on a minute."

"Yes ma'am," I said, patiently waiting for Jazzy. Her "minute" seemed to be more like several minutes as I waited on the phone, rehearsing what I should say to Jazzy.

Finally the phone was picked back up, but the voice on the other end wasn't Jazzy.

"Hello, John," her mom said.

"Yes, ma'am" I answered.

"Look, I'm sorry, sweetie, but Jazzy doesn't want to talk to you. You see, my daughter doesn't want you calling her anymore."

I guess I'd gotten my answer concerning where we stand.

Mrs. Smith continued, "You are a nice boy, John. I don't know what happened between you two, but I must ask you to respect her wish. You understand?" Mrs. Smith said in a gentle tone, careful not to break my fragile heart.

"Yes, ma'am." I understand."

"Hey, if it makes you feel any better, I like you better than this other guy she has started dating."

Dating? "Well, thank you, ma'am. Sorry to bother you."

"Goodbye, John."

"Goodbye, Mrs. Smith."

CHAPTER

23

The salt-and-pepper-headed pastor stood firm at the podium, looking out into the crowded sanctuary. Attendance at L3C had dramatically increased lately. A lot of young people had been attending service, due to the seven of us outreaching in our schools. Mainly Rachel, at Grand Lake High, had been inviting students to the Bible study after school and then to our church. Stephen, Hannah, Carl, and Tameka seemed to be doing the same thing at their colleges.

"Good morning, saints." Pastor Bruce's booming voice filled the sanctuary. "Could everyone turn in their bibles to Proverbs 3:5-6? On the two big screens behind him, the scriptures pulled up.

"Could we all read together?" he asked the congregation. Everyone stood in unison and read, **"Trust in the LORD with all your heart; do not depend on your own understanding. Seek his will in all you do, and he will show you which path to take."**

"Today I want to talk about 'Letting Go and Letting God.'" The title of his sermon faded in on the two big screens.

"Many of us are trying to take things into our own hands. We need to control them. We are afraid of totally submitting to God, because we are uncertain of what God wants us to do and not sure if it will be something that we want to do. But I am here to tell you to let go and let God.

"Some of you single folks are still holding onto that boyfriend or girlfriend who is unequally yoked, afraid to let go because you are comfortable. But I am here to tell you to let go and let God…"

While he was speaking, I was struggling to hold back the flood of tears that was creeping up, about to overflow the levee of my eyes. The pastor was preaching directly to me. It was confirmed — I needed to let Jazzy go. That day in the church pew, with my head hidden, I made up my mind to submit my will to God and let him take the wheel of my life. I turned to the back of the church, where I used to sit, and was surprised to see Jazzy there. She was audibly crying. But before the pastor could finish his sermon, Jazzy rushed out of the sanctuary.

He finished the sermon, and my face was drenched in tears, eyes bloodshot, and my nose running with snot. Pastor Bruce's message was right on point. I excused myself to go the restroom to try to clean up, wipe my face, and straighten out my clothes. As I exited the restroom and entered into the foyer, I saw Jazzy exiting the front doors. Triston Stewart had his car parked in front of the church, honking his horn, waving at Jazzy to hurry up.

Surprisingly, I didn't feel the anger or jealousy that I would normally feel watching them. I actually felt sad for Jazzy. What happened to the girl I knew? I was watching her head down the wrong path with this guy.

When I entered back into the sanctuary, I saw Tameka Wilson on the stage. *What is going on here?* Apparently, she had a testimony that the pastor wanted her to tell the congregation. I made my way back to my seat next to Carl, Stephen, and Philip.

Tameka had a wide grin plastered across her face, as excitement radiated from her.

"Well, good morning, saints," she said, excitedly.

A few in the crowd reply, "Good morning."

She continued, "God is so good. He is amazing. Two days ago, I heard the news that my cousin Terrance had been in a horrific accident. A drunk driver ran a red light and hit him on the driver's side. Terrance was in critical condition. By the time the news got to us, he had been in the hospital for a day already. So my mom, brother, and I rushed over to Truman Hospital to see how he was doing.

"He'd been upgraded from critical to stable condition, but there was serious cause for concern. Doctors were mainly concerned about his spinal-cord injury. X-rays showed that Terrace's T9 vertebra was severely damage and that he had less than a thirty percent chance of ever walking again.

"While I was welling up, I heard a voice from within say, 'Do you believe I can heal?' I did believe and spoke to Terrance, saying, 'I believe God is going to heal you today.' My mom cut in and said, 'Yes — we believe that he will make a full recovery someday.' I told my mom, 'No. God is going to heal Terrance today — completely. I know.'

"So I prayed for my cousin like I have never prayed before in my life, and, for some reason, I just knew that God wanted to heal him. I was commanding every ligament, every muscle, every tissue and bone to align itself back to its original place. While I was praying, I felt the power of God flowing through my hand.

"Once I'd finished praying, Terrance lay there, speechless. When he finally spoke, he asked me what I'd done to him. He said he'd felt a warm tingling sensation run through his body — like someone was moving his bones around. Fear and excitement came over him as he felt electricity shoot up and down his spine.

"I felt the boldness of the Holy Spirit, and I did something I would never do. I asked him to try walking. He looked at me like I was crazy. But he cautiously swung to the side of his bed and placed one toe on the ground, looking at my mom with a smile. He then placed the other foot on the floor, and, gathering himself, he began to walk. He began to *walk*, saints! He began to walk!" Tameka repeated loudly with overwhelming excitement.

Tameka pointed at her cousin Terrance in the back of the church and said, like a game-show host, "Terrance — come on down."

Some were in shock, while others screamed with joy and applauded loudly. The organist slid onto the organ and started playing some good old gospel, hand-clapping, feet-stomping, shouting music. The church went crazy. Some saints were circling the church like a track meet, while others were jumping in place. Carl pulled out his "Stank Face" look, and Stephen's hands went straight into the air, worshiping. Tameka "Tutu" started doing her thing, twirling in circles. It was amazing — this praise erupting in the church. I didn't know what to do, so I just stood there with a wide joker grin on my face. My cheekbones were beginning to hurt from all this smiling.

God truly used Tameka in a great way that day, but this was just the start of what was to come for us as a group.

* * * * *

It had been a little more than a week now, and love was in the air at Grand Lake High School. It was Valentine's Day. Giddy girls were in the hallways, in anticipation of what the day might bring. Flowers, cards, and candy were everywhere. I never did really understand this day. I mean, Valentine's Day should really be called "Ladies Day," because most men were not expecting any gifts.

This day was just another reminder to me that I didn't have anybody to call a girlfriend. Since I'd finally decided to let Jazzy go, things had been a little easier for me — it didn't hurt as much. However, that day was tough, since our relationship had never made it to this day, when I would have showered her with gifts. Instead, I pictured Triston giving her a withered flower and generic card for Valentine's Day. Jazzy would smile and accept his pathetic gift but would know she desires a lot more than that. I guessed that, someday, I would get a chance to participate in this day.

Philip arrived at school early again. As we passed the front office, we could see Mr. Boots and Principal Strudel holding hands and looking weirdly at each other.

"Oh brother," I said under my breath. The disturbing image of them looking like that when they rushed into the video editing room where I was hidden came to mind.

"You coming with me to get some breakfast?" Philip asked, interrupting my disturbing thought.

"Nah. I think I'm going to walk the halls and clear my mind," I replied.

Philip liked being early for everything, and, since I didn't have a car, I had no choice but to come to school early, too. So I liked to spend this time walking and talking to God to get my mind prepared for the day.

While I was walking, I spotted Trevor Jacobs sneaking up to Rachel's locker with a bouquet of flowers. He placed the colorful assortment of flowers in front of her locker, and, then, he wrote a post-it note and placed it on her locker.

Ah, ha! It is Trevor, just as I thought. He has a thing for Rachel.

I had to say something to him, because he had been doing this for a couple of weeks now. When Trevor finished placing his note on her locker, I was ready to confront him. I snuck up behind him and said, "Why don't you just ask her out?" I startled him, causing him to leap in the air. He turned to see who was speaking and looked at me like he had nearly wet his pants.

"I'm sorry. I didn't mean to scare you like that. I know that you have been putting notes on her locker for some time now. Just ask her out. Rachel is pretty cool," I said.

"No, no. I can't do that. What if she says 'No'?" Trevor said in a panicky voice.

"You will never know until you try," I said, trying to encourage him.

"I don't... I don't think I — I can. I don't think I can take her re–re–rejection," he said, softly.

I wasn't sure why he would go through all the trouble of placing all these gifts and notes on her locker if he never planned on talking to her. Anyway, I tried not to press him anymore. I did notice that he was carrying a medal or ribbon of some kind around his neck.

"What's that around your neck?" I asked.

Trevor proudly grabbed his medal and said, "This is the purple heart that my dad received when he was killed in service."

Not knowing what to say, I responded, "Sorry for your loss, man."

"He is my hero, and, someday, I will die in uniform, like him," Trevor oddly said. Trevor began to do something that I don't think that I had ever seen him do — smile. Now it made sense why he was involved in the JROTC.

The rush of students was coming into the school, and I could tell that Trevor didn't want to be near Rachel's locker when she arrived. So I decide to end our conversation by extending an invitation to him.

"Well, look, man. After school, if you have any time, why don't you come to our Bible study across the street? Rachel will be there. You'll see she's a nice person."

"I'll think about it," he said, with his eyes looking down to the floor.

"Alright, man. See you there."

"Hey, John could you keep this between me and…and you? Please don't tell Rachel or anyone," he asked, desperately.

"Look, man — my lips are sealed. Your secret's safe with me, but you need to tell her soon, or it will start to become creepy — you know? You don't want to be seen as stalking her," I said with a little laugh. But this didn't seem to amuse Trevor a bit. He just kept looking at the floor.

"OK. Thanks," he said, awkwardly, and vanished around the corner. *Strange kid.*

* * * * *

Our little room was beginning to fill up as students pressed in. We had come a long way from when we started. Then, it was just Rachel, Cassie, Philip, and me. Now this meeting is averaging about thirty people every day. Principal Strudel's attempts to silence the Christians in our school had only caused our Bible study to increase even more. Once everyone started to settle down, my brother stood in front and opened the meeting with prayer.

After my brother had prayed, Rachel came forward to begin the Bible study. Our study this week was on the book of Colossians. While we were opening our Bibles to the book of Colossians, someone interrupted our meeting. The wooden door behind us creaked open, and standing in the doorway was Trevor Jacobs. I couldn't believe Trevor had actually accepted my invitation.

"Come on in," Rachel said, smiling as she waved him forward.

The fragile, bashful boy came closer to the group. He was beet red and blushing from the fact that Rachel had spoken to him. I waved for him to sit next to me, up front, but he declined and sat near the back.

After finishing our reading of the word, our attention was now on the prayer board. The prayer board was our prayer list of things the group was praying for. Today's focus was on the release of Mr. Donovan, my history teacher who was accused of raping Tiffany Storm. When the news came out that Mr. Donovan raped Tiffany, I don't think anyone in our school really believed that it was true. The media painted Mr. Donovan as a religious monster preying on innocent girls, but everyone knew that Tiffany Storm was anything but innocent.

During our prayer, Rachel stepped forward and started declaring that Mr. Donovan would be set free. Then she started to prophesy to different students in the group. Trevor was starting to look uncomfortable, standing there and not knowing what to do. I could only imagine what he was thinking. I'm sure we looked crazy — people praying loudly. But he stayed for the whole meeting.

Rachel had always had a knack for knowing things about people. She was always trying to encourage someone. Thus the name "Psychic Rachel" was given to her. On the outside, she was a sweet girl, but when it came to the things of God, she was a fireball.

Especially since our night at Tameka's house. Ever since that day, she had been bold as a lion, speaking out against our principal and calling out the sins of students. Even in church, during praise and worship, you could feel God's presence when she sang. She did an awesome job of exhorting the people, getting everyone involved in worship.

I bet Trevor hadn't expected to see this side of Rachel. After our meeting was over, I rushed over to Trevor before he could vanish into thin air, like he always did.

"Hey, Trevor. Glad you could make it"

"Glad I came," he said, timidly.

Rachel was still hanging around. "Hey, Rachel," I said flagging her down to come talk to us.

"What are you doing?" Trevor whispered nervously to me.

"What's up, John?" Rachel said as she approached us.

As Rachel came toward us, Trevor's eyes shot straight to the floor, not wanting to make eye contact with her.

"Hey, Rachel. Do you know Trevor?" I asked, introducing the two.

"Yes. I've known Trevor ever since grade school," she said, smiling at him. *Wow! That was something I didn't know.*

"I am glad you came to Bible study," Rachel said to him, extending her hand for a handshake. This seemed to catch Trevor off guard. I nudged him to shake her hand. Rachel was awkwardly holding out her hand longer than she should have.

Trevor finally snapped out of his daze and raised his limp hand, giving her a weak handshake but still not looking into her eyes.

"I...I...am...G—Glad...I came," Trevor said struggling to get the words out as drool rolled down his cheek.

"Well, don't let it be the last time," Rachel said, cheerfully. "See you later, John," she said to me as she went to talk to Cassie.

"See — that wasn't all that bad, was it?" I proudly said to Trevor.

A tinge of anger surfaced as Trevor surprisingly looks me square in the eyes, with his lip quivering and said, "Don't ever do that again." He quickly exited the church doors and vanished like he always did.

I wasn't expecting that. I thought I was helping him out. What's his deal? Strange kid..

CHAPTER

24

The frigid hands of winter were starting to loosen their grip. Another month had passed, and the warmth of spring was starting to creep in. We were now in the last quarter of the school year — and what a sophomore year it had been!

I was at home, surfing my social media sites and enjoying the spring break. What a relief — no school for a week! As I roamed through cyberspace, rumors of Jazzy were starting to surface. Many were claiming that she was pregnant. I was getting messages from Eugene and Gary, my old cafeteria buddies. They were mocking me with comments like, "I guess you weren't man enough, like Triston." I wondered why I even hung out with those guys, those wanna-be's. I thought that they were jealous that I was with Jazzy and that they had no one. Even though I wanted to respond to their remarks. I didn't waste time replying to their negative comments.

Could Jazzy really be pregnant? Triston vehemently denied any claim that he'd gotten her pregnant, but there had been no rebuttal from Jazzy herself. She was silent, disconnected, and offline. She hadn't been active on any of her sites for weeks, removing herself from any social interaction.

A few weeks ago was when I started noticing her wearing over-sized clothes. Maybe I was naïve, but I figured that she was just dressing warm because of the weather — or maybe I was refusing to face the truth. I hoped the first was true and not the second.

A few weeks ago was when Jazzy's and Triston's relationship had taken a sudden turn. I used to hate my walks by her fourth-period class, because I knew that I would be seeing the two of them all cozied up. Lately I hadn't seen them together as often as before. I didn't know what had happened between them, but something had. To be honest, I can't say that I was particularly sad about the situation. I was trying not to focus on her anymore. I had been spending more time on personal video projects.

In my video-editing class, the students had been giving me high praise for my documentary of the riot. I had been selected as one of the finalists who would reveal their film at the end of the school year, in our auditorium. However, for some odd reason, my film had to be cleared by Principal Strudel before it could be shown. Mr. Spring did warn me that, before anyone could see my work, I had to prove that the footage of the shooter was authentic and not a recreation. He said that Principal Strudel had insisted upon this. I found it a little odd that our Principal was so involved in this process and that he seemed to be taking a particular interest in my project.

To me, it was obvious that my recordings were not doctored or recreated in any way — my video was what happened. But Mr. Spring said that, because no other cameras had captured the shooting event, I needed to have my recordings tested for authenticity. That didn't make any sense to me — something definitely was suspicious here. Hopefully, when we would meet with Carl later in the day, he could tell me who this guy was, and I'd have some proof of my work.

About two weeks before, I'd gotten an urgent call from Carl about who our mystery man was. Carl didn't want to talk about it over the phone or leave a trail of messages out in cyberspace. This was something that he wanted to tell me in person. However, I hadn't been able to get to his place, but Philip and I were supposed to be meeting with him today.

* * * * *

"Hello, boys," the slurred voice said.

"Good evening, Mr. Green. Is Carl here?" Philip asked.

"Carl — you got company," Mr. Green yelled to Carl after taking another gulp from the beer in his hand. "Come on in, fellas," he continued, with his breath reeking of alcohol.

As Philip and I entered into the apartment, Carl yelled to us from his bedroom. Following the trail of his voice, we entered his computer-controlled room. Carl's fingers were rapidly typing away, with his eyes glued to the screen, not even acknowledging our presence.

"Guys, take a seat. I want you to see this," Carl said, continuing to type away. Carl lifted his finger and tapped on the "enter" button. On his monitor, a picture of a man, probably in his late-twenties, came up.

"Borian Funar?" Philip said. That was the name under the guy who was on the screen.

"Who is he?" I asked.

"Fellas — this is our killer." Carl smiled with a sense of pride about his achievement in identifying this guy.

"How can you be sure?" Philip asked.

"I have run several test subjects with software of pictures of people that I know and covered their faces, revealing only their eyes. Every time, my software identified each person. So, I know that it works. After taking the frames that you gave me and scanning the perpetrator's eyes, from the database, this is the photo that came up every time — Borian Funar."

"Who is this guy, and why did he want the doctor dead?" I curiously asked.

"Ah — I wondered that, too. I did some digging on Mr. Borian and discovered that he is from Romania. His records show that he is a highly intelligent man. Graduated college with honors at the age of twelve. He has an IQ of 130, which only about two percent of the population has," Carl said.

"But still why would he kill someone?" I repeated.

"Where can we find him?" Philip said, sternly.

"Ah — I wondered that, too. This is the strangest thing about all of this. When searching for data on Borian, I couldn't find anything on him from the last seven years. No credit card transactions, pictures, or camera footage — "

"That is, until now," Philip cut in.

"It's like he disappeared without a trace. There is no evidence that he is even still alive," I added.

"And, according to his public record, he isn't alive," Carl said, soberly.

"What?" Philip questioned.

"Even though there is no proof of a body being found, records indicate that he was legally declared dead at sea. This guy was part of the Romanian military and supposedly died at sea," said Carl.

"Well, according to your detection software, he is alive and well," Philip said.

"But why would someone who is highly intelligent, lives in Romania, and is part of the military fake his death? And why show up seven years later to kill an abortion doctor? It just doesn't make sense," I stated.

"Maybe this is all part of a bigger plan," Philip chimed in.

"Maybe," Carl replied.

* * * * *

It was Wednesday, two days into spring break and two days after discovering who Dr. Macbeth's killer was. I was still trying to process the news about this guy, Borian Funar. It just didn't add up. A dead highly intelligent Romanian military officer resurrects himself seven years later to kill an abortion clinic doctor, among hundreds of people. What were we missing here?

Well, that wasn't the only strange thing that had been happening. Strange abilities are still manifesting themselves with the seven of us in the group. Now that we all had this week off, we decided to try to figure out what God was trying to do with us. Stephen finally set up a meeting with our Pastors, Pastor Bruce and Pastor Joel. We were scheduled to meet with them after Bible class that night.

Since the day that we were in Tameka's house and the Holy Spirit fell on all of us, all of our lives had changed. When that fire rested on my tongue, it was like I was being filled with something. I was speaking in a different language, and now I had a boldness about my faith like I'd never had before. Not only that, but, recently, I'd been given this ability to know things about someone or something. Like when I touched Trevor, I saw him in his room crying over his step-dad abusing his mother. God was showing me things, but I was still not sure what to do with this information.

All of us were starting to experience these supernatural occurrences. Carl seemed to occasionally have the ability to speak in different languages and to understand what others were saying when they were speaking another language.

Tameka shared her story about how God had used her to pray for the healing of her cousin, who couldn't walk after an accident. God healed him, and he was able to walk after her prayer.

Rachel, of course, had been prophesying to students at school, motivating them to change from their sinful ways and turn to Christ. "Psychic Rachel" was the name the kids were calling her.

My brother seemed to just know that God was going to do something before it even happened. Like the incident at church with the lady being framed for stealing the store's merchandise. Philip knew that God wanted to promote that lady and clear her name. Not only was Philip exercising a high level of faith, but another ability was starting to show.

The previous Saturday, L3C had held its annual "Let's Reach Our Community" event. However, the weather reports were not looking good. Severe thunderstorms were predicted to move in during the afternoon. Pastor Bruce was the lead pastor of this event and was left with the difficult decision whether to postpone the event or continue.

"Let's Reach Our Community" was a time when our church and surrounding churches in Grand Lake would gather outside together and go two by two to every home in the neighborhood, asking residents if they needed any assistance or prayers for anything. We would also pass out food baskets for the poorer neighborhoods and invite all the neighbors out to the big tent meeting that was set up outside.

There were free hot dogs, hamburgers, cotton candy, and nachos, with a variety of beverages. Some of the activities included basketball, large inflatables, dunk tanks, and many carnival-style games.

I looked forward to this time of year, but it was in question this year due to the approaching storms.

Pastor Bruce made the decision to continue with the meeting until the storm came. Little did he know that it was God who wanted this meeting to happen. Philip and I arrived at the site a little early to help set up the stage equipment.

Listening to the cautionary statements from the weather reporters and not wanting to put the saints in danger, Pastor Bruce was beginning to feel somewhat apprehensive about his choice. So, before we began our event, he grabbed the microphone and spoke to the workers.

"Before we begin our mission today, I feel led to really pray for the outcome of this day." The pastor paused, thinking to himself. Then he said, "Philip...Philip Mann, would you do me the honor of opening us up in prayer?"

Philip, shocked by the pastor's request, pointed to himself as if to say, "Who — me?"

"Yes, you, Philip. I sense you are a man of faith. Come to the stage, son."

Philip tentatively walked onto the stage and nervously clutched the microphone. While he was on stage, sprinkles of water were starting to come down. It seemed like the storm was coming in earlier than forecast. Sporadic raindrops were starting to fall; church members were beginning to search for their umbrellas and some for shelter.

Philip began his prayer. "God of heaven and Earth, we know that there is nothing too difficult for you. All of the universe is in your hands, and you command it to do what you will. I come before you, Holy Father, requesting that you would hold back the sky here over Grand Lake until we are finished doing your work in this community. May you be glorified and may people come to know you this day. Thank you, Lord, for hearing my prayer. In your son Jesus's name I pray. Amen."

Once Philip completed his prayer, the light rain had ceased, but people were still concerned about the second wave of thunderstorms that were supposed to come that afternoon. Pastor Bruce spoke to everyone.

"Saints, it seems we have avoided the early rain so far. I will let you know what we'll do if the storms come this afternoon."

Philip smiled, looked the pastor right in the eyes, and said, "It will not rain in Grand Lake until we are done doing God's work." The pastor was somewhat taken off guard by Philip's bold statement, but he also remembered the incident in church when Philip said that the lady would get her job back — and she did. He knew that God was speaking through Philip. So the meeting went on as planned.

All of the gang showed up to participate in the event. As people were trickling into the tent meeting, we could see the threatening clouds of the second wave of storms approaching. While the coordinators were organizing groups to canvas the neighborhoods, there was an abrupt shift in the weather.

Temperatures dropped ten degrees suddenly, as the grim clouds began to hover over us. Howling winds begin to sound as the gleaming sun was swallowed by the dreary clouds. Everyone was expecting a downpour of rain at any moment, but it never came. I pulled out my phone to check the weather report and was stunned by what I saw. The local weatherman was showing a map of the rain moving through the metro. Every city was being affected by the rains, and there were flash-flood warning alerts scrolling for every town but Grand Lake.

On the weather map, it showed colors of rain occupying the metro, but there wasn't any precipitation across the borders of Grand Lake. Church members who lived in Lee's Summit and Kansas City arrived at the meeting in amazement. While they were driving, a downpour of rain had come into their cities, making visibility very difficult. But once they crossed the city limits and entered into Grand Lake, the grounds were dry as the desert sand, with no water in sight.

That day an influx of people came into Grand Lake to avoid the rains. Many heard the news that the City of Grand Lake was not being affected by the thunderstorm. Large crowds gathered at the tent meeting, and many heard the gospel and gave their lives to Christ that day. As soon as the last prayer had been prayed, the seal on the heavens was removed, and the rains flooded the Grand Lake area, causing everyone to scatter. How did Philip know that his prayer would be answered? We were all surprised by the outcome of the day — but not Philip. He had a certainty that God was going to perform a miracle.

Out of the group, five of us had experienced these great supernatural occurrences, but Stephen and Hannah hadn't spoken of any such experiences — at least, not yet. However, Stephen and Hannah seemed eager to tell their story of what God was doing with them. Hopefully, the pastors could give us some insight as to what God was doing with us.

CHAPTER

25

Youth service had just ended. We were all hanging around the foyer of the church, just waiting on Pastor Bruce to finish mingling with the saints so that we could begin our meeting. The husky, red-mohawked youth pastor, Pastor Joel, also stood with us waiting on the pastor.

A jolly Pastor Bruce finally came out of the doors to the sanctuary.

"Good evening, everyone. Stephen — Hannah — Rachel — John — Philip — Carl — and Tameka, follow me. Let's go to my office. Stephen has told me that he wanted to meet with me about some strange occurrences."

We all looked at each other and chuckled. Carl said what we all were thinking.

"You have no idea, pastor."

"Oh, is that right? Well, I am excited to hear about what's going on," he said.

As we entered into his office, I noticed all the scriptures posted on his wall. Even though I had gone to this church several years, this was the first time that I had been in the pastor's office. He had photos of his twin girls lined up all around the top of his shelves and a huge wedding picture of a young-looking Pastor Bruce smiling as he dipped his wife, first lady Kimberly Marino. Looking at that picture, I could tell that the stress of leading a church had aged him, even though he was still considered young — in his forties. His hair was salt-and-peppered, with gray stubs surfacing from his unshaven face. In his picture, his hair was jet black, with a slender face.

Pastor Joel brought in some additional chairs to accommodate seating for all of us. When we were all seated, Pastor Bruce's jolliness switched to a concerned look, eager to hear our problems.

"Alright, kids. What seems to be troubling you?" Looking around, Stephen spoke up. "Well, Pastor Joel, a few months ago, you remember when you were calling the youth to repentance and to be sold out for Christ?"

"Yes, I recall," Pastor Joel said.

"Well, that convicted all of us here, causing us to go on this journey to find out what this Christian walk was all about. Many of us youth decided to consecrate ourselves, fasting and praying for ten days to hear from God. Our scripture was Jeremiah 29:13: '**You will seek me and find me when you seek me with all your heart.**'"

Pastor Joel interjected, "I have noticed a change with you guys — a fire — God's presence."

"Our group started strong, twenty-five deep, but over the days of fasting, it eventually dwindled down to this group now, the seven of us," Philip said.

"Yes, we had been meeting online for ten days," Rachel added.

Stephen continued, "Pastor, the last meeting that we had at Tameka's house, that's when things got — ."

"Scary," soft-spoken Hannah interrupted.

"Supernatural," Tameka added.

"Just plain weird," Carl said.

"So tell me what happened at your house, Tameka," Pastor Bruce

252

inquired.

"I think I speak for all of us when I say that, that day, we were all feeling a little discouraged — I know I was. So many of our friends thought that fasting was crazy and unnecessary. That night, we were pouring out our souls to God, pleading that he would manifest himself to us and — boy, did he ever! While we were all crying out to God, a rushing wind blew the windows wide open in the room. I thought that a tornado was coming. Then we saw fire forming and separating, coming toward us. The fear I'd had suddenly turned to peace. The fire rested on all of us, causing us to speak in different languages. I guess we were so loud that my neighbors came to my house to see what was going on. Many of them said they'd heard us speaking in languages that they knew. Even my mom said she heard one of us speaking in her native language, French."

"Wow!" Pastor Bruce exclaimed and then continued, "Your story sounds like a modern-day Acts 2, when the saints were in the upper room praying to God, and the Holy Spirit came and filled each one of them, causing them to speak in different languages."

I spoke up: "Pastor, that day was just the beginning. The following months after our upper-room experience, we all started to encounter some supernatural abilities. It's weird. Sometimes God shows me things about people — things that only they would know."

"Well, I can't explain it, but sometimes I just know that God wants to perform a miracle, and I have faith that things are going to happen. I just know," Philip said.

"Yes, I remember your prayer at the community outreach event. I am still amazed at the miracle that happened that day. What about the rest of you?" Pastor Bruce asked.

Carl added, "Sometimes I can speak in different languages and understand them, too."

"It is hard to explain what God is doing with me, but, sometimes,

I can see glimpses of a person's future and I have a compassion to speak life to them — to encourage them, build them up." Rachel proclaimed.

Tameka jumped in. "I just know that I felt the need to pray for healing for my cousin, and I knew that, what I prayed for, God would answer. The doctor said that he would probably never walk again, but, that day, he walked out of the hospital."

Finally Hannah spoke. "To be honest, Stephen and I didn't experience these phenomena until last week," she said. None of us had heard Hannah's or Stephen's experiences yet. This was Hannah's account.

Last week, Hannah had been preparing for her Philosophy 101 class. In this class, she had an arrogant, egotistical skeptic as a professor, Professor William Albright III. Even though Hannah didn't particularly like this class, she looked forward to going only because Stephen was there.

On that particular day, she arrived early to school and decided to get a bite to eat. She grabbed some bagels and a carton of milk and sat in the school's cafeteria with her Bible open on her tablet. While Hannah was seated, reading her Bible and eating her bagel alone, a tall, handsome -looking guy named Carlos Jones approached her. Now, she was used to boys trying to talk to her and would normally avoid conversation with them, but Carlos seemed like a nice guy.

"Hello," the tall, attractive boy said.

"Hi," Hannah hesitantly replied, still looking at her tablet.

"Do you mind if I sit here?"

Hannah didn't respond, so he took the liberty and sat down across from her.

"My name is Carlos. I usually don't approach people like this, but I saw you reading your Bible. Are you a believer?"

This got Hannah's attention. Barely raising her head, she responded "Yes...yes, I am."

"It's good to finally find another believer on campus. I just moved here from Michigan and was looking for a good church to visit. Do you know of any?"

Hannah finally stopped reading to look up at the attractive guy. "Life Changers Community Church is a good church," she proudly said.

"Is that your church home?"

Looking away, trying not to look into his apple-green eyes, she replied, "Yes."

"I know it's bold of me, but is it okay if I get your number? You know — to call you for directions to your church or to talk about anything else, if you'd like. Like I said, I am new around here. I'm just looking for someone to talk to who shares the same beliefs as me," he said as he smiled at her. Hannah normally wouldn't give her number out to guys she'd just met, but Carlos had her contemplating whether to or not.

Seeing that she was hesitant, Carlos spoke again. "I'm sorry — I don't think you told me what your name was."

"My name is Hannah," she replied.

"Hannah, mother of Samuel, meaning 'favor' or 'grace,' huh?"

Hannah was impressed by his knowledge.

"Yes, that's right," she said.

Carlos extended his hand to shake hers. "Nice to meet you, favored one."

When she reached out and touch his hand, Carlos' once-attractive looking face suddenly transformed. His face was contorting and twisting, looking disfigured. There was an evil aura around him. The touch of his hand sent shivers down her spine, and then she heard a voice — a knowing from within — saying, "He's a fake. He only wants to sleep with you."

Terrified by the sight of Carlos face, she dropped her milk, grabbed her Bible, and rushed out of the cafeteria, thinking to herself, "What was *that*?" After running outside, panting heavily and befuddled by what she saw, Hannah took a moment and calmed herself down. She decided it was best to head to her class, get there a little early, and wait.

This was the story that Hannah told the group as we sat in the pastor's office. After Hannah spoke, Stephen also began to tell his story.

"That same day, something strange also happened to me. Hannah and I attend the same class, Philosophy 101, with Professor Albright." Stephen said. This was Stephen's account.

CHAPTER

26

Professor Albright trotted over to the door to close it so that class could begin.

"Good morning, class. Hope you had a good weekend and are ready to put your thinking caps on. We are going to have some fun today. I would like to continue with our discussion about faith and philosophy."

Professor Albright, with his arms folded and head down, began pacing across the room like he was in deep thought. He lifted his head, showing a wry smile, and then began his lecture.

"Faith — oh, the concept of faith! And when I say 'faith,' I am talking about religious beliefs. Faith, religion, God — all are man-made ideologies. Yes, I said God is someone that was created to help men cope with reality. This notion of God is something that people want to worship but can't seem to agree on who is being worshipped.

Whose faith is right, anyway? Christians? Muslims? Hindus? Buddhists? Some other faith? We have been indoctrinated with a set of beliefs given to us by our upbringing. Today, my goal is to free you from this brainwashing called 'religion' or 'faith.'"

While the professor was talking, Hannah and Stephen looked at each other, thinking the same thought: *Why did I take this class?*

Hannah began to see a dark image around the professor and felt an evil presence seeping from him. She could detect pride and hatred in the professor's demeanor.

As she was studying his countenance, the professor suddenly turned and looked directly at her.

"You, young lady," the professor said.

Surprised by his abruptness, she replied, "Yes."

"If you don't mind, I have a few questions for you." He was looking at the cross that was dangling from her necklace.

"Are you a Christian?"

"Yes, sir. I am."

"As I thought. I bet you grew up in a Christian home."

"Yes. My parents are missionaries."

"If you don't mind me asking, were you born here?"

"No. From what I'm told I was born in China, somewhere in the Jiangsu Province. My mother abandoned me, placing me in an orphanage, and that's where I was adopted. Now I live here."

"Interesting. So you could've very well grown up in a home in China and believed in Buddhism."

"I suppose so, but — "

Professor Albright cut her off.

"You just helped me prove my point. Because of your parents, you believe in Christianity. If your upbringing had been different, you would have been believing in Buddhism. Your upbringing determined your religious path," he said.

"Well, my upbringing may have started me on this path, but there still came a point in my life where I had to believe in Christ for myself. I believe that Jesus is Lord not because my parents are making me be — "

"Young lady, please don't try to preach to me," the professor said, cutting her off again.

Hearing the name of Jesus made him cringe. Trying to control his annoyance, tapping his fingers together, he responded.

"Okay, let's see if your faith can answer my questions. Hypothetically speaking, let's say there is a God. Is your God loving and good?"

"Yes, sir."

"Okay, then why does your loving, good God allow so much evil, pain, and suffering to exist in this world? Is it because maybe he is loving and good but not powerful enough to prevent evil acts from happening. Is that it?"

"No. My God is an almighty God?"

"Then why would a loving, good, and all-powerful God not stop evil acts, when he has the power to do so. Is it possible that he is not aware that evil acts are happening? Is that it?"

"No. My God knows everything"

"So a God who supposedly loves children, sees and knows that a little girl is about to be raped and murdered — and you said he has the power to stop it from happening — but he chooses not to do anything. Why? Would an omni-benevolent, omnipotent, omniscient God allow this? If God does exist, he must be either impotent, ignorant, or just wicked. Explain this to me!?"

The professor spoke with fervent disgust toward God, waving his fist to the heavens as he spoke. Hannah knew now that he was speaking from a personal hurt that he had experienced. Even though she knew that God was a just God, she couldn't think of an adequate answer to give the professor. She was feeling defeated and intimated by the barrage of questions. The professor gave his crooked smile and said,

"Just as I thought. No answer from the Christian."

Meanwhile, as Stephen was listening to the professor's accusations, a righteous anger was brewing in his spirit. He could not contain himself anymore, raising his hand and speaking at the same time, he said,

"Mr. Albright, may I answer your questions and ask you some of my own, sir?"

"Ah, you want to come to the defense of your fellow believer, huh? Alright. This should be interesting," the professor chuckled.

"I am assuming that you are an atheist," Stephen said.

"Your assumption is correct," the professor replied.

"Sir, do you believe in evil?"

"Yes, I believe in wrong. By the way, I know where you're going with this. Why do Christians think that we atheists need God to have a moral code and live civilly with others? I have my own set of moral laws I live by."

"Well, your moral law may require you to live civilly with others, but what about the one whose moral law doesn't. Who is to say who is right and who is wrong? How can we know what is wrong unless we see what is right? How can you know what is evil unless you see what is good? If there was no common moral law, then the words 'evil' and 'good,' 'right' and 'wrong' would mean nothing. Everyone would do as they please, with no justification of consequences.

"In other words, if there is wrong, as you say, then there has to be a law saying what is wrong or right. And if there is a law, then there has to be a lawgiver. 'Who is the lawgiver?' is the question — you or someone greater?"

The class was amazed at Stephen's wisdom and how he was challenging the professor. Hannah was beaming with joy as she watched Stephen articulate his answers.

"OK. You still have not answered my original question, son. Why does an omni-benevolent, omnipotent, omniscient God allow evil to happen?"

"The problem of evil. This is how I understand it: I will try to break it down in two parts. Part One: God is love, as you say, but we fail to realize he is also holy. We like to ask the questions about how can a loving God allow this or that to happen, but we don't ask the questions about how a holy God can continue to allow us to keep living when we have offended him.

"We breathe his air every day and enjoy his sunlight and gentle breezes. Do we say thanks? Only a few do. We don't like to hear this, but God can do as he pleases with us, but thank God, because his character is patient with man, in providing us a chance to come back to him.

"Part Two: Mankind was created by love, for love, to love. God is all knowing, as you say. He knew that, in order for man to truly love him back, he had to give him a free will. Love wouldn't be love if God *made* people love him. Love had to be voluntary. But, by doing this — giving man a free will to choose God or evil — God risks men choosing evil.

"And He knew that we would, but it had to be this way in order to receive love. As a result, men chose not to love God and put their wills above His will, which produced sin and separation from him.

"God is all powerful, as you say. Because of his love for us, God provided a way to appease his holiness. His Son, Jesus, came to Earth to reconcile us back to God the Father by paying our penalty of sin on the cro — "

The professor stopped Stephen before he could finish the word.

"Alright — this is not a church pulpit. Answer the question: Are you saying that, because of man's disobedience to this God, evil exists in this world? Well, this is where your logic is flawed.

"Even though you may answer the question of moral evil, what about natural evils — natural disasters that happen every year and claim so many lives. Why does he allow that? This is not a result of a sinner's actions," the professor said, tapping his fingers together.

"Sir, I am not going to pretend like I know everything, because I don't, sir. What I know is that, as a result of Adam and Eve's sin, we live in a broken, fallen world, where everything is affected, including nature.

"Just like darkness comes into the world when the earth rotates away from the sun, so evil comes when we turn away from God. Why kids starve, why people are born with deformities and disabilities — I don't have a full answer, but I believe that God is still just."

"There we go again — belief, faith — coping mechanisms to help ease man's conscience," the professor stated.

Stephen answered, "Professor, you assume that the human mind is governed only by reason — what we can make sense of. But faith is also a big part of everyone's life, including yours."

"Oh, how is that?"

"This morning, when you came to work you had faith that you would make it to this school safely. If you didn't have that faith, you would've stayed home. Even though people die every day from car accidents, you believed you would make it here with no problems, not thinking twice about possible dangers. Your thoughts were only on the lesson you had prepared for class today.

"You had faith that your chair would support you when you sat down — even though it could only be one loose screw away from collapsing."

At that moment, when Stephen made his comment, the leg of the professor's chair gave way, causing it to collapse to the floor.

Sounds of astonishment rang through the classroom. The professor, looking over at his chair, was also shocked but tried not to show it.

What were the odds of that happening at that precise time? Stephen continued with his speech as though nothing had happened.

"Everyone is given a measure of faith — some greater than others. It's not a matter of *if* you have faith but rather *what* your faith is *in*. Professor, it doesn't matter how much evidence I present to support my worldview. If you are determined not to believe that there is a God, you will not be convinced. It is only when you are open to finding out the truth that you will discover and find that the evidence leads you to Christ."

The end of class was nearing as the professor looked at his watch.

"This has been a very interesting discussion today, to say the least, class, but our time has ended. I need for everyone to complete their chapter reading on philosophy of religion. We will complete this topic next session."

As the students were leaving, many passed Stephen giving him a thumbs-up or a head nod gesturing their approval on his stance. There were a few haughty students who sneered at him as they passed. Stephen turned and was about to talk to Hannah, but, before he could speak, Professor Albright interrupted them.

"Young man," looking at his attendance form, searching for Stephen's name.

"Is it Stephen Ortega?" he said.

"Yes, sir."

"Mr. Ortega, I'll admit you brought out some interesting points, but let's get one thing clear, I am the teacher in this classroom. There is nothing that you have said that I haven't heard before."

"I meant no disrespect, sir. Just trying to defend my faith," Stephen replied.

"Well I have a proposal for you. Every year, our school host a series of debates on differing worldviews. You seem to have some knowledge about your religion. How would you like to be a part of a panel defending your Christian beliefs?"

"Well, I need to pray about it first."

"Pray? The professor said as he tried to suppress his laughter. "Of course, you do. Okay — you do that. I need to know by next week."

Stephen told this story to all of us as we sat amazed at him challenging a professor.

"Really, I didn't know what to say to the professor, but, when I started to speak, it was like words and scripture were coming to my mind. I just knew how to apply all of this information and put it into an articulate answer. It was amazing."

"Yes, it was. He made me proud to be a Christian," Hannah said, smiling at Stephen. Stephen was trying not to blush, but he wasn't doing a good job at it. His cheeks were rosy red.

Pastor sat there quietly with an intense look on his face trying to process what he just heard, all of our accounts of supernatural occurrences. Then suddenly like a light just went off in his head. He said "I Corinthians 12:7-11. Yes, that's it," he said with excitement like he just discovered the cure for cancer. "That's it!" he repeated again.

Pastor Bruce straightened up in his chair, rapidly thumbing through his Bible to find that scripture. He read, **"7. A spiritual gift is given to each of us so we can help each other. 8. To one person the Spirit gives the ability to give wise advice; to another the same Spirit gives a message of special knowledge. 9. The same Spirit gives great faith to another, and to someone else the one Spirit gives the gift of healing. 10. He gives one person the power to perform miracles, and another the ability to prophesy. He gives someone else the ability to discern whether a message is from the Spirit of God or from another spirit. Still another person is given the ability to speak in unknown languages, while another is given the ability to interpret what is being said. 11. It is the one and only Spirit who distributes all these gifts. He alone decides which gift each person should have."**

Pastor Bruce leaned back in his plush chair, smiling. "Yes that's it. I have been praying to God that he would manifest himself in this church. God is starting to answer my prayers." He sat back up again and began to speak to each of us.

"Stephen, I believe the Holy Spirit has given you the message of wisdom. John, it sounds like he has given you the message of knowledge. Tameka, you have been blessed with the gift of healing."

Pastor Bruce turned, looked at Hannah, and said, "Be strong. You have been given the gift of discernment. Rachel, the Holy Spirit is working with you in the gift of prophecy." Then the pastor smiled and said, "Carl and Philip, it sounds like God has given each of you two of these gifts. Philip, you have the gift of faith and miracles, and, Carl, you have the gift of speaking in different languages and interpreting them also."

"So what does this mean? Why has God given us these abilities?" Stephen asked.

"Well that's something that you all will have to ask him about. The Holy Spirit is the one who has chosen to give each one of you these specific gifts. I believe that Jesus' return is now nearer than ever and that God is about to move in supernatural ways, one last call to his saints. A great awakening is about to occur. You guys are a part of this plan. Seek him, and he will guide you."

CHAPTER

27

We were nearing the end of the school year. For almost the entire school, year Pete had been in a coma. The week before, there was some sign of hope: He actually moved his hand once. I knew he was in there somewhere, just waiting to surface. All I could do was keep praying.

There were only two more months left in this crazy school year. Prom night was approaching soon, and all kinds of creative proposals were being made. One senior took his girlfriend to Clear View Lake, and they went coasting on the water, in his boat at night. He had hundreds of candles floating in the water with the candles forming words that said, "Will you go to the prom with me?" Of course, she accepted. I don't think many people could've topped that one.

Thank God I was not old enough to go to the prom this year — too much pressure. Not to mention I would have had to find someone to go with. However, Philip was of age, and I knew the person he wanted to invite to our prom was Tameka, but I didn't think that he had the courage to ask her. She was still in denial about how much she really liked him, referring to them as only "friends." I could tell that Philip got annoyed at the fact that she always said that he was like a brother to her, but Philip was afraid to make his feelings known to her.

Another person in our school who was afraid to make his feelings known was Trevor. He was still leaving notes on Rachel's locker, but he was still too afraid to even say "Hi" to her when she walked by. Finally, I confronted Trevor again about his stalkish obsession with Rachel.

"Hey, man. You'll never know until you try," I said to him. He was unaware that I was standing right behind him.

"Huh?" he said, startled by my abrupt appearance.

"Look, man. Prom is coming up, and she hasn't been asked out by anybody. It's your senior year. Don't regret not asking," I said to him, getting his attention.

"I don't know," he said softly.

"Don't wait too long," I said as I walked away.

* * * * *

The winner of the film project in Mr. Spring's class still had not been announced. Even though I seemed to be the favorite, the process was taking a lot longer than normal. While I was in my video-editing class, Mr. Spring got a call and instructed me to go the Principal's office. *What did I do?* I thought. Taking the long walk to his office, I tried to think of what I possibly could have done this time. Maybe he was accusing me of saying, "God bless you," to someone again.

I couldn't come up with any reason for this visit. I just know that the last time I'd been in his sterile office, it wasn't a pleasant experience.

I sat in his office, looking at his academic achievements, awaiting my fate. Finally Principal Strudel strolled into the office with his cat Matty, the mean one. Not far behind him, Mr. Boots also entered the room with Rocco, the other cat, and closed the door shut. I must admit a little fear rose in me, as the nature of this meeting seemed odd.

"Well, Mr. Mann. I must say, I have seen your work on your film. What is it called again?"

"The Zealot Movement: Whose movement Is It?" I answered.

"Interesting title. You make a compelling argument, trying to defend your Christian brothers, even though your views are distorted. Nonetheless, I brought you into this office to personally let you know that I can't show your film to the school, for numerous reasons."

"What — why!?" I exclaimed.

"The primary reason I chose not to show your film is because it is fraudulent. Do you really want us to believe that someone framed this Pastor Henry fellow? Do you?"

"A mystery man?" Mr. Boots, who rarely speaks, chuckled at the thought.

"Your film's authenticity is in question here," Principal Strudel stonily stated.

"What's on the film is what happened. I didn't change or add anything," I pled with them.

"Then why are you the only one who captured this so-called 'mystery man'? There were several news stations in attendance, and no one recorded this but you?" he said with a smirk. "Your footage makes for a dramatic documentary, but I am afraid that it is fiction."

Frustration rose in me as I tried to plead my case to deaf ears.

"What would you say if I could tell you who this killer is?" I said.

"I know who this killer is. His name is Pastor Henry Joseph," Principal Strudel said, rudely.

"Nope. I know the real killer's name," I retorted.

My statement seemed to unnerve the Principal a little. I could swear that I saw beads of sweat starting to form.

"You're bluffing," Mr. Boots spoke up. He steadied the wobbly Principal.

Then I heard Mr. Boots speak to Principal Strudel in a different language, trying to calm him. I don't know what they said, but it seemed to put Principal Strudel at ease. After the Principal composed himself, he looked at me and said:

"Have you taken this film to the authorities?"

"No. Not yet."

"Good. Then I advise you to destroy this slanderous film. It should not be shown at my school, and I advise you not to show this fictional film to anyone. Trying to put your spin on what actually happened…." He said, murmuring, as his voice trailed off.

Mr. Boots whispered something else to him in another language. This was the first time I heard them speak in another language.

"But, Bo Bo?" Principal Strudel said, in English.

They both turned to me, having forgotten that I was still in the room.

"That is all, John. You may leave," the Principal said, brushing me away like a piece of discarded trash.

"Bo Bo." That name again. Then a light switch clicked on, and the lid to my mind was uncapped. The memory of me hiding in the video -editing class came back to me — when the two of them had barged in. I remembered the words that they said.

"I know you can't talk about your work, honey, but what is going to be done about this? She is rising in the polls."

"All I can say is we also have ways of convincing the public who to vote for. Don't worry — the Senator will win."

The dots were starting to connect in my mind. *Could it be?*

* * * * *

It was Wednesday night, and Bible study was almost over. Pastor Joel had given an amazing word to the youth on activating our gifts. I was sure he'd been inspired to teach on this because of the recent revelations by our group. God had given each one of us gifts to help glorify him and help each other out in the church. Today, after church, the group planned on meeting at Stephen's house to further discuss our discovery of the gifts that the Holy Spirit had given us.

Once service had ended, I was out in the foyer, just waiting on Philip to finish talking to our parents. He was letting them know that we were going over to Stephen's for a little while. It was a school night, so we couldn't stay that long.

While I was waiting, the church was starting to empty out, and everyone in our group was already on their way over to Stephen's. I was stuck, still waiting on Philip. While I was standing in the vestibule, I felt a tap on my shoulder, and, then, I heard a familiar voice — a sweet voice that I hadn't heard in a while.

"Hey, Johnny."

I turned around slowly and saw an oversized-bellied Jazzy. There was no doubt that she was pregnant. Her once-radiant face looked worn out, with a puffy nose. Her eyes were blood red from crying. She looked vulnerable, and my heart broke for her.

"I bet you didn't expect to see me like this," she chuckled, nervously.

She was right about that. I hadn't seen her in at least a month, and my suspicions were finally confirmed — she was pregnant.

"Well, I have something for you," she said, timidly. "I thought it would be best if I wrote it down." She handed me an envelope, and I could see tears starting to form in her eyes. Suddenly, Jazzy lunged toward me and gave me a tight hug. I could feel her rapid heartbeat as her body convulsed from weeping on my shoulder.

Not knowing how to respond, I gently patted her back as the few church members who were left walked by. She whispered in my ear, "I'm going to miss you." Then she kissed me on the cheek and exited out the door. I sensed that the hug she gave was one that said, "I don't want to let you go, but I am going away for a while."

I stood in the middle of the vestibule, surveying her envelope, seeing that there was a letter inside. As I was about to open it, Philip came out the sanctuary doors.

"Ready to go?"

"Yeah. I guess so," I said, solemnly.

"Whoa! What's wrong with you, bro?"

"Jazzy."

"What — Jazzy was here?" Philip said, looking around.

"Yeah... she just left."

"I haven't seen her in a while. Why you lookin' so down?"

"She gave me this."

Philip looked at his watch and said, "We have to go. Dad is letting us stay for only a little while. Why don't you read that letter in the car?" he said as we hurried to the car.

We jumped in the Camaro and started our drive toward Stephen's place. Looking out into the dark sky, I pondered why Jazzy looked so sad and what she meant by, "I'm going to miss you." My attention went back to the white envelope.

"You going to stare at it all day or open it?" Philip said, snapping me out of my depressing thoughts.

I slowly and carefully opened the envelope. Like I suspected, it was a letter — a long letter — written in Jazzy's hand. I guessed that it must have been important enough that she didn't want to send it in an email or text but wanted to put her personal touch on it.

"What does it say?" Philip eagerly asked. I began to read.

Dear John,

My Johnny, the boy who made me feel welcome when I came to this town. You were always nice to me, and, over time, I have grown deeply in love with you. Our friendship meant the world to me. The times that we spent at the lake skipping rocks and talking about our school day are priceless. Looking at you scrunch your nose when you were lying or were nervous was so cute. Where did those days go? How did things change so much between us?

When we broke up, I was so hurt by what you did. Leaving me alone like that when I made myself so vulnerable to you. At first, I thought that I would pay you back by going out with Triston. I admit it felt good watching you be jealous of us, and I actually enjoyed the attention that I was getting from Triston.

After a while, though, I began to see who he really was. I knew that I didn't love him. I still loved you, but I felt bad for Triston, and he used that against me by tricking me to sleep with him. One time — that's all it took. Just one freakin' time! As you now know, I am pregnant. You were right, Triston is a jerk, and he is denying that this baby is his, but he is the only one I have ever been with.

As a result of my pregnancy, my mom and I have been arguing a lot. She looks at me like I'm a disappointment. Kids are posting all kinds of mean comments on my sites. Now is the time I need my mom, but she ignores me and seems to worship my stepdad. I miss being able to talk to you about things like this. I just want to let you know that I can't live here anymore. Can't live in a place where I am not wanted. My dad said that I can stay with him in Texas, and my mom didn't even put up a fight about it. Since we broke up, I have no reason to stay here anymore.

Remember that time when we were on the roof of my house? You said to me, "Wherever you go, even if it's to the moon, I'll find some way to get there." Well, John, I'm going to the moon. I am finally moving to Texas. Hopefully, one day, I will see you again.

Love always, Jazzy.

* * * * *

"Hey — what took you guys so long?" Tameka said to us as we entered Stephen's house.

"I had to let my parents know where we were going." Philip answered.

"Why the down face, John?" Hannah said, sensitively, seeing through my attempt to hide what I was feeling at the moment.

"Nothing. I just got some bad news. That's all." I said, nonchalantly, trying to downplay my true emotions.

"Anything you want to talk about?" she asked, gently.

"No — not really."

"Alright," Hannah said, seeing that I wasn't in the mood to discuss Jazzy.

Carl jumped in and changed the conversation. "So are any of you guys going to your school prom?" he said, bluntly. Looking at Rachel and

Philip, the only two in the group who might be going. Both were silent, and the glances between Tameka and Philip were awkward.

Hannah, who seemed unusually talkative today ask Rachel, "What about your secret admirer? Has he asked you out yet?" she asked, which caused her and Tameka to smile and Rachel to blush a bit.

"You have a secret admirer?" Stephen asked, clueless as to what had been going on. Everyone's attention was on Rachel.

"Well, I don't know what's going on. I have been getting a lot of love notes and flowers lately. This week, whoever has been writing theses note did something different. On Monday, I got a note that just said, 'Will you'?"

"'Will you'?" Carl said.

"Yes," Rachel continued. "Then, on Tuesday, I got a note that said, 'go to,' and, today, the note said, 'the prom.'"

"Hmm, it looks like someone is about to ask you to the prom," Tameka said, gleefully, giving a quick glance at Philip. But my brother failed to pick up on her hint.

"I don't know if I even want to go to the prom," Rachel said.

"Girl — why not?" Tameka inquired.

"When the time is right, I will meet who I'm supposed to be with. Right now there is no need to hurry love. I was reading that in the Song of Solomon."

"What chapter and verse is that?" Hannah curiously asked.

"Chapter two, verse seven tells us not to arouse or awaken love until it so desires," she explained.

"That doesn't mean you can't go to the prom," Tameka said.

"I know — but I just don't want to go just to go."

"Well, to me, it's a time to have fun. You can't get that experience back once you leave high school," Tameka said, like she knew what she was talking about. Obviously Rachel and Tameka had different views on the matter, and they had both brought up good points.

My talk with Trevor must have worked. It looked like Trevor was starting to make his move. However, after this conversation, I wasn't so sure that Rachel would accept his invitation.

While the girls were going on and on about all this prom and love stuff, we boys started our own conversation.

"Have you guys got any news on who the killer is?" Stephen said, diverting his attention to Philip, Carl, and me.

"Well, through my program, I discovered what the killer's name is, or was."

"'Was'?" Stephen said with an inquisitive look.

"Yeah. According to Carl's program, this killer — Borian Funar — is a dead Romanian military officer," Philip cut in.

"Hey — my program is accurate. This guy is still alive. He must have faked his death or something."

While my brother and Carl were arguing over the validity of the detection program, I spoke up.

"I think I know who the killer is," I said, softly, causing everyone in our group to stop talking and turn to me with a look of astonishment.

CHAPTER

28

"It happened just a couple of days ago — on Monday. While I was in my video-editing class, I got a call to come to the Principal's office. Principal Strudel called me to the class to discuss my film project about the riots that had taken place at the abortion clinic.

"Our school has a film competition, and the winner of that competition shows their film at the end of the year to the entire school. I was favored to win this, but, for some reason, Principal Strudel wanted to approve my film first, even though my teacher, Mr. Spring, had already approved it.

"While I was in his office, Mr. Boots was also there — him and their two cats. Principal Strudel told me that he couldn't show my film."

"Yeah — probably because it was defending Christians," Philip cut in.

"Well, I'm sure that's part of the reason, but what he told me was he couldn't show my film because he questioned its authenticity — the part where I show footage of the real killer — just because no other camera caught the killer in the act but me. He stated that I'd *created* this scene, even though I have no idea how I could even do that.

"So, now I'm disqualified from showing my film — a film that tells the truth about what really happened at the rally. I was furious, and when I told him that I knew who the killer was, Principal Strudel started to get oddly nervous. I swore I saw him begin to sweat. I touched something in him. *Then*, the Principal and Mr. Boots started to talk in another language."

"'Another language'?" Rachel questioned.

"Yeah. They were speaking to each other like I wasn't even in the room. But what got my attention is when Principal Strudel called Mr. Boots 'Bo Bo.' That's when my mind started to put the pieces together. Philip, do you remember when I told you about my encounter with those two in the video room when I was hiding from them?"

"Yeah, I remember."

"Well, when they were talking, Mr. Boots called Principal Strudel 'Richie.' 'Richie' is short for 'Richard,' and the Principal called Mr. Boots 'Bo Bo,' which, I believe, is short for 'Borian' — Borian Funar."

"That's kind of stretching it — don't you think?" Philip said.

"I wouldn't doubt that Mr. Boots is the one," Rachel jumped in. "There is always something eerie about that man around the school. I just know that he is the one with the bloody boots in our dream, John. Killing seems to come easy to him," she said, anxiously, looking at me.

"It would make sense," Tameka said. The girls were now engaged in our conversation.

"When I was hiding in that room, I remember Principal Strudel saying that he would take care of Mr. Donovan and Ms. Rand — and now both of them are no longer at our school. Mr. Boots told the Principal that he would take care of Senator Wright becoming President."

"So you are saying that he planned to frame Henry Joseph and the Christian community of being killers, of being... Zealots... who would kill for what they believe in?" Philip asked, incredulously.

"He knew that President Copperfield was a Christian, and, if he could get the public to turn on Christians, they would turn on her," Carl said, with his hands clasped together in a thinking position. I could see the wheels turning in his head.

"I don't know if he was working for the President, but this was a carefully planned event," I stated.

"All this may be true, but we still have no proof — nothing that we can give the police besides our theories," Stephen said, putting a damper on our excitement of discovering who the killer was.

"Stephen has a point. Even with your software, we can't prove this. Besides the picture that you have of Borian Funar looks nothing like Mr. Boots," Philip said, throwing more dirt on our fire.

They were making good points, but I just knew that Mr. Boots was the killer.

That's when Carl said, "Wait a minute! Remember that we are dealing with a highly intelligent man. He could have had facial reconstruction after faking his death. If he did, that would explain why none of the facial-recognition software even came close to putting his name on their list. But if my belief is true — that he didn't change his eyes — then all I need is a picture of this Mr. Boots. Then we can compare eye scans of Borian and Mr. Boots to see if they match. Does anyone have a photo?"

"Our yearbook!" Rachel exclaimed. "Maybe he's in one of our pictures."

"This year's yearbook hasn't been released yet," Philip said.

"What about last year's?" I suggested.

Rachel pulled up last year's yearbook online and scrolled through multiple pages before landing on a picture of Mr. Boots' eyes peeking out from behind a door.

"There he is," Rachel said, excitedly.

"Here's another one," Philip said.

Carl copied both pictures and dragged them to his tablet. Typing feverishly, he opened his program and placed the picture of the young Borian, the picture of the killer in my footage, and the two pictures that Rachel and Philip had found all next to each other.

"Ah, ha! You see — if I can just match the points on the iris with the pupil and the corneal limbus and then look for similar blemishes on the sclera. Then, if I can measure the distance between the eyelids and the spatial distance between the two eye sockets, I think I can narrow this down," Carl excitedly rambled off.

"English, please," Stephen said.

"Yeah — we don't speak geek," Tameka said.

"We haven't been given the gift to interpret geek," Philips added as he and Tameka laughed at their jokes.

"Ha, ha!" Carl replied, sarcastically. He lifted his finger for one final stroke. Hitting the "enter" key, he said, "According to my data, it shows that Mr. Boots has a ninety-eight percent chance of being our guy. All eye photos matched each other. The two you gave me and the one on the footage is a one hundred percent match. There is a blemish or a scar that is on the sclera of his eye that showed on those pictures. This is our guy."

"What's the 'sclera'?" I had to ask.

"It's the white part of your eye," Stephen answered for Carl. Then he continued, "We have to bring this information to the police, and John, you have to upload your film online. He may prevent you from showing it in school, but he can't stop you from showing the truth to the world."

* * * * *

280

It was early Friday morning, and we were on our way to another dreadful day at school. Since our discovery at Stephen's house, Philip, Rachel, and I had been fearing for our lives, with Mr. Boots still at the school. The day before, we'd told my parents about my footage of Mr. Boots — or I should say, "Borian Funar" — murdering the doctor.

Of course, my dad reprimanded us for not taking this to the authorities earlier. We did, however, take all of our information that we'd gathered that day about the murder and reported it to the police. The police didn't seem to take us seriously but did say that they would look into it.

I also took Stephen's advice and uploaded my *Zealot* film to all my social accounts. If I couldn't show my film to the school, I would show it to the world. Everyone needed to know what had really taken place at the abortion-clinic protest. I checked my video to see if anyone had seen it so far. Surprisingly, my film had gone viral! More than one million views already and steadily climbing!

This was good, but it was also scary: What if the Principal and Mr. Boots see this and then retaliate against us? Knowing that I am dealing with a killer in my school frightened me.

On our way to school, the radio was on, and a news update came through. News about the President's bill was being announced. Congress had approved his newly revised hate-crime bill, which would restrict the freedom of religion if it is deemed to be intolerant speech toward any group. The President also seemed to be pushing for revision of what it meant to have freedom of speech and religion.

We pulled into the school parking lot, and our day was about to begin. Walking through the ominous school doors, we were about to look a killer in the eye.

"You ready for this?" Philip asked.

"Let's pray," I proposed. We both prayed that God would give us wisdom and protection in school.

"Hey, Rachel wants to meet with us at her locker. She seems to be really shaken up about this whole situation. We need to strengthen her," Philip suggested.

"Alright."

As we approached Rachel's locker, she looked like she was in a good mood. She was talking with Cassie, and both of them were giggling about something.

"What's up, ladies?" Philips said.

"What's so funny?" I asked. Rachel didn't seem to be shaken up to me.

"Well, we're waiting to see what note the secret admirer will have today," Cassie said, cheerfully.

"What did the note say yesterday?" I asked.

"It said 'with,'" Rachel said.

"OK?" I said, puzzled by her reply.

"Yes — put them all together," Cassie said, excitedly. "Monday, the note said, *Will you.* Tuesday, the note said, *go to.* Wednesday, the note said, *the prom.* And yesterday, it said, *with.* So today…"

While Cassie was speaking, we heard rumbles from the students nearby; then laughter ensued. In the distance, I saw a scrawny, pimple-faced boy with an oversize suit on and his hair slicked back with gel. The fragrance of Cool Breeze cologne was preceding him. The crowd parted and there came Trevor, shaking, with a single red rose in one hand and an eight-by-eleven in a half piece of paper in the other that said *Me.*

He was doing it. Trevor was actually going to ask Rachel out in front of everyone. The trembling Trevor wiped the saliva from his mouth and began to stutter through his words.

"W...Will y...you go to th...th...the p...p p prom with me?" he managed to utter. I could see the sigh of relief on his face as the words came out. This was something that he had been wanting to ask her for some time now.

All eyes were on Rachel, as everyone was silent and waiting on a response. Rachel paused for a long time. I could see the nervousness on Trevor's face as sweat poured down his forehead.

"Ah, Trevor — this is so sweet. You are so sweet. I appreciate all your gifts and kind words, and I know it must have taken a lot of courage to do this for me."

What was she doing? The way she was looking, I could feel a "but" coming.

"But I decided that I am not going to attend prom this year. At this time in my life, I just want to dedicate myself to the Lord. I hope you can understand that. Sorry for your trouble."

The dejection on Trevor's face said it all. She'd just crushed his spirit. I felt bad for him and angry at Rachel. How could she do that?

Tears were starting to shape in his eyes, but he sucked them up and replied:

"I — I understand. This rose is for you." Trevor handed her the rose. Then he turned and walked out the school doors.

Most students were laughing, while others had tears in their eyes, sympathizing with the pain that Trevor must have been feeling at that moment.

Rachel rejected Trevor in front of everyone in the school. I wasn't expecting that. It wasn't supposed to end like that.

* * * * *

It'd been more than a week since Rachel embarrassed Trevor in front of a crowd of students, leaving him limping away like a sad puppy. I hadn't seen Trevor since he walked out the school doors. A lot had happened since then. Detective Rogers — the same detective who'd questioned me after my car wreck with Pete — had called us earlier in the week. Apparently his forensic team had analyzed my video and determined that it was authentic, which caused the FBI to get involved in the investigation. They also tested Carl's new eye-detection feature that was part of his improved facial-recognition software. They were impressed. The FBI had been trying to track down Borian Funar for years, and, all this time, he had been hiding out in little old Grand Lake.

Borian Funar was a Romanian spy and top fugitive on the FBI list. About three days before, I'd had the privilege of seeing Borian — Mr. Boots — arrested. While we were at school, the police swooped in and cornered Mr. Boots, causing a big scene. Principal Strudel had to be carried away because he was weeping hysterically, speaking to Mr. Boots in their Romanian language and spewing out curses at me and the policemen. Mr. Boots didn't try to resist — he just willingly let them cuff him.

As he walked past me, he smiled and said,

"You have no idea who you're dealing with kid. I'll be out soon. What I'm doing is way bigger than you can imagine." He stared at me with a sinister look before the police officers shoved him into a police car.

Rachel, Philip, and I had all witnessed this event. Relief was on Rachel and Philip's faces, but I knew better. Things were just getting started with him. Rachel was convinced that Mr. Boots was the school shooter in our dream. This, however, didn't make any sense to me — it just didn't add up. Someone with that IQ, in the top two percent of the population. It seemed that someone like that would have had a master plan. He would be a few steps ahead of everyone. A school shooting didn't seem like his style.

It took him seven years of planning, changing his identity and his appearance, and traveling to the United States to pull this off. And if it hadn't been for my videotape of him committing the murder, his plan would have worked.

For him to go on a rampage and randomly shoot down students at our school didn't seem right. I told Philip this, but he and Rachel were convinced that God was just trying to warn us of what could come if Mr. Boots wasn't arrested. I hoped that they were right.

After Mr. Boots was arrested, the news reporters were swarming our school in a frenzy. News vans were everywhere, and Principal Strudel took a leave of absence. With the arrest of Mr. Boots, Tiffany Storm finally felt safe to confess that she'd falsely accused Mr. Donovan of raping her. She played to the cameras, looking distraught, placing the full blame on Principal Strudel. She confessed that he'd put her up to it, promising her a scholarship to any school she desired.

Mr. Donovan and Henry Joseph had both been released yesterday. Our prayers at the after-school Bible study had been answered.

On this day, I was sitting on the sofa with my family, with everyone in their usual spots. The evening news appeared on the television, and Grand Lake was the top story. Our high school had been getting all kinds of coverage lately.

Breaking news had just come in. The news anchor cut to live action. Cameras from a helicopter view were zooming in on a home. It was Principal Strudel's home. The SWAT team had surrounded his place and barged in on him. A cameraman who was fully armed with a bullet-proof vest and a helmet followed the team into the house.

We could see them going from room to room, trying to locate the Principal. As they approached his bedroom, there were sounds of water and blaring music. The camera showed a silhouette of Principal Strudel singing in the shower behind a foggy glass door. Then the camera quickly cut away as the police announced their presence, which caused the Principal to let out a high-pitched scream.

After the officers made him cover himself, the camera turned back to a terrified Mr. Strudel. In an effort to defend their master, the Principal's two cats, Rocco and Matty, attacked one of the SWAT members, causing him to shoot and kill Matty. On camera, we could see Principal Strudel letting out a horrific cry as he wept at the death of his beloved Matty. He exited his house in just a pair of boxers, swearing and crying at the camera, causing four officers to subdue him.

"Wow! Look at him," Philip said, shaking his head at Principal Strudel squealing and swearing.

What's going on? I pondered. Surprisingly, I felt bad for our Principal. Poor Matty.

"I am still curious as to why they went through all this trouble to make sure President Wright was elected," my dad said, somberly, still bitter about the outcome of the election.

"Good question." Mom chimed in.

All of this was taking me back to earlier in the year, when, on one early morning, we saw Principal Strudel, Mr. Boots, Triston, and Tiffany meeting together. Now we knew what they were planning — everyone except for Triston. I was still wondering what his role had been.

CHAPTER

29

Another week had passed since all the mayhem at our school. Principal Strudel and Mr. Boots were both in prison, awaiting trial. Since his release, Pastor Henry Joseph had been trying to sue the City of Grand Lake for wrongful arrest. Mr. Donovan decided to give up teaching and began work as a director for a local museum.

God had been moving at our high school Bible study. Attendance had steadily increased, especially since all the drama that had occurred that year. Many students were now starting to profess their belief in Christ.

Things had finally calmed down, and prom preparation was scheduled to begin the next week. Philip still hadn't asked Tameka out, and it had been more than two weeks since anyone had seen Trevor Jacobs. I was starting to get worried, concerned that he may harm himself. I knew Rachel felt bad about the situation. She didn't regret her answer, but she wished that she would have answered him privately and not in front of everyone.

I awoke this morning with images of those blood-stained boots from my dream. If Mr. Boots was the killer, then why was I still seeing these images? I thought everything had been settled, but, that morning, I awoke with an uncomfortable feeling. Something just wasn't right. So, before we went to school, I asked my brother to join me in prayer. We prayed in the spirit for a long time, and I knew that, in this prayer, I had to keep praying until I felt a breakthrough. I felt the Holy Spirit groaning on my behalf.

After feeling at peace, we jumped into our trusty red-rock Camaro and headed to school for another day. I don't know how to describe it, but this day felt weird. It was a calm, serene day — almost *too* calm, like an eerie calm before a storm. I thought my brother noticed this, too.

While we were driving to school, I checked my phone and saw that Mrs. Woods had been trying to contact me. As I looked at my phone, it started to ring. On the caller ID was Mrs. Woods's number again.

"Who is it?" Philip asked.

"It's Mrs. Woods. This can't be good," I replied.

Not wanting to click the green "accept" button, I did anyway.

"Hello" I answered.

"John. Is this John?" she asked.

"Yes, ma'am. This is John."

"Good. John, something has happened to Pete."

My mind raced with negative thoughts. *My friend has stopped breathing. He's dead,* was all I could think.

"John — are you still there?"

"Yes, ma'am."

"Pete has just opened his eyes!" she exclaimed.

I could hear the joy in her voice, and I felt sudden relief, as I was prepared to hear the worst news possible.

"My boy Pete is awake!" I shouted to Philip.

"Praise God," he replied.

"I will be there as soon I get out of school, Mrs. Woods," I said, excitedly.

Mrs. Woods was starting to say something else, but I didn't hear what was said. I was so excited that I hung up on her while she was still speaking. "Pete opened his eyes" was all I heard.

We arrived at school early, like always, and, for some reason, we saw Rachel at the school also.

"Why are you here so early?" I asked.

"I couldn't sleep last night, so I just woke up early and came here. I don't know what it is, but something doesn't feel right about today," she commented.

"We were feeling the same way this morning, before we prayed." I said. "Do you want us to pray about this?"

"Yes, please pray for me."

As we were praying together, I heard the words, "Fear not, for I am with you."

"I feel that God is telling you, Rachel to fear not, for he is with you," I said to her.

A look of disbelief was on her face. "Those are the words I heard over and over in my dream last night," she confessed.

Amazed at this but not knowing what to do with this information, we continued to pray for God's strength. After our prayer, Rachel and Philip headed to the cafeteria for breakfast, but I decided to take my daily walk around the building to meditate on this day. As I was walking up the stairs, I saw Triston in the distance, all alone, just leaning against a locker — Jazzy's old locker. He was reading something — maybe a letter.

Normally I would've just turned around and kept walking, but I could sense that God wanted me to talk to him. As I approached him, I saw his jaw tighten and his fist begin to clench.

"What do you want, church boy — Zealot?" he spewed out.

"Look. I don't want any trouble. I just saw you up here by yourself at Jazzy's old locker."

"So, you won, man."

"I won?" *What is he talking about?*

"Yeah, she was always in love with you. Even when she was with me. I knew that she was using me to get back at you. So I used her to have sex with." He tried to laugh, even though I knew that wasn't true.

"I think that we both care about her."

"What does it matter? She went and ran away to Texas anyway."

"Look, man. She's having your baby. You need to be there for her." It hurt me to say that, but I knew that he needed to be involved in her life.

"Why you trying to be nice, church boy?" he asked, genuinely.

"I know we've had our moments, and I don't know where your life is headed, but I do know that God has a plan for your life if you submit to him."

"God? I don't believe in that stuff."

"God loves you more than you can imagine, Triston. He loves you so much that he urged me to come to talk to you today. To be honest, I didn't want to come over here, but I needed to tell you that he loves you, and he wants you to know him." The words that came out of my mouth were not my own but truly from the Lord.

For the first time, I was seeing Triston through the eyes of Jesus. He wasn't the monster I painted him as. I saw a vulnerable, scared boy who masked his pain with aggression and retaliation against others. I didn't think that he had ever heard someone genuinely say that they love him. Triston finally was starting to let down his defenses, and I could see his tough exterior begin to soften.

"How can I experience this love you talk about?" he asked, humbly.

"You must believe and receive what Jesus has done for you. Would you like to pray with me?"

Triston just stood there, still leaning against the locker, contemplating my invitation. An inner struggle was raging inside of him. Then, suddenly, just like I had seen him soften up, he began to harden again. His eyes became steely, and he stood erect, glaring at me.

"I will never accept this God," he said, defiantly. "I've heard that line before. I don't love him. You think you are slick, John. You don't care about me, and you almost got me, too. You can keep your God. I'll be fine by myself," Triston said, slamming his hands against the locker and ripping up the letter that he'd been reading.

"Get out of here, Zealot, before I make *all* of you Zealots disappear." I had seen Triston angry plenty of times before, but this time was different. It was like he was demon possessed — he had so much hatred toward God.

So I just turned, wiped my feet, and walked away.

* * * * *

Seconds seemed like minutes as I listened to my English teacher go on and on about using prepositions, what they were, and why they were needed. I was just waiting for this class to be over because I needed to get to the library, so I could pick up my vintage projector. Moments earlier, I'd received a notification that my projector was finally ready for pickup. I had been waiting on this item for some time, and, for some reason, others had been, too. I needed to get in and out of the library before my next class started.

I had a final coming soon in my history class. My final project was going to be on the history of film. This vintage projector would be a nice addition to my final work, showcasing the beginning of film.

The bell finally rang, and I rushed to the library to get my projector. I was met with a bright, smiling librarian. She was not your stereotypical librarian — the one who has her hair in a bun and wears black-rimmed glasses. This woman had a pleasant smile with long, auburn hair.

"May I help you, young man?" she asked.

"Yes. I'm here to pick up the vintage film projector."

"Okay. What is your name, sir?" she asked as she scrolled through her database.

"John. John Mann," I answered.

"Okay, I see you. It has just been shelved. You are the third person this month to check this out. Must be a popular item."

"Must be," I replied.

"Okay, John. I'll be right back. It may be a while, so, if you need a pass to class, I can give you one."

"Yes, ma'am. That would be helpful."

Good. I didn't have to rush to class. While I was waiting, I noticed a *Persons* magazine on display with my title, *The Zealot Movement: Whose movement Is It?* On the front cover was a picture of Mr. Boots firing his gun at the doctor. *What? They stole the picture from my film!* I didn't know that they still made magazine prints, but I guessed they did. Intrigued by this, I grabbed the *Persons* magazine and decide to sit and read some of the article while I am waiting for my projector.

I found a table, and I was surprised to see Rachel a few tables away. We looked at each other, and I got a sudden sense of *déjà vu*. We had experienced this moment before. Terror was on Rachel's face, as she was thinking the same thing I was. *No this can't be! Mr. Boots was arrested!* And, just as in my dream, my phone began to vibrate, and what followed next confirmed my suspicions.

A loud, crackling sound went off — like fireworks. It has begun. "Jesus" was the only thing I could say. Things were happening so fast and on cue. The boy…the boy who was about to be murdered came running through the library doors yelling "Run! Run" I whispered along with the boy as he yelled the words out in terror. I ducked under my table.

A single shot rang out, dropping the boy in front of me. A cacophony soon followed. The water sprinklers came on, and the pulsating warning alarm was going off. Screams were echoing throughout the library, and the presence of fear was thick. I looked at the fallen boy next to me as his eyes looked back with a blank stare, indicating that the life had left his body. I turned and looked at Rachel, across from me, huddled under her table in fear. She was mouthing a prayer to God.

As water began to trickle down the sides of the table, I saw them — those same, hideous boots, covered with blood, were coming toward me. Things began to slow down for me as my senses were heightened. I could hear the thud of my heart and the flow of adrenaline traveling through my veins. The crunch of his boots was getting louder as he came closer. He stood at my table. *If I am going to die, then I am going to die fighting*, I thought.

The killer reloaded his gun as shells fell to the floor. I looked to heaven to tell God I would see him soon. Just one more step closer, and then I would pounce to attack. But, instead of taking a step forward, the killer took a step backwards. He turned in the direction of Rachel.

"Rachel," I whispered to myself. "No."

The killer stood in front of her table and spoke:

"Rachel, come — come out," a quiet voice that I'd heard before was now speaking loud and with rage. I peeked out from my table and see the scrawny, pimple-faced, shy boy named Trevor. Trevor was standing there with his full JROTC gear on. He had his father's Purple Heart around his neck and two guns strapped on his body.

Trevor pointed the gun at Rachel and angrily repeated himself:

"I — I said, 'come out.'"

The trembling Rachel made her way out from under the table and was standing a few feet in front of him, looking right into the muzzle of Trevor's gun.

Trevor was so overcome with anger that he began to cry.

"Look at me. Rachel. *Look at me!*" he screamed. "I bet you didn't see this coming, "Psychic Rachel" — did you? You did this. You made me do this. I — I love you. I — I have loved you for a long time. But you just p… p… played with me, pretend — ing to b — be nice to me and then crushing my heart." Along with Trevor's stuttering rant, he was seething and huffing as drool ran down his cheeks.

"You have to believe me. I didn't mean to hurt you," Rachel pled.

"But you did. I — I am tired of taking crap from people, tired of hearing the laughers. Today is judgment day — just ask my stepdad and Triston," he said, with an evil grimace.

What has Trevor done?

"They won't be messing with me anymore."

"What are you doing, Trevor?" Rachel asked.

"Quiet. You see, Rachel, you and I are supposed to be together. Don't let God come between us."

Something strange began to happen to the trembling Rachel. She stopped shaking and stood tall, looking into Trevor's evil eyes.

"Nothing is going to come between me and God," she boldly answered.

Her answer enraged Trevor. He lifted his gun at her and spoke with no stutter.

"How much do you love your life? Choose now — me or God?" He cocked his gun back and aimed it at her.

CHAPTER

30

As I was peeking out from under my table, I looked into Trevor's eyes as he uttered those words, and I saw emptiness, and haze in his eyes. He looked like a shell of himself, like someone else had taken over his body. While I was looking at him, something strange was beginning to happen to me. It was happening again — a vision, a flashback into his life. Like our first meeting when I was giving him back his backpack, God gave me a glimpse into his life. He was sitting with his back to the door, crying as he heard his mother being abused by his stepfather.

The same thing was happening again. Time seemed to stop, and, this time, I was standing at the school doors, looking at Trevor walking toward me, after Rachel had just rejected his invitation to the prom. I heard the laughter of students as he came closer to me. I could feel his pain, the same pain that I felt after Jazzy had broken up with me — that crushing, hopeless, and heartsick pain, which I so desperately wanted to get rid of. I was feeling it again as he walked by me on his way out the door. I followed Trevor to his house and saw him lock himself in his room. He lay on his bed crying for days. The sad thing about this was that his parents didn't even care.

In this vision, I stood there day after day, watching him do nothing but sulk, wondering to myself, *Why I am looking at this*? Then the day came when Trevor finally decided that he was going to end things — that he was going to take his life. The pain that he was feeling was unbearable. That day, he wrote a lengthy suicide letter. He knew that his stepdad had a vast collection of guns and figured that he could use one to shoot himself and that no one would care. He just wondered how long it would take before someone would even discover his dead body.

After he had written his final letter, he turned on the television, and, on the movie channel was the movie *Soulless Corpse,* the same movie that my dad wouldn't let me see. As you may recall, this movie was about a girl who'd been cyber-bullied, which caused her to take her own life. In the movie, this girl was resurrected from the dead on the anniversary of her death. She had no emotion — she was a soulless corpse on a mission to seek out and kill everyone who had ever posted any negative comments about her.

As Trevor watched this film, he could identify with the girl. Trevor's plans to take his own life now became plans to take others' lives. He was going to get revenge on all those who had hurt him, especially Rachel.

The day of the shooting, he awoke early and dressed in his army attire, with his dad's purple heart around his neck. He thought he was a soldier ready for battle. Trevor's first target would be his drunk, abusive stepdad. He waited until his mom left for work before he made his move. His stepdad was still asleep, passed out on the couch, with an empty bottle still in his hand from a night of drinking. Trevor went to the garage, where the collection of guns were stored. He took a shotgun, a 9mm and a 995 Carbine, loaded them, and exited the garage.

I watched, powerless to stop him, as Trevor stood in front of his abusive stepdad. He stood there recalling all the painful memories and hurtful insults. He saw flashes of his mother calling for help as she was being beaten — and then thoughts of his stepdad telling him that he was a "nobody" and wouldn't amount to anything. With each memory, Trevor's anger was boiling. I could see a murderous rage overtaking him. His stepdad was beginning to awake from his slumber, startled to see Trevor standing over him. At first, he laughed and thought it was a joke.

"Look at you, kid. What do you plan on doing? You gonna shoot me?" he said, laughing at Trevor, who barely had enough strength to hold up the gun.

"You don't have the guts to pull the…"

Before his stepdad could finish his words, Trevor fired the shotgun into his chest. This marked the beginning of his rampage. That moment is when I saw him turn into a possessed man.

Next, he drove to the school and entered through the gym doors. With Mr. Boots in jail, there was no security at the school. Trevor easily entered the school and appeared on the gym floor with a fully loaded shotgun. Triston was playing basketball. Trevor cocked his gun and shot Triston. Mr. Thomas, our PE teacher, tried to stop Trevor, but he was also gunned down.

The library was his next target. He must have known that Rachel was a library assistant at this time of day. *Why was God showing me all of this?* I thought as I continued to follow him.

A few more teachers tried to reason with Trevor, but he just responded with gunfire.

Trevor was about to open the library doors, and that's when I was suddenly sucked back to the present, looking into Trevor's evil, hate-filled eyes. What seemed like hours that I'd spent peering into his life was only seconds in real time. I was back under the table, looking at a possessed kid.

"I said, how much do you love your life?" Trevor repeated, glaring at Rachel. "How zealous are you for your God, Zealot? Choose now — me or God?" His finger was on the trigger, ready to fire.

Rachel didn't even blink. She didn't hesitate or reconsider her position. She looked directly into his eyes, and with a Godly boldness, said, "I choose God."

"You chose wrong," Trevor said, coldly. With his gun aimed at Rachel's head, a loud crackling sound resounded as the gun fired. The bullet was traveling straight for Rachel's head.

"Rachel!" I screamed.

For some reason I couldn't look away. The look on Rachel's face was an indescribable look of peace — a peace that said, 'Whatever the outcome is, I'm okay.' As the bullet was traveling toward Rachel, time began to slow down as if someone had pressed the slow-motion button on the TV. I could see the bullet spinning slowly through the air. The hairs on my arms begin to rise. Something other worldly was happening.

A piercing brightness enveloped the library. A quick flash of lightning struck the room, and I couldn't believe what I saw next. A gigantic being, standing about ten feet tall, was illuminating the room. This being was standing in front of Rachel, guarding her. The bullet that was coming toward Rachel was easily deflected by this heavenly being, this angel. A glowing angel had appeared. He appeared out of nowhere, and time returned to real time.

Trevor was initially frightened, but then the evil look in his eyes returned, and he began to unload all of his bullets on the angel, switching guns and doing the same again. However, the angel just stood there, expressionless, as each bullet bounced off him.

Judging by the reaction of others in the library, it appeared that Trevor, Rachel, and I were the only ones who were able to see this angel. I could hear screams and whimpers from students nearby as Trevor — now a madman — was shooting wildly. I turned to my left and saw the sweet, auburn-haired librarian holding her arm. She had been nicked and was bleeding from Trevor's gunfire.

The few students who dared peek at what was going on were perplexed as to how Trevor was shooting at Rachel, but nothing was hitting her. They couldn't see the angel like we could.

The angel finally spoke in a booming, thunderous voice, causing the ground to shake. The tremors from his voice caused Trevor to cease firing and fall flat on his face.

"Stop! You do not have permission to harm God's anointed!" The rumble of his voice echoed off the library walls.

Trevor was now lying prostrate on the ground, trembling in fear. As I watched the scrawny boy, I thought I knew, an uncanny thing began to happen to him. A dark, ghostly figure was rising from him, coming out of his body, leaving him limp and weeping hysterically in a fetal position. The dark, grotesque creature hovered over him, hissing like a lethal snake ready to strike. This demon's searing eyes were filled with hatred. I couldn't understand why he hated us so much. I could feel the hate emanating from him. He was chanting repeatedly into Trevor's ear.

"Kill yourself. Just kill yourself. Kill yourself. Just kill your — "

"Silence!" the angel commanded the demon. "Murder, you have no authority here! Release him!"

The demon hissed one last time. Then, he turned, with his searing eyes looking directly at me.

"I will return," he said before he vanished into thin air. His words sent chills down my spine. The name the angel called that demon was "Murder." I had a feeling that one day he would return.

Trevor was still sobbing and drooling uncontrollably. He rose to his knees, with his hands on the ground, fumbling and reaching for his gun. He found a gun, grabbed it and pointed at the temple of his head.

"Trevor — no!" Rachel yelled. "It's not too late. God can forgive you. Give yourself to Him," she pleaded.

Looking at Rachel, in a soft voice, Trevor muttered the words, "Look at what I've done. He can't forgive this. It's too late for me." He closed his eyes, with his trembling finger on the trigger. He squeezed it, and I could hear a click....

*****

Caves of Palestine

While John was telling his story, he was interrupted by what he believed was a group of poisonous spiders crawling right for Sergeant Jake's hand.

"Hey — watch out!" he screamed to the sergeant. John took off his shoe, ready to squash the spiders crawling toward the sergeant. Sergeant Jake leapt from his sitting position, turned, and took a second look, carefully examining the spiders.

"What are you doing?" John questioned.

"Look," the sergeant said as he let one of the creepy spiders crawl up his finger. "This isn't a spider — it's a Spiderbot. My boys are getting close, John!"

Almost as soon as the sergeant had finished speaking, they heard rapid fire outside the cave. Shots were ricocheting off the stone walls. They heard cries and yells of English mixed with Arabic.

"They're here, kid!" Sergeant Jake said with excitement. "You'll have to finish your story on our way home." He smiled, rejoicing at the possibility of being rescued.

The back-and-forth sounds of gunfire went on for about thirty minutes before a loud boom rattled their cave. Stone dust filled the air as a bomb went off.

"They must be breaking down the walls," Sergeant Jake said, gleefully. Strength was starting to return to the weakened sergeant. The thought of being rescued was energizing both of them. After the bomb went off, there was a long period of silence. Finally, John and the sergeant could hear a faint voice calling. They couldn't identify whose voice it was, but the sergeant assumed it was one of his men.

"It looks like we're going to get out of here, kid. Don't forget to tell me more about your God and what happened to you, kid," the sergeant said with a smile.

"Yes, sir," John replied.

The two were relieved at the thought of leaving that dingy cave and being reunited with their loved ones, but they had no idea of what was to come.

Reginald Wattree Jr.

ABOUT THE AUTHOR

Reginald Wattree Jr. is a Kansas City native who now resides in Lee's Summit Missouri. He is a devoted husband and father of three. A graduate of DeVry University, currently works in the field of information technology.

Despite his training in management and information technology, Reginald likes to make up his own stories complete with real life, real drama and cliffhangers. In this debut novel, *The Zealot's*, Reggie keeps the readers engaged on every page. With this introduction to the Christian Fiction genre, his Gifted Generation Series is sure to gain audiences of all ages, teens to adults. Reggie is securing his place among the list of Best Sellers.

Look for more from Reggie and the Gifted Generation Series and stay connected online.

Contact Information:

Email: giftedgeneration@mail.com

Web: www.giftedgenerationseries.com

@giftedgenseries

Gifted-Generation-Series